"What have you got there? Come on, Filbert, let me see."

Belle was on her hands and knees half under a table, head next to the cat's as he pawed at something, something she could not see, between the drapery and the wall. From behind them, all that Gore could see was two bottoms wriggling as they worked, one upholstered with fur and finished with a plume, the other covered with sprigged blue lawn. On the whole, he decided that he preferred the one without the tail.

"Ahem."

"What? Ouch!"

Belle struggled up, rubbing her head, which had struck the table, further mussing her cap, and glared at her guest. "I might have known it was you."

"What a warm welcome, Lillie." He grinned. "Here, let me." He stepped forward and straightened her frilled cap. "That's better. You look quite charming in that."

"Thank you, I think," she replied suspiciously.

"Can't you accept a compliment?"

"Oh, well, I never can be sure when you say things that they *are* compliments." She busied herself setting her skirts to rights.

Gore realized that this was true. He did always seem to be teasing her or picking at her about something. No way to treat a lady, he chided himself, especially not one as pretty and nice as she. The fact was, despite their being at daggers drawn twenty minutes out of every hour, he had come to enjoy their time together and found her easy, yes, comfortable, to be with.

Still, he was not about to be taken in by her. In the beginning, he had wanted to see just how far she would take the whole thing, just what she would do. But now? Oh, devil take her, he decided. She is not harming me, after all. Nor Lillie. My mad cousin is cavorting somewhere in Italy with little care for what happens here in London, so why am I worrying?

"You have the right of it, Lillie, I suppose I do tease you horribly, don't I? I promise to do better. Pax?"

Belle looked at him askance. She wanted to believe him. She wanted to look in those eyes and see admiration, not teasing or suspicion. She wanted . . . too much, and she knew it. Well she would take what he offered and be glad of it.

"Pax."

<u>BOOK YOUR PLACE ON OUR WEBSITE</u> AND MAKE THE <u>READING CONNECTION!</u>

We've created a customized website just for our very special readers, where you can get the inside scoop on everything that's going on with Zebra, Pinnacle and Kensington books.

When you come online, you'll have the exciting opportunity to:

- View covers of upcoming books

- Read sample chapters

- Learn about our future publishing schedule (listed by publication month *and author*)

- Find out when your favorite authors will be visiting a city near you

- Search for and order backlist books from our online catalog

- Check out author bios and background information

- Send e-mail to your favorite authors

- Meet the Kensington staff online

- Join us in weekly chats with authors, readers and other guests

- Get writing guidelines

- AND MUCH MORE!

**Visit our website at
http://www.zebrabooks.com**

THE CAT'S BRACELET

JESSIE WATSON

Zebra Books
Kensington Publishing Corp.

http://www.zebrabooks.com

To Kitty and the rest of the menagerie,
past and present

ZEBRA BOOKS are published by

Kensington Publishing Corp.
850 Third Avenue
New York, NY 10022

First Printing: June, 1998
10 9 8 7 6 5 4 3 2 1

Printed in the United States of America

ONE

"No, ma'am, the coach to Beaconsfield won't be leaving today. Hasn't even come in. Most like it hasn't been able to leave from West Wycombe, or broke down on the road betwixt there and here, what with this terrible storm. No more coaches be comin' in, I'd say. Don't know how you made it this far, and that's a fact. It's a testament to your driver and his team, I can tell you."

"You are right, of course, it would be foolhardy to attempt it, for I never thought to make it safely this far." She shifted her soaked feet in the puddle forming from the rain that ran off her cape. Her ruined boots did little to protect her feet, and her clothes clung like a cold, wet shroud. Her bonnet had all but fallen apart in the short distance she had to run between her public coach and the inn, and she was well aware that she must look a perfect fright.

The inn door suddenly shot open with a blast of wind which carried with it buckets of rain, debris from the yard and her coachman. "Damn this foul weather, Fred, I haven't seen the like in years of driving this road!" he cried, heading for the taproom.

"Aye, a proper tempest it is, Tom. Ask Hilda for something hot and tell her it's with my compliments."

The driver nodded his thanks and disappeared into

the adjoining room. "Hilda m'darlin', save my life and get me a toddy!"

The woman pushed a dripping curl from her forehead and continued. "Well, I suppose I must make the best of the situation and wait out the storm. Might I have a room, please, and a private parlor? Or I can certainly eat in my room, if there is nothing private available."

"Oh ho! Bless you, ma'am, that's a good one!" the innkeeper chuckled. The joke was lost on the sodden mass before him. "No, no, there's no rooms to be had. The storm, you know," he explained kindly.

Blast! Again, this dreadful storm. Wasn't it enough that she and her fellow passengers had only barely survived the trip? It had taken ages to extract the coach from the mud several miles back, and they had at last dragged into the yard of The Rose Revived hours behind schedule, only for her to learn that she would not be able to complete the next leg of her journey. And now, no room. She had begun to shiver. Ah well, doubtless she would not be the only stranded traveler making do on the floor of the inn. Hardly a welcome thought. She hoped that, at least, she might find a place near the fire.

"Perhaps I could be of assistance?"

She turned to see a smiling woman of about her own age, that is to say nearly thirty summers, standing nearby. The two women bobbed their heads, and the weary traveler returned the smile.

"Good day. You are most kind to inquire. My name is Annabelle Makepeace and I find myself stranded by this storm. It would seem that I am not alone in my predicament, usually a comforting thought, but in this instance, it appears to mean that my fellow travelers have had the good fortune to take all the rooms in the inn." Despite her distress, her smile broadened in response to the other woman's grin.

"Yes, I have no doubt you are too late. The place is absolutely teeming with wet, disgruntled wanderers, who have had to break their journeys here. I among them. Not," she charmingly assured the innkeeper, "that your establishment is not of the best quality." He smiled and nodded his thanks.

"Well, but that still leaves you in the cold, quite literally, does it not? Oh dear, I might have the grace to introduce myself. I am Lillie Broadhurst, and I shall save you. You will share my room."

"Oh, I—"

"Nonsense. You would appear to be an upright gentlewoman," she said, raising a brow comically to survey Belle's pathetic person.

"Good heavens, how could you possibly tell? I might be any manner of cutpurse," Belle said with a small, rather nervous, laugh. And you might be goodness knows what, she said to herself.

"I have an eye," her would-be rescuer assured her dryly. "In the event, neither of us has the ability at this moment to observe the usual niceties, no manner of proper introduction nor vetting of our respective pedigrees via the village tabbies, neither, so we must accept one another on faith, as it were. I must confess, my motive is not entirely altruistic. I have a desperate need for company so, please, allow me to help you. You must, you know," she smiled, "for I am quite used to managing things and have not a thing to put my hand to. You, dear Miss Makepeace, must save me from myself. Will you not come?"

There seeming little real choice, Belle smiled warmly. "I shall be most pleased, thank you."

"Good. Mr. Hapgood can have your case brought up

to my room, although I daresay its contents will not be fit for much until we can get the dampness out. Mr. Hapgood, please have hot water brought up at once, so that Miss Makepeace can refresh herself."

The Rose Revived, in its previous life, had been a private house, and Belle soon found herself in a quaint room nuzzled under the eaves. The chamber was larger than she might have expected, and its windows gave onto a small garden where steps led down to the Thames. The room's situation was a boon to anyone staying there in the warmer months, when the windows open from other chambers over the courtyard would allow the sounds of comings and goings, greetings and orders, cattle and people to invade their tenants' every waking, and especially nonwaking, moment. The innkeeper's boy deposited her bag before the fire and departed. Belle removed her rain-soaked cloak and stepped quickly toward the warmth.

"Miss Makepeace, this is my abigail, Warner."

The maid dropped a curtsy.

"Warner, I have asked Miss Makepeace to stay with us. Perhaps for the next forty days and forty nights," she added dryly, as she cast an eye at the rain sluicing down the window. "Not that she had much choice in the matter, poor thing."

"Would that be because of the storm, ma'am?" the maid inquired, failing to contain a smile.

"Ah, Warner, so aptly named, and so droll. I will have you know that I already have cautioned Miss Makepeace of my tendency to, um, manage things, so I assure you, winks and nudges of warning behind my back are quite unnecessary," she pointed out with a chuckle.

Warner grinned. "Well, that's all right, then. We had better be getting you out of those wet things, Miss."

"Yes, and I shall find you something to wear, before you perish."

Belle had observed this exchange with amusement, such bantering not being the usual discourse between a lady and her maid. "You are most kind."

Lillie inspected her guest. "We seem to be of a size. That is a blessing." She extracted a pretty round gown from the clothespress and held it aloft for approval. "What do you think of this? Or this?" The voice was somewhat muffled, coming as it did from amidst a large number of gowns, night shifts, spencers, pelisses and bandboxes. At length, she managed to wrest another gown from the stingy cabinet.

A knock announced the arrival of the hot water, delivered by a maid looking quite frazzled by the demands of an inn full of querulous travelers. Once Belle had washed and her hair had been dried and repinned by Warner, she felt much more the thing. Lillie had insisted on dragging what must have been every frock from the clothespress for her approval.

"Oh, they are all lovely. That pretty bottle-green one I think, if you are certain you do not mind."

"Green it is. An elegant choice, if I may so, madam." Her hostess gave her best impression of an ingratiating modiste. "It should be perfect with your coloring." Warner helped Belle into the gown, and Lillie surveyed her again. "Do you know, we have the same complexion, same hair, same eyes—such a boring shade of brown, do you not agree?—same figure . . ." She paused, her mind working busily, and continued with a peculiar look in her eye. "You know, we actually look rather alike." She stood beside Belle in front of the glass.

Belle blinked in surprise. Now that she was dry and properly dressed, it was quite evident. Lillie's nose was not as strongly punctuated as her own—ironic, that, given her admitted proclivity for managing things, Lillie's lips were fuller, and Belle's hair was not fashionably cut and styled, but there was a remarkable resemblance. They even were the same height.

Her hostess said, "Well, I am famished, and I am convinced you must be also."

"Indeed I am."

"Then, Warner, do go down and tell Mr. Hapgood to send up a very large meal."

After the abigail had left, Lillie confided that she had been with her only a few months. "But we are getting on famously. At least she has not left me yet." She grinned.

"Oh! What was that?" Belle cried.

"What's wrong? What is it?"

"I don't know! Something ran under the bed. Could it be a rat?"

Lillie laughed. "Quite a large rat, I should say. That is Filbert. A cat, not a rat, if you will forgive the rhyme. He is traveling with us." As she was flushing him out from beneath the bed, the last words were somewhat stifled.

"You have a cat? Here?"

She replied quite nonchalantly. "Oh, yes. One simply arranges the necessary accommodations. As to your first question, I cannot be altogether certain that *I* have him, rather I should say that *he* has me, for he certainly behaves as if he were the one putting all the food in our mouths."

A very large cat with enormous feet was, at length, extracted from his hiding place. "There," Lillie smiled, huffing from the exertion, "this is Filbert."

"Yes, so he is."

Filbert had rather long hair, mostly white, with a char-

coal grey tail and grey markings splashed along his back
and the top of his head. What might have been a dignified cat face was denied by a single large grey spot
on only one side of his upper lip, giving the comical
appearance of one half of a moustache. He escaped his
captor, sneered at the indignity of it all and waddled
toward Belle. Filbert sat calmly and deliberately, staring
with knowing yellow eyes and waiting for the introduction to be completed. Lillie obliged.

"Oh, do go away," Belle told him.

"Why, Belle, don't you like cats?"

"No, I do not. That is, I have not had much experience with them. They have always seemed rather, well,
untrustworthy to me somehow."

"Well, I do sometimes get the feeling that Filbert here
talks about me with the other cats and the dogs when
I have left the room. But, truly, he is a dear." She
reached down and hefted the large bundle of rather
scrubby fur that was Filbert. His bulk spilled over both
her arms, and four feet in the air, he snuggled into her
embrace. Purring loudly, he peered shortsightedly over
his prosperous tummy at Belle.

"I think he is smirking at me, Lillie."

"Oh, I should not be at all surprised, for he is quite
pleased with himself. Actually, do you know, I think he
probably had a hard life before he came to me."

"Well, if he did, then he certainly has made up for
it. Clearly, he is always home at mealtime."

Belle chuckled to herself. Really, Lillie seemed such
an independent soul and here she was, absolutely potty
about this ridiculous cat.

Lillie laughed abashedly. "I know what you are thinking, but I adore animals. The house is simply full of
them. Aunt Eulalie brought Filbert up to us on her last
visit, just over two years ago. She had found him hang-

Jessie Watson

ing about Randolph's London house—that is where I am going—and, for some reason, decided he would have a good home with us. She was right, of course."

"Of course."

"You will not mind sharing the room with him, will you?"

"Not so long as he keeps to his own bed."

Lillie smiled inanely down at the cat. "Oh, he is such a darling, I know you will get on beautifully."

"Mmm. A darling. Yes, I am sure he is," Belle replied with an arched brow.

Later, after the two women had done great justice to their supper, they lingered before the fire, chatting as easily as two old friends. Belle drew her borrowed Norwich shawl closer about her and sat back in her chair, breathing a sigh of satisfaction. The surroundings were so much better than she had dared hope just a few hours before.

Lillie had explained that her carriage, a private one on its way to London, had limped into the inn yard much earlier that day.

"Do you live in London, in the house you mentioned?" Belle asked.

"In a manner of speaking, that is, temporarily. I reside in Burford, which is not far from here, actually, but I have had the house opened up for a few months. This will be my first visit to London." She seemed oddly undisturbed by the interruption to her journey.

"You do not seem very anxious to continue your trip. I have never been to the Metropolis, either, but I am sure I should be champing at the bit, were I in your shoes."

Lillie gave a tinkling laugh. "But you are, dear Belle."

"Pardon?"

"In my shoes, silly!"

"Oh! So I am!" Belle joined in the laughter.

"Now, your turn. What is your destination?"

"Well, I am supposed to be in Beaconsfield tomorrow afternoon. I am taking up a position as companion to an elderly lady."

"Oh, what untrammeled joy. Must you? That is, if I may ask, do your circumstances require you to do so? Forgive me, but your speech, your carriage—well, you would appear to be gently born." She spoke this, not in resentment that Belle might have put herself forward as something she was not, thereby placing Lillie in the uncomfortable position of sharing her accommodation with someone beneath her own station, but rather out of straightforward interest.

Belle shrugged. "Well, yes, I am, but I am widowed, you see, I am actually *Mrs.* Makepeace. I lived as long as I was able on what Gilbert left me, he died nearly three years ago, and now it is time for me to earn my bread."

"But you do not relish the thought?" There was sympathy in the voice.

"I concede I do not. Not so much, I *hope* because I do not wish to work, but rather that I fear the work will be tedious, one long day yawning into a lifetime of days spent fetching and reading and, oh my, listening. If I could somehow be productive, if it all actually *meant* something, I think I should not mind so much. But there, I am not fit to do anything else. Except perhaps governessing. Well, one must persevere. And things could be much worse, after all."

"But then, who among our class is fit to do anything of real merit? We women are not seen as worth educating, and our fathers do not seem to consider that changing circumstances, such as yours, can thrust us upon the world with no real knowledge of how to make our way in it. And heaven protect the woman who does not choose to marry!" A disgusted sniff followed this last remark.

"But, what of you? Who is this Randolph you mentioned? Your husband?"

"My late husband. I, too, am widowed. Almost two years. But, we had many years together, for I married when I was young. That is, I suppose I was young in years, but not in life, if you know what I mean. Being the only child and with a cousin living with us, after my mother died, all the domestic responsibilities devolved to me, and I detested them. I wanted to ride and flirt with boys and shoot. Damme, I would have gone to war if I had been a man. Instead, I found myself walled up in Oxfordshire like a heroine from a silly novel, only my prison was a manor house and I its mistress!

"When Randolph offered for me, I am not certain which I found the most appealing, him or the freedom I believed marriage would buy me. Oh, I knew I should be going from running one household to another, but I still was young enough to believe it would be different. That being mistress of my own house, with a husband at my side, would make me happy." Lillie sipped at the last of her cold tea and made a face.

"I was wrong. Oh, it was not the house, for it is lovely, and I can say that I ran it ably. God knows I had sufficient experience. And it was not Randolph, for he was a good husband and a caring, kind man. Still, what I thought was love was, to some extent, desperation. Desperation which, together with my youth and inexperience, convinced me that I could be happy in such a life. I was quite fond of Randolph, but I grew weary of trying to be happier than I was. Do I sound hopelessly shallow and selfish?" Belle smiled. "Oh, I suppose I must but, Belle, I must have my happiness! I have always had to care for others, and I never had much time for myself. Still, you mustn't think that anyone was cruel to me, neither my father nor my husband, for nothing could be farther from the truth. It is only that our life was so boring. We rarely even entertained because Randolph preferred the quiet life. I have never traveled, which I yearn to do, or had anything interesting happen to me. I should love above all things to visit Italy, I have read so much about it."

Her long story finished, Lillie leaned back with a sigh, and they sat for a time, sharing the joys and tribulations of their prior lives, eventually falling quiet, as they watched the fire.

"We could change places, you know," Lillie said softly. "I could go to Italy as Belle, and you could have your independence as Lillie."

"What? Are you joking?"

"No, I do not think that I am," she replied soberly.

"But—that is impossible, it's preposterous . . ."

"Why?"

"Oh, come. Surely you must see that. Why, it is something done in books, I make no doubt, but for us? Really!" she chided.

"I am in earnest. No one else need know. And it would be for just a few months. Then we could change back, each of us having got what we want and *need.*"

"No," Belle responded firmly.

"You have never visited London, you said so. Nor have I, therefore no one knows me there. Well, almost no one. There is Randolph's Aunt Eulalie, you know, the one who brought Filbert to me."

"Oh, yes, I am on tenterhooks to meet *her,*" Belle interposed sarcastically.

"Oh, she's really a dear. And we have only ever met

a few times, you see, over the years. The last time was when she brought little Filbert to me. Eons ago."

"Two years, if I remember correctly," Belle felt the need to point out.

"Exactly. Anyway, the poor thing's eyesight has since become very poor, so it is unlikely she would notice any significant difference between us. She would never question your identity. You need only join in the Season, if you wish, go shopping, to the theatre, nothing difficult, I promise you."

"You are mad!"

"Desperate. Listen to me, Belle. Before today, before we met, each of us was prepared to live a life we did not want, because we had no choice. Now we do. Belle, I believe that everything happens for a reason. We were fated to meet. I know it. We cannot cast aside this opportunity. Do you want to spend the rest of your life catering to the whims of others? Do you?"

"But, Lillie, you are an independent woman. If you want to go to Italy, why do you not just go? Why enter into such a havey-cavey business in order to do what you have the right and means to do? It seems quite simple to me."

"Believe me, Belle, that sounds a great deal less complicated than it is. I mean, I broached the subject with my father. His house and mine are just a few miles apart, you see. I wanted to tell him what I was thinking of doing. Good heavens, I might as well have said I was running off to join a band of Gypsies! He is a dear man, but very conscious of the opinions of others. He fears that the neighborhood would think my going off to Italy much too daring, even for a widow. Well, it is a small village, so perhaps he has something of a point. It is absurd, I know, but I love him very much and he has a weak heart. I could not knowingly upset him. Seeing how disappointed I was, he suggested that I travel to London for the Season, instead. At the time, it seemed better than nothing." She sighed deeply.

"A pity," Belle said, her tone only a little dry, as she did sympathize with Lillie's evident disappointment.

Lillie blushed. "Gracious, I know how it sounds, and it is very kind of you not to ring a peal over me for my ingratitude. I am aware that I am a most fortunate woman. Still, you can help me, Belle, if only you will."

Belle walked to the window. The black night cast her image back at her, and she looked into her own eyes to see resolve weakening. She drew a deep breath.

"No. . . . I could not possibly let you support me in that way, I could not accept money from you."

Lillie crossed to her side. "Not even for helping a friend? For you would be helping me, you know."

"Especially not then. You have helped me today, did you expect payment from me?"

"Certainly not!"

"There."

"But it would not be the same."

"It would."

"No, honestly. First, I have simply pots of money. Randolph was rich beyond any maiden's dreams and left me obscenely well-fixed. Then, I had quite a large fortune of my own to begin with. To say I would never miss a comfortable sum for you would be greatly understating the case." She placed a hand on Belle's shoulder. "Second, taking my place for several months is hardly comparable to a night's shelter from a storm and the loan of a gown."

"Indeed, I do not think a new wardrobe and joining in the whirl of the Season qualifies as a hardship."

"Perhaps not for you, but I should hate it. Well, not exactly, I suppose, but only after I have had my turn, my adventure. Then, I think, I could enjoy that life. And there is one more thing." She paused, a teasing smile on her lips.

"What?"

"The Bracelet."

"What bracelet?"

"The one in the London house. The Cat's Bracelet."

"Lillie, do explain, please, all of this is giving me the headache."

"Let us go back to the fire, it is too chilly by the window. I really do not know much. No one seems to."

Belle sat down, groaning, and rubbed her temples.

"It is said to be a very old piece. Some long-ago ancestor of Randolph had it made up for his wife. Dozens of diamonds. Anyway, it disappeared one day. The story goes that Ethelbert made off with it."

"Ethelbert?"

"The cat."

"Oh, for pity's sake!"

"I am only the storyteller, my dear. Apparently, Ethelbert was the descendant of a long line of Broadhurst cats. Anyway, he was a favorite of Virginia—that was the ancestor's wife—and he was something of a magpie—always making off with oddments and such, and hiding them. Apparently, he was especially fond of anything that sparkled. He had snatched a few pieces of her jewelry in the past but nothing as dear as the diamond bracelet."

"I daresay."

"Well, the thing just went missing one day and they could not find it! They always assumed that Ethelbert pilfered it, but he never would own up to it—nefarious creature. They looked everywhere, all his usual hiding places, but never discovered it."

"Good heavens. Well, what happened then?"

"Old Sebastian Broadhurst, Virginia's husband, had fits, of course. So did Virginia, come to that, she was fond of The Bracelet. But not as fond as she was of Ethelbert."

"Sounds familiar. Are you sure she was an ancestor of Randolph and not you?"

"Oh, hush. Sebastian threatened to strangle poor Ethelbert . . ."

"Poor Ethelbert?"

"Yes, poor Ethelbert," Lillie cooed and hugged Filbert who sat, dignified, on her lap looking askance at Belle. "As I was saying, old Sebastian swore he would have the cat assassinated or murder him himself, but Virginia swore she would leave if he put a hand on him. Sebastian would not stand for a scandal and so, very grudgingly, he relented. Ethelbert won a reprieve, Virginia remained, and she and Sebastian never spoke to one another again."

"Oh, that is, is . . . hilarious!" The two went off into gales of laughter. "Dear, that was unkind of me, what a sad end."

"Not really. Evidently, Virginia and Sebastian managed quite nicely in their respective armed camps. They were able to behave like civilized people at family gatherings and on public holidays, and things ran rather smoothly. Fortunately for the future of the Broadhurst line, they had already filled their nursery."

At this, they went into whoops again. After a few moments, Lillie continued. "Family legend has it that the bracelet, which came to be known as The Cat's Bracelet, is still in the house. Somewhere." Filbert gazed out from shuttered, inscrutable eyes, purring loudly and, Belle suspected, smugly.

"It is there for the taking, my dear. Whoever finds it

gets to keep it, or so the story goes. Find it and it is yours."

"This is fantastic!"

"Isn't it? And so, Belle, I shall, of course, pay all of your expenses whilst you are 'me,' but if your pride makes you stick at accepting remuneration, find The Cat's Bracelet, if you can. I have no need of it, and it could support you quite nicely for the rest of your days, I should think, for Sebastian was quite extravagant. Or so they say," she finished coyly.

She rose and put Filbert down gently on the hearthrug. "I am to bed. Please, please, Belle, think on what I have said. And please, please, say yes!" She hugged her. "Give me your answer in the morning. Good night."

"Good night, Lillie."

A short time later, Belle crawled into bed beside Lillie, already soundly asleep, as if nothing out of the ordinary had occurred that day. She longed for sleep, but her mind refused to come to rest, as thoughts popped in and out of her head like fitful raindrops at the beginning of a summer storm.

Could she possibly do this? Would anyone discover her lie? Lillie swore not, but could she trust her newfound friend's complacency? She should just go on to Beaconsfield. And a life of boredom, at best, she reminded herself. If she did take Lillie's place, at least she would have a few months' memories of life among the *ton* before she went out to make her living. For she could not accept the gift of The Bracelet. Could she? Clearly, Lillie neither needed nor wanted it. Hmm. A diamond bracelet. Ethelbert's bracelet. Where could it be? Perhaps in a dusty cupboard that had been overlooked? Or maybe inside an old shoe? No, she could never accept it, but it might be fun just to look for it.

Something large and warm curled up heavily against her. Her attempt to push Filbert away was somehow interpreted as a desire for him to nestle closer. She heard a deep, sonorous purr—definitely smug, she decided groggily—felt a tickle of a proprietary whisker at her nose and slipped into a deep sleep.

By the time the rain stopped and the roads became passable, two days had passed and Belle was on her way to becoming quite familiar with her new friend's life.

Lillie had taken over the responsibilities of running the household at Burford at an early age. She had managed the staff, the household accounts and the menus. The family was small, Lillie having been the sole child of Matthew and Marguerite Charteris, and there remained only she, her father and cousin, Gore Lindley, after her mother's death. Actually, he was not a real cousin, but the child of close friends of Matthew and Marguerite. Following the deaths of his parents, he had come to live at Burford when he was just a boy, and Matthew Charteris had looked on him almost as a son. Gore had taught Lillie to ride, shoot and swim and they were as close as brother and sister. She had described him as a Corinthian who had bought his colors and been serving in the army on the Continent for many years, and she spoke with deep regard.

Whenever she could, Lillie would sneak away to follow Gore about, galloping across the fields or swimming in the nearby Windrush River. When she was not running wild, as her father put it, she had her head lost in a book about knights or far-off places. And, while her father indulged her, he often expressed his concern that she would never outgrow her hoydenish ways.

"But, my governess somehow made a reasonably respectable young lady of me. Then I met Randolph at one of our local assemblies. He had recently moved into the neighborhood, having tired of London, and was very popular with everyone. I had not really thought of marriage, because I wanted to travel and see exciting places, all the ones I had read about in my books. At the same time, I knew that such a choice was not open to me. I fell in love with Randolph, and when he offered for me, I decided to accept him and make the best of things. And I did. We were happy enough together in our fashion, although neither of us, I think, would have said we enjoyed a *grande passion*. Then, when he died— so young, just like his father before him—I grieved." Lillie drew a deep sigh. "More than I would have expected." She looked up to gauge the reaction of Belle, who smiled and nodded her understanding.

"Ah, I did love him, Belle."

"I know." Belle patted her hand.

"And so, after a time, that passed . . . into another place in my heart. That is when I began to think of going to Italy. I thought I had lost my chance, but now I am truly going! Oh, Belle, I do not know what I shall find there. Perhaps nothing. Perhaps everything. But, soon I shall know!"

Belle, too, shared stories of her past, but clearly Lillie would have little use for such information far away in Italy. Eventually, Belle protested that she could not fit another bit of Lillie into her head.

Lillie laughed. "You will make a wonderful 'me.' And you will have Warner to help you with my more recent history." She slewed her eyes toward her maid, who tried to contain a grin. "Just be certain not to believe everything she tells you! Had I but known I should need you for a testimonial, Warner, I should have increased your wages," she drawled.

"Well, it is too late for that, ma'am," Warner's eyes twinkled. "Now you can but trust me."

"Hmm. Of course, I would never stoop so low as to remind you of that ridiculous bonnet I gave you just the other week. Or the time you stayed in Bath with your weak chest whilst I muddled through without you all those weeks, or—"

"Oh, cut line, dear Mrs. Broadhurst." Warner chuckled. They laughed together, and Belle could see how fond they were of one another.

Belle had been most relieved to learn that she was to have Warner at her side, but had been concerned about Lillie. Surely she could not, would not, set out for Italy alone? It appeared at first as if Lillie would do just that, but as it happened one of the maids who served them at the inn had confided to Warner her desire to quit the place. She was a decent, well-spoken, middle-aged woman who had gained some experience as a lady's maid at The Rose Revived. Warner had advised her mistress of the situation and, before Belle knew it, Lillie had acquired Millicent as companion for her journey abroad.

The rain which swept through Oxfordshire and threatened to greatly expand the boundaries of the Thames, extended clear down to Newbury. A very bored gentleman sat at a table at the overpriced Pelican and stifled a yawn as he played his next card. Only boredom could drive him to cards, a pastime he otherwise considered fit for fools eager to part with their money, not that he did not have plenty to lose, sharps and nitwits. Having thankfully lost the hand, he ran long fingers through dark hair, tossed a few coins onto the table, and walked slowly upstairs to his room. Hooded green eyes glanced briefly out the window before Gore Lindley threw himself onto the bed. God, would this damnable rain never cease? At this rate, he would never reach Burford.

TWO

Belle leaned closer to the mirror, her breathing short and shallow. Before Lillie had left, she had felt a certain competence, had even entertained the thought that she might successfully play this role over the coming months. But all that had vanished when her caller was announced.

Aunt Eulalie. Here. God, she was not ready. Perhaps a few days from now, or next week. She could not for the life of her have said in what ways she could have further prepared herself for this moment during that hoped-for reprieve, for did she not know by now almost as much about Lillie as she did about herself? Yet, she had hoped to have enough time to attain a certain ease with her surroundings, never mind that Lillie had been as much a stranger in this house and in London as she.

During the few days Lillie had spent in the house in Berkeley Square before her emotional leave-taking of Belle, Warner and Filbert, she had demonstrated as little familiarity with her surroundings as did Belle. Still, Belle had hoped for just a bit more time to settle in, to brace herself for her coming trial, as at this moment, she was convinced it would be. She had only just begun to take on her new identity, to try it out on the world. Only yesterday she had ventured out to Grafton House to select fabric for new draperies, half expecting the proprietor to catch her out and publicly decry her masquerade. That, of course, had not occurred. He had accepted her, as had the household staff Aunt Eulalie had hired in anticipation of her niece's arrival, just as Lillie had assured her they would. She put her hands to her face, which was white with apprehension, and let out a tremulous breath. Dare she ask the Almighty for help in their deception? Belle decided that she did, then she pinched her cheeks ruthlessly, straightened the tucker at her bosom, took several deep breaths, stepped back from the mirror and walked to the drawing room.

Eulalie Broadhurst Singleton's spine, as straight as it had been in her girlhood, never touched the back of the chair on which she sat, parasol tightly furled, its sharp tip impaled in the rose-colored carpet on the floor. A companion of somewhat younger years sat close to hand. The older woman's outfit was of the latest stare, dark blue silk, almost black in a certain light, flounced at the hem and high at the neck, lathered in three rows of soft, expensive lace. Belle entered, took another deep breath, forcing a smile to her face, and crossed the room. "Aunt Eulalie! How good it is to see you. Only I would have come to you, you know."

The elderly woman raised rather cloudy blue eyes and squinted. "Lillith. Wait for *you* to come to *me?*" she retorted tartly. "I am not certain I have that many years left in my dish. If Constance Stevenson had not heard the clerk mention your name at Grafton's yesterday, I should never have known you had arrived in town. Ah, come here, my dear, and give me a kiss," she finished warmly.

Lillith! Lillie had neglected to mention her christening name. Belle complied but, when she tried to draw back from the kiss, Eulalie held her fast and peered closely into her face, squinting even harder. Belle froze. Would she lose all so soon? Eulalie held her gaze for some moments, then patted her cheek and smiled. "Pretty as ever, you are."

Belle, torn between guilt at her deception—she would have to get accustomed to that—and relief at its success, impulsively hugged the older woman. "Oh, Aunt Eulalie, you are kind to say so," she smiled. "You are looking wonderful."

"Nonsense, dear," she smiled in return, "I have not managed 'wonderful' in years. At my age, one strives merely to look presentable and fit, otherwise one is invited nowhere. This is my companion and friend, Barbara Tallboys. You will remember that I wrote you of Tabitha's passing," Eulalie said with a sad sigh of her previous companion.

"Yes, I was sorry to learn of it, Aunt. How do you do, Barbara?"

"I am pleased to make your acquaintance, Mrs. Broadhurst." The companion had a sweet smile and looked on her employer with fond patience.

They sat for a time drinking tea and talking of all that had passed since last they had met. Belle decided that she acquitted herself well enough. She had responded correctly to the mutual acquaintances and shared experiences of which Eulalie spoke—at least, she saw nothing in the older woman's demeanor to suggest that she had put a foot wrong. They spoke, too, of Randolph, and here Belle actually found the going the easiest, in that Eulalie contented herself with speaking lovingly of her nephew, necessitating only the merest murmurs of response. But, if Belle found relief at passing this part of her "test," she also again experienced a sense of shame and guilt at fooling the kind, old lady, and in such a matter. She shook her head and returned her attention to the conversation.

Presently, they heard a beating sound that seemed to emanate from the hallway off the morning room. When Belle opened the door to investigate, Filbert strode in, quite purposefully, walked without hesitation to Eulalie, and jumped into her lap. Evidently, he had been drumming his large back feet against the door to be let in; he had done much the same thing just the other day, when he had been accidentally shut in a closet. Thinking that Eulalie might take exception to this familiarity, not to mention the fur that he deposited wherever he sat, or the snags that his claws would inevitably produce in the fine fabric of her dress, Belle stood up.

"Oh, Aunt Eulalie, I am sorry. Filbert will do just as he pleases, and . . ." When she noticed the smile that wreathed that lady's face, she hesitated.

"Not at all, Lillie. What an elegant, little man you are, eh, Filbert?" "Elegant" and "little" were not words Belle generally used to describe the cat, who now stood in Eulalie's lap, rubbing his head against her chin and purring, not a claw in sight.

Belle looked from them to a portrait hanging on the newly painted wall, her eyes wide. The painting was of a lady past her middle years, in the dress of more than one hundred years ago. In her lap lounged a big cat. Belle had seen the painting before, but had not paid it much attention. The cat was white and grey, just like "little" Filbert, and he sported the same unfinished moustache. She blinked.

Eulalie followed her gaze. "That is Virginia and Ethelbert."

"He reminds me of Filbert."

"Of course he does, Lillie. There have been Broadhurst cats almost since there have been Broadhursts. Have you not seen the other portraits?"

She had. Paintings of long-past Broadhurst women were scattered about the house. Each of them portrayed a lady posed with a large cat. Belle had supposed it to be a tradition—the first Broadhurst lady who sat had been pictured with her cat, a real one, and subsequent artists had simply painted in similar felines to carry on the custom. It was only coincidence that Filbert had the same grey spot on his lip. Wasn't it?

"Do you mean that all of these cats were real?"

"What a silly question. Naturally they were real!"

"But, they all look rather alike." Eulalie smiled. "Oh, come, Aunt, you are not suggesting that the cats were related, too?" Come to think of it, they also had the same smug look that Filbert adopted when he had his own way.

"And why should they not be?" She stroked the cat lovingly. "Filbert here comes of a very noble line, as you can observe. Let me see," she closed her eyes in thought for a moment, "there were Lambert and Velbert," she paused. "And Flaubert, but he was on the French side of the family and, so, of no account." She dismissed him and his keepers with a sniff. "Oh, and Egbert, of course, to name just a few."

Belle choked back a snicker. "Noble" was another word at odds with her perception of Filbert. She saw him more as a large, fur-covered pillow, with feet and a sneer. She wondered if all the Broadhurst women had been mad—at least on the subject of cats. Lillie must have fit in quite well with her husband's ancestors. Well, there seemed no point in pursuing the matter. "Of course, Aunt Eulalie."

"Do you mean to look for The Bracelet, now that you are here?"

Her face lit up. "I do. I like treasure hunts."

"Good. Let Filbert help you. It could be that he knows the hiding place. The secret may have been passed down to him. As I have told you before, Filbert *knows* things, I can see it in his eyes." Belle contained a giggle. "Probably you have only to ask him in the right way and he will show you."

"I shall keep that in mind, Aunt."

"And so, my dear, what are your plans for your stay in London?"

"Well, I plan to keep rather to myself, you know. There is a great deal to be done here in the house, and I would like to work in the garden—it is in sad need of attention—then, of course, I shall visit the museums."

"Yes, that is all very well. So many people of our class come to town only to imbibe the heady wine of the Season, without a thought to partaking of the real treasures to be found here. I heartily recommend that you—did you say 'garden'?"

Too late Belle realized her error. Lillie loathed gardening, she knew that. Oh, how could she have forgotten? Her own enjoyment in caring for growing things had made her careless. Yesterday, she had closely examined the small, walled garden behind the house. It was overgrown, but she could see that it must once have been lovely and her hands itched to dig into the soil and restore it.

"As I recall, Lillith, you never cared for gardening. Said it was too much trouble for too brief a reward." She raised an inquisitive brow.

"Ah, well, Aunt, you are right." Eulalie's brows rose higher at this seeming contradiction. "Um, that is, I was *used* to feel that way, to be sure, but I have, of late that is to say, come to enjoy it enormously. So gratifying." She smiled a silly smile, praying that her explanation sounded plausible.

"Now, Lillith, that is quite enough. There is more to be said, certainly," Eulalie replied with some sharpness in her tone.

Belle gulped. Good Lord, Eulalie did not believe her. What should she do? "Why, Aunt, whatever do you mean? I have simply learned to appreciate the pleasures of growing things and I—"

"Yes, yes, so you said, my dear, I heard you. I mean, however, what else do you plan to do whilst you are here? I am the last one to encourage an existence given over to mere revelry, but neither do I spurn the myriad pleasures available to the *ton.*"

"Oh! Of course, Aunt! You are right. Absolutely." To Eulalie, Belle's relief had sounded like an eagerness to join in the Season—something she had never intended to do.

Eulalie went on, "Good, I am gratified to learn that you will be accepting invitations. There are so many things to do." She grinned and rubbed her hands together with anticipation.

"Oh, but Aunt Eulalie, I do not wish to go out much. As I was saying, the museums, the art—"

"Stuff. You are contradicting yourself, Lillith. You just told me you are itching to attend your first London ball," she exaggerated with an innocent smile.

"But, Aunt Eulalie—"

"Not another word, dear. I am convinced you are still knocked up from the journey. You must rest, and you will call on me in a few days. Then we shall sort through some invitations I have received, for you will be welcome wherever I am invited. And, soon, you will be deluged with invitations of your own, once it is generally known that my niece is arrived in town." Clearly, Eulalie intended to see to this accomplishment herself.

"But, Aunt, I only want—"

Helped to her feet by Barbara, Eulalie shook out the hem of her dress and peered closely at Belle. "And you should spend this brief respite seeing to a new wardrobe, for you will not have a moment once the Season is underway. Those things," she sketched a dismissive arc with her arm in the direction of Belle's plain gown, "just will not do here in town. No, no, not at all." She shook her head slightly and frowned. "Tsk, really, Lillith," she chided softly at Belle's apparent lack of sophistication. "I shall look for you on Monday. You know the address."

Belle's mouth was agape. Lillie had never mentioned just how forceful the old woman was. Belle had the feeling she would be saying the words "Lillie never mentioned" to herself many times over the coming months. She looked toward Barbara, who gave a sympathetic smile and shook her head, as if to tell her she was wasting time in protests.

"Yes, Aunt, I shall be there." Belle sighed.

After her guests' departure, Belle decided to go outside to escape the confinement of the house. She gathered gloves and a basket of small tools, and stepped through the French doors which gave onto the sunny garden. Two shallow steps brought her to a meandering stone path punctuated with Corsican mint, thyme and, now, weeds. The yard was oval in design and enclosed by a mellow brick wall. While not large, indeed it was almost intimate, the space was carefully planned to allow the inclusion of a variety of herbs and roses and two or three small trees.

She began the work which she hoped would calm her nerves but, if her hands were busy, her thoughts re-

mained on her predicament. Lillie had stayed only a
few days in London before departing on her adventure,
as they had all come to call it. The two had explored
the house in Berkeley Square together, examining the
rooms and furnishings, discussing new paint and wallpaper, color schemes, necessary repairs and furniture
arrangements. The stocks of linens, dishes and cutlery
were looked over with the aid of the housekeeper, and
Lillie had asked Belle to see to the necessary household
refurbishments in her absence.

Over the days before Lillie's leaving, Belle had marveled at her friend's handling of the difficulties they
encountered as they planned their campaign. She
would boldly attack a problem head-on. "Oh, come,
Belle, he is just the family banker, he does not know
me, nor I him. We shall just present ourselves in reverse,
as it were, and make the necessary arrangements. Don't
be such a goose!" Lillie's brash confidence had done
nothing to ease Belle's nervousness about that meeting,
and the former's reaction had been smug and gleeful
when they came away having easily arranged for Belle
to draw on Lillie's accounts and for Lillie to draw on a
letter of credit in Belle's name. On other occasions, she
simply refused to acknowledge the realities of her situation, such as when, how, *if* she would take her place
in London, once she returned from abroad. "How I
shall manage to reclaim my place here after all of this
is over, I cannot imagine." That she uttered these words
with grinning relish gave the lie to her seeming concern. "But, it is not as if I ever have to live here or, if
I should, it need not be for a very long time." Belle
wondered if Lillie had always approached obstacles in
such a fashion, or if this behavior were simply a dem-
onstration of her single-minded intention to have her
adventure.

As the time for her departure drew nearer, Belle grew more agitated. Time after time, she would ask Lillie to repeat "just once more" some detail of her past, and Lillie would patiently explain the asked-for details once again.

"Lillie, we may both have always lived in the country, but your life was far grander than mine. How shall I know how to go on? If I had a particle of sense, I should run while I still have the chance."

"You will do splendidly, just be more confident. And listen to Warner, for, believe me, she will tell you how to go on! And do trust Filbert."

"I beg your pardon?"

"Well, you can see he has already begun to take to you."

The feline in question reclined at the moment in Belle's lap, and she could not have run off if she tried. She looked down at him. "Yes, and I cannot tell you how pleased I am to have won his esteem." Her tone was very dry. "But, pray, tell me why I should trust him."

"Well, as you just agreed, he quite approves of you, Belle, and that counts for a lot."

"Good heavens."

"No, honestly. You see, Aunt Eulalie told me that she thinks Filbert 'knows' things." She held up a hand. "I know, I know, but I have come to rather agree with her."

Belle put her head in her hand. "Oh, heaven help me."

"Actually, I think he is very wise. He is a good judge of character . . ."

"Is he?"

"Yes. We once had a footman who had pilfered a few small items that we had never missed. Well, Filbert never liked that man, and one day we heard this terrible crash and what do you think we found?"

"I tremble at the thought."

"We found Jackson on the floor in the dining room, and in his pocket was a silver salt cellar. Filbert had caught him in the act and tripped him so that he fell into a jardiniere which, when it shattered, brought us all on the run." She looked pleased with herself following this long-winded tale. "So, you see, Eulalie was right, Filbert does know something. Well, actually, she seemed to mean something entirely different, although I cannot claim to know what. But, Filbert does know people, and you can trust to his judgment."

"Thank you, Lillie, I feel so much better."

Incredibly, this was lost on her friend. "Good, I made sure that you would."

Lillie's litany of encouraging words had continued unchecked, even as she stepped into the coach that would bear her to the coast, where she and Millicent would board ship for the Continent. It seemed that none of Belle's apprehensions had been able to dull Lillie's exuberant mood as she at last took the first steps of her journey. Still, when the two women faced one another and said their goodbyes, both drew ragged breaths. Lillie twisted her reticule between fussing fingers. This was the first evidence Belle had seen that she harbored any anxiety about what they were about to do. While she was relieved to find that Lillie actually seemed to grasp the gravity of the matter, she had not the heart to send her away downcast, and strangely, she herself began to feel a glimmering of anticipation.

"Oh, Belle, are we mad, do you think?"

"Yes, very like we are, dearest Lillie!"

Lillie gasped. "Should we . . . call it off? Belle, if you are truly set against this, I cannot force you to it. We can go away, the two of us, and have a wonderful, long holiday. I am certain that we should have our own sort of, of—adventure."

"You'll not fob me off with a few weeks in Brighton, my girl! You promised me a stay in London with all the trimmings, and I intend to have it!" Belle grinned broadly, hoping to set her friend's mind to rest.

"Oh, Belle!"

Both women laughed nervously and clung together. "Well, I suppose the horses must be restless. We must not keep them waiting any longer. Dearest Belle, take care. Do not worry! Just be happy and enjoy yourself!"

"And you, too, Lillie. Please do not do anything, well, too adventuresome!"

"I promise. And remember, I shall write and let you know where I can be reached. Depend on Warner to help you go on, she is a stout-hearted old thing." Warner gave a wry smile and patted her mistress's hand. "Goodbye, 'Lillie.' "

"Goodbye, 'Belle.' "

And, after a last crushing hug, "Belle" was off and the masquerade was on.

"Mrs. William Rafton to see you, ma'am."

"Oh. Thank you, Thomasina."

The maid bobbed her head and closed the door softly behind her. Belle wondered who her caller could be. Her time, of late, had been taken up with the purchasing of more fabric, meeting with the seamstresses who were stitching new draperies for several of the rooms, and directing the many workmen applying coats of paint and wallpaper and repairing various items. It had seemed that she could not turn around in the house without tripping over, or answering questions put by, any number of craftsmen. Thus it was that she had found no opportunity to meet anyone, let alone expect any callers. Whoever it is will just have to take me as I am, Belle decided, as she straightened her apron and her frilled cap.

A tall, lanky woman, simply but yet exquisitely dressed, rose when Belle entered. "Mrs. Broadhurst, how good of you to receive me. I know that we have not been introduced. I am Mrs. Cecily Rafton, your neighbor, just down the road," she smiled, "at No. 12."

Thank God, a stranger. "Not at all, Mrs. Rafton. It is very good of you to come. I fear I have been remiss in my calls."

Cecily Rafton had dusty blond hair, sparkling grey-blue eyes, which graced an otherwise rather homely face, and an easy grin. "But, how could you pay calls with things being as busy as they are here? Oh my, how rude. I fear you must think me a complete nosebody, and of course, I am, or so William, that is my husband, tells me. Only I could hardly help but notice all the workmen coming and going here. The place is a veritable beehive! I am convinced that I should not be bothering you."

Belle laughed. "Pray, do not feel so. With so much bustle here, one could not help but notice. And to say the truth, I am quite pleased to be taken away from it." She called for tea and bade her guest to sit.

Mrs. Rafton apologized for not having called sooner to welcome Belle to the neighborhood. "You are only recently come to town?"

"Yes, and for the first time. But all I have seen so far are the fabric warehouses."

"Dear, we shall have to see to that, though I must confess that being a conscientious neighbor was not my only reason for calling."

She looked about the morning room, the only place where the painters had finished. The walls had been painted a hyacinth blue and the decorative plaster-work sprays of roses which cascaded from the tops of the window frames and doors were a silky white. This room was Belle's favorite. In another light, this shade of blue might have appeared too cool, but the room caught the morning sun, which gave the color an almost sapphire cast without being overwhelming. The satinwood furniture gleamed in the sunlight, and the garlands of blue and pink in the thick carpet were the perfect accents for the blue walls and white flower trim.

Mrs. Rafton smiled widely in appreciation and nodded. "Oh, this is so lovely. I take it you have just finished in here; I can still smell the paint."

"That is correct. I am pleased that you like it. The color is rather unusual."

"Oh, yes, but it is perfect. I adore it! Well, as I was saying, I do have something of an ulterior motive." She hesitated, glanced at Belle, and laughed. "Mrs. Broadhurst, I am not one for roundaboutation, as you shall doubtless come to know if we are to be friends, and I hope that we shall. I am come looking for advice. There!"

"You wish me to advise you? In what way, Mrs. Rafton?"

"Why, this!" She waved long arms about her to take in the circumference of the morning room. "You see, No. 12 also is in need of work. We have not done anything to it in simply ages, well, apart from some furniture. I was hoping that you might share with me your recommendations for painters and such. But, now that I have actually seen the work, I must beg you for your own assistance, for I am sadly without a jot of taste or sophistication in such matters."

"Surely not," Belle exclaimed, admiring her caller's poplin gown of rich yellow and cream stripes, and her jonquil bonnet. "Why, just look at your gown. It is not only of the first stare, but elegant and perfectly suited to your coloring and figure. Never tell me this was all the work of your modiste."

Flattered, her caller replied, "No, that is true, it is my doing. When one is, ahem, blessed with a long, narrow figure such as mine, one learns to make the best of it." This in a very dry tone. "But I thank you. I enjoy all the shopping and planning for my wardrobe, and I do love to look nice. Sadly," she drawled, "this is where my accomplishments in the decorative arts begin and end. William agrees."

In response to Belle's raised eyebrows—really, this William did sound rather like a tyrant—Mrs. Rafton added, "Oh, do not think my dear William mean-spirited. If anything, he is overindulgent. Anyone who voiced no complaint—well, hardly any—about that hideous sofa with the sphinxes, is truly a man to be treasured. No, dear Mrs. Broadhurst, he loves me dearly and will let me have anything I want. Only now, he begs that I please have someone else do our decorating!" She grinned impishly.

"Certainly, I shall be pleased to give any assistance I can, but," Belle added quickly, "I have had little experience and can offer only my own opinions, that is, those things that I should like, which may not be what you and Mr. Rafton would care to live with. As to the other, I will gladly give you the names of the workmen and seamstresses."

Cecily and William Rafton were a true love match. This fact manifested itself in frequent, intimate smiles, a touch on a shoulder, the clasp of a hand. That these glances and gestures occurred no matter the company, and elicited neither discomfiture nor snicker from those about them, was testimony to their sweet naturalness.

They had been married some twelve years when, to their delight, they had at last produced a child, Phillip, who had just departed to spend several weeks with Cecily's mother. The couple spent the usual months of the Season and Little Season in town, and the remainder of the year at their estate in Gloucestershire, where each could pursue his and her particular interests. Where William was an indifferent rider, athletic Cecily was a born horsewoman and enthusiastic driver, who kept her own perch phaeton in town. Since her husband preferred birdwatching, she confined the use of her bow and arrow, which she enjoyed prodigiously, to stuffed targets. Each was possessed of an amiable, generous disposition and great sense of humor, often socializing and giving and attending entertainments with a wide circle of friends.

Upon her admittance to No. 12 later that day, Belle could hear laughter coming from upstairs. Entering the drawing room behind the maid, she saw Cecily and William, their heads together, as they looked out the window at some birds squabbling in a tree just outside. Her hostess jumped up from the bench in the window embrasure. There was becoming laughter still in her voice.

"Mrs. Broadhurst. Welcome. Please meet my husband, William. Dearest, this is the neighbor I told you about. Mrs. Broadhurst."

William Rafton was somewhat taller than his wife, and his dark hair was punctuated with premature strands of grey. He was comfortably dressed in merino trousers and morning coat, a scarf tied casually about his neck.

With an easy, genuine smile, he shook her outstretched hand.

"Ah, Mrs. Broadhurst," he gestured her to a chair, he and Cecily sitting opposite her. "You would be the very tasteful Mrs. Broadhurst of whom my lady wife spoke. Cecily has told me of the wonders you have wrought at No. 7. She also tells me of your generous offer to assist in our redecorating efforts. Not a moment too soon, ma'am."

"Mr. Rafton!" his wife slapped his arm playfully.

"Only tell me, Mrs. Broadhurst, in what way I may repay your kind efforts, for indeed you have agreed to assume a heavy burden," his eyes twinkled. "A new carriage and pair? No? Our son, perhaps?"

Cecily jumped up, arms akimbo. "William, you fiend! Stop! What will Mrs. Broadhurst think?" But she could not keep from joining in his and Belle's laughter.

Belle had not relaxed or so enjoyed herself in some time. She was pleased to find how easy she felt with these two people. "No, no, Mr. Rafton, I assure you, it will be no burden. Only," she added, sobering, "I must tell you that I have no particular gift for such an undertaking. I can only tell you how I have gone on at No. 7, and give you the odd suggestion and put you in the way of the appropriate shops and tradespeople."

"Good God, Mrs. Broadhurst, surely you see that I have had a surfeit of odd suggestions?" he gestured toward a table supported by a bizarre mythological beast. "I depend upon you for more than that!"

"Very funny," his wife drawled, and the three laughed again.

Grinning, he kissed her cheek and rose. "Mrs. Broadhurst, I hope you will forgive me, but I am engaged elsewhere this afternoon. I shall leave you both to your plans. My wife knows what I like—believe it or not!" His eyes sparkled.

"Oh, you!"

He put an arm about her and squeezed her gently. "Cecily . . . just try to think of our furnishings on a more, oh, well, mundane, level. Yes, yes, mundane, that should do it."

"Do you see what I must put up with, Mrs. Broadhurst? He is too impossible, is he not?"

Belle laughed all the harder. She liked her new friends, liked to see the affection that was so natural between them. She and Gilbert, too, had enjoyed a love match, but theirs had been a quiet, uneventful marriage, and she had sometimes yearned . . .

"I hope that we shall all be great friends, do you not, William?" Her husband nodded his agreement. "All right then, off with you. Do you stay at your club for supper?"

"I do."

Cecily took Belle on a tour of the house. The rooms were well proportioned and in good repair. While the drawing room had been expensively decorated, much of the furniture was to be replaced, she explained, pointing for emphasis at a rosewood side table whose legs were ornamented with snake-tailed goddesses. A few of the pieces were of Chinese taste, but most were of the Egyptian style. The latter had been all the rage a few years earlier, and Cecily had made her purchases based upon the popularity of the pieces, with little thought to either utility or their effect on their surroundings or the residents. Gaping lions, coiling serpents, clawing crocodiles and menacing sphinx heads and dragons glared at one another from various points in the room. The internecine conflicts amongst the furniture at No. 12 were waged without notice or interference by Cecily. Her friends did not tell her, since the same kinds of furnishings occupied the rooms of more than one of her set. And those whose preferences tended to less ostentatious chairs, quieter couches and tables without lotus leaves were too fond of her to report the war. William was too preoccupied with his ornithological pursuits to pay more than passing attention, and when he did, he was inclined to indulge his wife, rather than question her efforts.

Not long ago, however, he was heard to curse roundly, after barking his shin on a protruding mahogany wing.

"Oh, William, what happened? Did you bump into the table?"

Rubbing his damaged limb, he growled from between clenched teeth, "No, I did not. The damn thing attacked me. And it is not the first time!"

In the face of his discomfort, she tried to contain her chuckle, but was not entirely successful. She made a show of inspecting the table in question. "Well, at least *it* is not damaged."

"Would that it were!"

And then had followed William's confession that he found the furniture both uncomfortable and unpleasant in the extreme to look at, but had been too considerate of his wife's feelings to say so.

Cecily was contrite. "But, William, you promised me that you loved the furniture!"

"Not to say 'loved' exactly, my dear. Even for you I could not have gone that far. I believe I said that I 'liked' it. How could I not? It had been bought and paid for, after all, and it would be totally wasteful to redecorate all over again. And, besides, I did not want to hurt your feelings." She blinked and hugged him. "We shall change it all soon enough, my dear." He patted her shoulder. "Who knows, perhaps I shall grow used to it."

He chuckled, and although he did not refer to the subject again, Cecily, who now saw the furnishings through his eyes, came to detest them even more than he did. Some time later, she had seen all the work going on just a few houses away. With her outgoing nature, it had never occurred to Cecily to hesitate before calling on her new neighbor seeking advice and assistance.

The two women now sat in the morning room, sipping tea. The atrocities of the drawing room had not been committed here, but Cecily pointed out her desire "to just freshen the place—it has a decidedly shabby air, don't you think?"

"Not to say shabby, Mrs. Rafton, but as you say, you could just brighten it up a bit." Belle looked at the rather faded paper on the walls. "What would you think of yellow? That would brighten it considerably, I should think. The room does not seem to get as much sun as it should."

"You are right, it does not, because that tree has grown so that it blocks too much of the light. And I think yellows would be just the thing. We can look for fabric for draperies for here as well as the drawing room."

"I found Grafton House to have a nice selection of good quality material. Shall we try there? Would tomorrow suit you? I get the distinct impression that you wish to get this done as soon as possible."

Cecily laughed. "You are quite right, I am itching to get started. And Grafton House tomorrow sounds fine. Oh, and afterward, if you like, we can go to Layton and Shear, where I get most of the material for my gowns, and then to my dressmaker." Belle nodded her assent. "What do you think might be good colors for the drawing room?" She eagerly awaited her new friend's reply.

"Well, what do you and Mr. Rafton like?"

"Lord, Mrs. Broadhurst, do not trust it to me. After all, I chose that hideous gold you see in there now."

"Let's see." Belle tapped her chin thoughtfully. "Does a soft green appeal to you? You could accent it with white and a darker green, if you wish. That could look very nice."

"Good. Now, about the furniture . . ."

There followed a good deal of discussion concerning the desire for comfort and less ostentation, and the merits of Sheraton, Hepplewhite and Adam. As they talked, the afternoon slowly and companionably wore on.

Belle and Cecily departed Grafton House in New Bond Street, leaving behind a sizeable portion of the latter's household money, then spent a couple of hours at Layton and Shear choosing fabrics for Belle. After refreshing themselves at a tea shop, they visited Mrs. Niven, Cecily's favorite modiste. The shop was small, exclusive and very à la mode. Mrs. Niven gushed over Cecily, one of her most frequent and extravagant clients, declaring herself greatly pleased to have the dressing of Mrs. Broadhurst.

They were ushered into a tastefully decorated dressing room, where Belle's outer clothing was removed and her measurements taken. Mrs. Niven and Cecily circled her critically, murmuring their observations to one another. Belle stood "very still, please," gazing at the beautiful furnishings. This was a far cry from Mrs. Peabody's, the establishment of the seamstress at her home in Whichford. Her wardrobe here would be far grander than what she had been used to, and even though she hoped to keep her socializing to a minimum, her clothes must reflect Lillie's station and the fact that she was in London now, not a small town in the country. She was startled out of her reflections by a sharp clap, clap of the dressmaker's hands.

"We are finished, Mrs. Broadhurst. You still have a good figure, although you are rather petite." She smiled. "I shall dress you beautifully."

Cecily beamed, and Belle breathed a sigh of relief that this close examination was ended and she had been deemed acceptable. For some time, they discussed the newly purchased fabrics and colors, and pored over patterns and fashion plates in magazines. Cecily's suggestions were well received by Mrs. Niven.

"Mrs. Rafton has impeccable taste, Mrs. Broadhurst, you are most fortunate to have such a fashionable friend."

Belle herself offered only a few suggestions, realizing that she was rather out of her depth in matters of such finery, and most of her comments were restricted to preferences concerning color and fabric. By the time they left, the modiste had orders in hand for dozens of items, from exquisite undergarments to a complete range of day and evening wear. Mrs. Niven promised to have the bulk of the order ready as soon as possible, with several items to be delivered in a day or two. In the meantime, Belle would wear the things that Lillie had left behind, since the latter planned to augment her country wardrobe when she stopped in Paris.

She was taken aback by the cost of all this luxury, but was under strict orders from Lillie to disregard expense, and she forced her shock to the back of her mind. When she lived in Whichford, Belle had dreamed and sighed over back issues of *The Ladies' Cabinet*, never thinking she would ever have the chance to wear such lovely things. Goodness, looking at current copies of that magazine as well as *Ackermann's Repository*, and all the fashionable women she had seen since arriving in London, she realized how outdated had been her ideas of what was *à la mode!* Belle looked forward to wearing her new clothes. She was especially taken with a walking dress of Circassian cloth in a pale pistachio green. The long sleeves were capped with white lutestring epaulettes, and the same fabric formed two *rouleaux* just above the flounce at the hem, and trimmed the front and back of the high bodice.

After leaving the establishment of Mrs. Niven, there were more stops to be made for shoes, bonnets and fans at Covent Garden and, finally, at the recently built Burlington Arcade. Here, under the arched glass roof, they meandered back and forth across the nine-foot-wide aisle from one tiny, exclusive establishment to another. A beadle patrolled the area to ensure that no one broke the Arcade's code of conduct, prohibiting such unacceptable behavior as hurrying through the long passageway, whistling, singing and carrying bulky parcels. By the time Belle returned to Berkeley Square, she was too tired to worry about the expense that had so plagued her earlier. Indeed, she could not at that point imagine herself with sufficient energy to attend the myriad social events that required such a wardrobe.

Belle dutifully presented herself to Aunt Eulalie in Queen Street on the appointed day. A fire burned in the grate, and a white-haired man in a Bath chair sat near it, a colorful, long paisley shawl wrapped about his shoulders and extending to cover his knees. Uncle Aubrey, Eulalie's husband, had been confined to the chair since suffering an apoplexy many years earlier and, blessedly for Belle, had never been able to make the journey to Burford to meet Lillie.

He raised bright blue eyes. "Well, well, at last we meet. Or, have I been having another dream, Mother?" He looked inquiringly toward his wife.

"No, Aubrey," she smiled, "you have not. Lillie really is here, at last, as you say, and happy we are to have her."

"Uncle Aubrey, I am so pleased to finally meet you." Belle leaned down and placed a kiss on his cheek.

"Sit down here next to me, Lillie. Eulalie has been telling me of her plans to introduce you about. I hope you are well rested, my dear, for she has talked of all manner of balls and routs and such. I do not doubt but that she will have you cutting ribbons on statues with the Regent, himself. I think she wants to make up for lost time."

Eulalie chuckled and patted his hand, then sniffed. "Prinny is perhaps the last sort of person I would wish my niece to spend time with."

"Couldn't agree more. He is rather an arrogant clown, but that's something of a contradiction in terms, is it not? At any rate, Lillie, Eulalie was quite the society belle in our day, used to like to dance her shoes off. Haven't had much fun in years, now have you, dear?"

"I get about quite enough, Aubrey, do not fret."

"Pah! You would say that anyway. Spend far too much time cooped up in this house with me. Should get out more. And now you have good reason to do so!"

Belle detected a reddening of Eulalie's cheek. Of course! She was looking forward to the Season with Lillie. Well, she could hardly refuse the old woman's *entrée* now that she knew that, could she?

"I look forward to the Season and to spending time with Aunt Eulalie and with you," she assured him.

"Good. Come to see us often, I hope. Always welcome." He turned to his wife. "My dear, I am tired and want to sleep. Please ring for Parker."

After he had left, Aunt Eulalie sighed. "He likes to tease me about liking balls and such, which I do. What he does not say is how much he liked them. He really never leaves the house any longer, and strangely, he seems content with that."

"His illness does not seem to have affected his mind."

Eulalie nodded. "Thank heaven for that blessing. Actually, we have been talking about selling this house and moving to the country. I think he would like the fresh air and scenery."

"So, this will be your last Season in town, then? Well, I must tell you I am eager to begin, Aunt Eulalie. It is very kind of you to help me."

"Oh, not at all, Lillie. We shall have a marvelous time. Now, I have been going through my invitations." She reached for a small stack of vellum envelopes at her elbow and sifted through them, annotating as she examined them through thick spectacles.

"I think that we should start by attending the tea Mrs. Templeton is giving on Wednesday." She peered at Belle over her spectacles. "That is the day after tomorrow, you know. What have you done about your wardrobe, Lillith?"

"I went shopping with a new friend, Cecily Rafton, last Friday, Aunt. Everything is in hand. In fact, I must go for a fitting tomorrow. I am sure I shall have something suitable."

"Good. If your friend did not tell you, J & J Holmes in Regent Street is very good for shawls. Now, Mrs. Templeton's is a very smart set, so this will be a good place for you to begin." Lillie nodded. A tea sounded harmless enough.

"Then, the Deverells are having a small rout that evening. You will like them, and it will be a good chance for you to get your feet wet, as it were, at a society party." She glared at the next invitation and tossed it aside with disdain. "Good heavens, how did that get in here? *Not* people you want to know, dear." She turned through more of the cards. "Ah, here. The Binghams. Fine people. They are having a musical evening on Friday. That will be quite nice, I am sure."

Belle was feeling overwhelmed, but remembered that this was Eulalie's last chance to enjoy life among the *ton* in London. She smiled. "It all sounds wonderful, Aunt Eulalie."

THREE

Since Gore Lindley had an old acquaintance with the Bingham family, he was readily admitted to their house for the musicale. He had been in town only a couple of days and had called on his "cousin," Lillie, in Berkeley Square earlier that day, but found her from home. Belle had fortunately been at Mrs. Niven's shop for another fitting. Having other matters to attend to, he could not await her and said he might return that evening, but the parlormaid had explained that her mistress had been invited to an entertainment at the Binghams'. He decided to seek out Lillie there.

"I wish to surprise Mrs. Broadhurst, so please do not mention that I called," he advised the maid.

Now he stood, eyes searching, and at last spied her across the room. He smiled with old and deep regard and began to walk toward her, when he was stopped momentarily by an old friend.

At the last minute, Eulalie had decided she should stay at home with Uncle Aubrey, so Belle had come to the Binghams' alone. She had felt out of place at first, but the company was friendly, and she had begun to enjoy herself. She now sat with a glass of punch, listening to the aria being sung and casting her eyes about the room. Goodness, that was a devilish handsome man, she thought, catching sight of Gore and admiring the natural dark waves of his hair. Not wishing to be seen staring, she inclined her head more toward the singer, but turned her glance sideward to catch another glimpse of him. I wonder who he is?

Gore halted his progress two or three feet from Belle and looked more closely at her. Damn funny, he considered, somehow she looks rather different. Oh well, it has been many years, old man, he told himself, she is just older, that is all. As are you! But, as he approached, her appearance became more troubling. He could not put words to it, she looked very like Lillie, but something was a bit off. Come on, old son, who do you think it is? How many people could look just like Lillie—for she did—and not *be* Lillie?

Belle looked away quickly. Gracious, the man seemed to be walking her way. What should she do? She fanned herself. For heaven's sake, stop thinking like a schoolroom miss. After all, you have conversed with many men, and he is not likely to bite. She turned and gave him a formal smile, as he reached her side.

"Lillie! Lillie, don't you know me? Has it been so very long? Or, is it because I am such a poor correspondent that my infrequent letters have made you cool toward me?" he bantered. His eyes sparkled with wit, but watched carefully for her reaction, for he was now certain that this woman was not who she claimed to be.

Belle swallowed. Who on earth was he? She flew desperately through her mental catalogue of friends and acquaintances, that is, all those people whom Lillie had assured her she would "have so little chance of encountering."

She could hear her friend's laughing voice, "Mr. Paxton Blount. A nice gentleman, several years above our age and rather pleasant to look on. But, oh Belle, the clumsiest man alive, I do swear it. He trod on my flounce, not once mind you, not even twice . . ." Her handsome inquisitor stood watching her, with natural, athletic grace. No, this was not Mr. Paxton Blount.

Oh, Viscount Fremont! Yes! ". . . such a dedicated sportsman, shooting, riding to hounds. And so handsome, hair as fair as can be and . . ." This pest looked as if he spent every waking hour exercising out of doors, but his hair was as black as coal. Well, not the Viscount, then. Oh, why did he not just go away?

She skimmed madly through more names and descriptions as he gazed questioningly at her. It had to be Lyman Newley. Was he not ". . . dark as a Spaniard, my dear, and the greenest eyes. . . ." So far, so good. ". . . terribly handsome . . ." He certainly fit that description. ". . . but, my dear, he barely came up to my chin!" Belle blinked up at the gentleman who so patiently awaited her response. "Oh, dear," she breathed, then gasped, not having intended to speak aloud.

"I am sorry, Lillie, what did you say? Do stop quizzing me for heaven's sake!" When he tilted his head, suiting movement to his question, the light caught a small scar at the top of his left cheekbone.

"And, Belle, one day when he was teasing me, I threw one of my dolls at his head, clobbered him with it, actually. Well, for pity's sake, I was no more than five or six, Belle! It did leave a little scar though, just above his left cheekbone."

She smiled. "Gore, how good it is to see you again."

He threw back his head and laughed. "You do know me, minx."

He wondered at that, but guided her toward a sofa in a far corner that would afford them as much privacy as they were likely to find in the crowded room. "She's quite good, is she not?" Gore said.

"Who? Oh, the singer, yes. Mrs. Halliday. She seems to have a gift one seldom hears in an amateur."

Across the room, Mrs. Halliday stood elegantly beside the piano which was played by a much younger woman, in fact, her daughter. Her voice, clear and clean as a bird's on a spring morning, sang of love in the Italian of Rossini.

He looked closely into Belle's face. Just as pretty as Lillie. Really, the likeness was extraordinary, he noted, but she was definitely not Lillie, he could feel it. Then, who is she, he wondered. And where is my cousin? Is this one of Lillie's mad pranks? No, not in her line. Could this woman be an actress? Had she brought some harm to Lillie and was now trying to take her place? Could this all be for Lillie's fortune? These thoughts all collided in his brain like so many billiard balls after the first stroke. It seemed unlikely to him that his strong-minded, old friend could have been gulled, that she would have been foolish enough to let someone take advantage of her. Lillie would give as good as she got, he knew. Then, what was it? He had to get to the bottom of this.

"Well . . . Lillie," he nearly choked on the name, "after returning to England I traveled to Burford only to find you had come here. Your father sends his love, by the way."

"Oh, dear Papa. Was he well when you left him?"

"Quite well and missing you a bit, I think. When did you arrive? How did you find the journey?" Anything to draw her out.

"I arrived almost two weeks ago. The journey went well, apart from being stranded a day or two in Newbridge due to a storm. The roads were impassable, but the inn, a lovely old place called The Rose Revived, was very nice. We all liked it quite a lot."

" 'All?' Did you have traveling companions?"

She recovered quickly. This was beginning to get easier. "Oh, Warner and I. She is my maid."

His eyes narrowed. "Your maid?"

"Yes."

"But, you said 'all,' Lillie, that generally means more than two. Was there someone else with you?" He tried to keep his tone light.

She hesitated. "Of course not, Gore, who else would be traveling with us?"

Her hesitation was just long enough to plant a seed in his already suspicious mind. "I have no idea. A friend, perhaps?"

"No, no, it was just us, I assure you." This time, her response was a little too quick.

"Of course, my dear. Just the two of you. Well, how do you like London? Is it all you had imagined?"

She smiled. "I like London, although I confess that I have not seen much of it."

"Not to worry. Now that I am arrived, I shall take you to see all the sights. You may depend on me, old girl. And I shall happily escort you to all the usual society functions. That is," he grinned, "until you find another gentleman whose company you prefer more."

Belle groaned inwardly. "Too kind," she managed, "but, you see, I had not thought to go out much into society, I—"

Gore laughed. "Do not gammon me, Lillie, I know you too well, remember? You wrote me how confined you felt at Burford, and Uncle Matthew told me that, actually, you had desired to go to Italy, but he talked you out of it. He rather regrets that, incidentally. Since you settled for London, I make no doubt that you must wish to take full advantage of all it has to offer. I promise to keep you very busy."

Belle did not seem to be able to exhale. Good God, he sounded like Aunt Eulalie. How could she extricate herself from this? To demur further would be rude. "I . . . I suppose that I might."

"Good, but you do not seem exactly enthralled at the prospect. Am I not a presentable escort?" he teased.

"But of course you are, Gore!" What woman would not be thrilled with his company? Oh dear, she was getting in deeper and deeper. "Tell me, have you left the army? After all these years?"

"Yes, I have had my fill of the barracks. It is time I found a wife and settled into a comfortable country life."

Belle knew that Gore had little fortune to boast of. Perhaps he was hanging out for a rich wife. She glanced at his smart clothes. Money well spent on the right wardrobe, and his good looks and manners would assure him at least a head start with many a young miss. "Ah, and about time, too. If I should come in the way of an eligible young woman, I shall tell you."

Yes, he thought, I suspect you will be on the lookout yourself for a rich husband, in the event your present endeavor is unsuccessful.

"Splendid. My dear, business calls me away for a few days, but I shall call upon you when I return."

"I shall look forward to it."

Gore left soon after, and Belle collapsed against the back of the sofa, her fan fluttering as rapidly as her heart.

Gore's arrival and departure, and everything that went in between, had not gone unnoticed by the Binghams' other guests, particularly the females. He was rather above average in height, and his movements and figure suggested that he would strip to great advantage. And then, he was of a pleasing, though hardly garrulous disposition, a man who would bend a respectful ear to dowagers, share a joke with his peers, and cast a very appreciative eye to a well-turned ankle.

He had left England with a subsistence, but years of wise investing had made Gore Lindley a very rich man, not that he intended to let on the extent of his bank account to the matchmaking mamas or the fortune hunters. No, he planned to let everyone think he was no more than comfortable, and in that way, he hoped to find a woman who would love him for himself.

Thus, those at this evening's entertainment, those who had a particular interest in his potentiality as a husband, and, consequently, his finances, would glean over the next day or two only that he was merely comfortably set, and with no title to recommend him, neither. As this information flew through Kensington and was passed from street to square in Mayfair, more than one parent with a daughter who needed to marry well sighed and crossed another name from the list of eligibles. Luckily, the crop of gentlemen the past couple of Seasons had been bountiful, now that the evil Napoleon was, at last, a name to be mentioned only in history books or war anecdotes. And so, Gore would have his wish, the fortune hunters would leave him in peace and he would be at his leisure to find his wife.

Early the morning following the Bingham party, he took himself off on the "business" he had mentioned, to Newbridge to visit The Rose Revived. He was, ostensibly, a traveler breaking his journey at the old inn. It was easy to engage "Frederick Q. Hapgood, Prop." in conversation. Over a pint in a quiet corner of the taproom, Gore explained that he had chosen the inn at the recommendation of a friend's sister, a Mrs. Broadhurst, who had stayed there recently and very much enjoyed its amenities.

"Oh, yes, Mrs. Broadhurst," the man said thoughtfully.

"You recall her?" Gore could not believe his luck.

Hapgood nodded emphatically. "I do. Indeed I do. Be hard not to. That would have been during that awful rainstorm we had. She was here. She and her cat, that is."

"Did you say, cat?"

"That's correct, a cat. Big bruiser of a feline he was, too. Wouldn't have minded having him as a mouser, I can tell you. Oh! Er, that is, not to say that we have such vermin in this establishment, you understand."

"Of course not," Gore assured him smoothly. "Still, it is odd that you should remember her."

"Not a bit, sir. It was a somewhat . . . unusual . . . turn of events, you might say. She and that other lady and all."

"Other lady, did you say? Was she traveling with a companion, then? Her maid, I assume?" he inquired, although it was unlikely that even an innkeeper would describe a maid as a lady.

"No, no, not her maid. Well, that is to say, she did, of course, have her maid with her. She was a lady of quality, after all. No, I meant that other lady that she met here, after she arrived."

"Ah, I see. I expect they had arranged to rendezvous here to continue their journey to London together."

"No, no, that wasn't it, either. She didn't know the other lady and the other lady didn't know her. Not at first, that is. You see, that day—and the next, and the next, come to that—we were full to overflowing, I'm happy to say. Because of the storm, you know. And, then, we're a small inn, as you can see, sir. Good for business, although I suspect the travelers weren't so pleased about it. Had them sleeping everywhere, we did, 'cause we ran out of rooms early on. The Maybush, just over the road on the other side of the bridge, was full-up, too. Why, there was this one dandy who . . . Well never mind, that's another story for another day, as they say. No, this lady, the second lady, that is, arrived after your friend's sister. All soaked she was—the second lady, not your friend's sister—and nowhere to go, as none of the coaches could travel any farther.

" 'I would like a room, if you please,' she says, real polite. 'Well,' I says—and not for the first, nor the last time that day, I can tell you—'there be no more rooms, we're full up.' Just then, your friend's sister, Mrs. Broadhurst, showed up and offered to share her room. Just like that! Can you imagine? I was that amazed, I can tell you. Well, to make a long story short." Gore managed not to laugh, "she took her in and they seemed to become fast friends."

"Extraordinary."

"Didn't I tell you? Another strange thing. They looked almost like twins."

"Remarkable! Do you recall the other woman's name?"

"Hmm, let me think. Macintosh, was it? No. No." He drummed a finger against his chin. "Began with—wait, ah, Makepeace, that's it. Don't remember her given name, though."

"Was she in a private coach, also?"

"No, she was on the public stage. And she was a lady, but not well-off like Mrs. Broadhurst. She had just the one case and her clothes were good, but plain. You know, not fashionable."

"My friend never mentioned such unusual circumstances."

"I daresay she didn't tell him. He probably would have had a fit if he'd known she was taking in strangers. But wait, Mrs. Broadhurst was going on to Italy. How did she come to tell you of her stay here?"

Gore nearly choked. *Italy?* "Oh, uh, well, she wrote to her brother and, um, mentioned this place. When I found that I would be journeying in this direction, and not knowing the neighborhood, I decided that Mrs. Broadhurst's encomium was good enough reason for me to stop here. So, yes, Italy. Well, er, I knew that she was there. But, how did you? Did she mention it?"

"Mention it? I should say she did. Quite excited about it, she was. Deprived me of a good maid too, in the bargain, her and her trip to Italy."

Gore pondered this information all the way back to London. It was fantastic. Lillie had left Burford to spend the Season in London, met with this stranger, evidently switched places with her and had gone haring off to Italy, leaving said impostor in her place. As a girl, Lillie had pulled more than one prank, doubtless rebelling against the restrictions that her responsibilities placed upon her younger years. But, this was the outside of enough. How could she do something so mad? She did not, apparently, even know this woman and yet she had entrusted her with her very identity. And her fortune! Gore knew that Lillie was a very rich woman, and this creature, who clearly was not, could do God knew what with all that money whilst its rightful owner was away. This Makepeace woman must have taken advantage of her somehow.

He knew that he needed more information. Gore and Lillie shared the same banker. He had not yet been there since his return to England, so a visit to Faraday and Prine was necessary for his own affairs and, at the same time, he would see if they could, or would, tell him anything of this insane matter.

In the event, once his own business was concluded, it was not difficult to get Mr. Prine to indulge his curiosity. The size of Gore's account with the firm and the gentleman's return home after so many years of serving his country only to find his cousin flown to Europe were sufficient to loosen the banker's tongue.

His tone and manner were obsequious. "Ahem, you will appreciate, I know, that I should not discuss another client's affairs, but you are family, sir. Actually, as it happens, I know very little. Mrs. Broadhurst came to me a couple of weeks ago with her friend, Mrs. Annabelle Makepeace. The latter lady was to leave for the Continent in a day or two, to visit Italy for a short time, and Mrs. Broadhurst arranged for a very generous letter of credit for her. She also made the necessary arrangements for drawing upon her own account during her stay in London." He sniffed with some disapproval. "As I understand it, a local Burford firm handles her household accounts in the country." He paused. "Rather startling, really."

"In what way?"

"Their appearances, sir. They look very like one another. I thought at first that they must be related."

"I see. And can you tell me, has Mrs. Broadhurst had occasion to draw yet upon her accounts? Ah, as her oldest friend, I feel a certain, well, responsibility you understand. Her first visit to London, and on her own at that. Women can be notoriously profligate, can they not, especially without a man to guide them." God, he thought, Lillie would murder him for that.

"Of course, of course. Well, I must admit—but you did not hear it from me, you understand?"

"Naturally not."

"Well, I must say that she has been spending rather large sums, as it happens."

"Has she indeed?"

Gore considered all he had learned, as he sipped his brandy that evening. Annabelle Makepeace. A good name for a schemer, he decided illogically. He never would have believed that Lillie could be such a wantwit. Well, Mrs. Makepeace had enjoyed her last day of un-fettered abandon at his cousin's expense. He intended to expose her, and in the process, he would see to it that she sweated for every farthing she was so gleefully spending. He also reminded himself to find another banker. This one had a loose tongue.

Belle dug happily in the hardened earth surrounding a large, long-neglected clump of germander. Working in her garden at home in Whichford had been a plea-sure, and she had been most capable. Since arriving in London, she had spent happy hours weeding, pruning, weeding, cutting back and *weeding*. It seemed her efforts were definitely, her lips curled in a happy smile, going to bear fruit. The day was sunny and warm, and she had been toiling for some time. Sitting back on her heels, she used her apron to mop the dampness from her brow and neck, carelessly smearing both with dirt. Oh, well, she decided, it is a good thing that this garden is walled, so no one can see me.

Surveying her work, she gave a smile of satisfaction, for the plants really were the better for her efforts. The lavender—her particular favorite—myrtle, everlasting, and purple sage showed definite signs of promise for recovery, although what appeared to have been yarrow probably would not survive, or would give a poor show-ing, at best. There was a variety of roses, some climbing up the brick wall, but most were old roses—damask, cabbage and musk. They had grown lanky and scraggly over the years, but Belle believed her pruning would yield good results when they bloomed in midsummer. A specimen medlar tree was planted slightly off-center in the garden, its unruly branches beginning to display its white and blush pink flowers. In the late fall, she could pick its small brown fruit, finish the ripening on a shelf in a cool place, and try to make a preserve. But, she remembered, I will not be here then. Perhaps Lillie . . . She chuckled to herself, trying to picture her friend preparing the preserve. Highly unlikely. It was not that Lillie was lazy, simply that she did not have the patience for such a task. Oh, well, she might have one of the staff do it. Belle had read that the medlar made for excellent preserves, and it would be a shame to waste the fruit again this year. In any event, both the medlar and the fruit tree espaliered on the wall were in need of pruning and shaping, but that work she would leave to an expert.

Belle returned to the germander. Its glossy, dark green leaves would be dotted with tiny flowers in the summer. If all went well, the whole garden would be a profusion of color, texture and fragrance. Lemon and peppermint fragrances would waft upward as she walked along the garden path, bruising the thyme and Corsican mint that pushed their way up between the stones. The myrtle which decorated another section of the brick wall would be sprinkled with white flowers whose perfume would mingle with the roses in July. She planned to spend much time here on the bench reading or just throwing the doors open to enjoy . . . Belle stopped in mid-thought and again reminded herself that she might not be here then. For one thing, Lillie was uncertain just how soon she would return. And what if I make a muddle of things, she wondered. If I am found out, probably by that awful cousin of hers, I shall have to leave here. It makes me feel a bit like Cinderella.

Despite Gore's assurance that he would call on her in a few days' time, his continued absence after more than three days led her to indulge the foolish hope that he might never come. In her less desperate moments, she felt that, since he had accepted her in appearance, surely her training under Lillie would see her through the rest of the way. Now I know how an understudy must feel when the leading lady cannot take the stage, she told herself dryly. If only I do not succumb to a fit of nerves, I can play this role. Her relationship with Aunt Eulalie was sufficiently difficult and volatile, but at least she had been prepared for it, for all that she had dreaded it. And it seemed to be progressing well. Once Gore met the old lady, as certainly he would, and saw her acceptance of Belle, it could only add to her authenticity. Her village life had been so quiet and simple, it had not prepared her for such subterfuge, and the tension from it all was beginning to tell on her.

Well, in the meantime, she decided, I think I shall follow Lillie's instructions and enjoy myself. Or try to. Perhaps, I shall accept some of those invitations which have begun to arrive—not that Aunt Eulalie will allow me to do otherwise. She sighed. And I shall be able to wear some of my beautiful new clothes, just as Lillie insisted. For her sake, I have to present myself fashionably, that is, present Lillie fashionably, or myself as Lillie, or . . . Oh dear, sometimes I am not sure that I remember who I am or who I am supposed to be! She dug more vigorously. And, of course, I would not want Gore to think that Lillie has become a dowd in her advancing years. That would never do. A gentleman as handsome as he would certainly expect her to be presentable, would he not? She could hardly be seen with him unless she looked her best, er, Lillie's best. Oh, there I go again, she realized. "Damn!"

"My, my, such language from the lips of a lady."

Belle froze at the sound and peeked reluctantly over her shoulder back at the steps into the house. Gore. She shut her eyes in mortification and drew in breath to still her suddenly fast-beating heart.

"Gore. I did not know that anyone was there."

"Apparently." He smiled, his brows raised. "Was it that pathetic-looking weed you were cursing at?" He took the two shallow steps in one stride and stood at her side.

"What? Oh, no. This is germander, teucrium is its Latin name, and it is not a weed at all, but a lovely flowering plant. It has just been sadly neglected." She stood and tucked some stray curls under her straw bonnet, adding to the grime she had deposited on her face earlier. Nervously, she smoothed her apron and removed her gardening gloves, while attempting to gather her wits. She looked at the gloves covered with soil and realized what she had just done, then remembered the dirt she already had on her face and neck. Her composure, what there was of it, disappeared. She raised a hand to try to rub off some of the dirt and caught his eye. He was chuckling, and she wasn't sure if she wanted to kick him or bury herself beside the germander.

He removed a pristine square of white linen from a pocket and with one hand held her chin, and with the other brushed off some of the now-dried dirt. "You present quite a picture, cousin." He laughed.

"Oh, indeed, I make sure that I do," she retorted with a wry smile. Idiot, she told herself. Here you were not five minutes ago planning for him to see you only in fine gowns, while you cannot even present him with a clean face and apron. "I got carried away, you see. I always do when I garden, it is so calming, you know." Oh, really, Belle, how would he know? The man probably did not have a nervous bone in his body.

"Yes, I can see what you have been doing, Lillie. What I do not understand is why."

Belle blanched. She had done it again and with the same thing, the blasted gardening! I swear, she promised herself, if I ever get out of this, I will never pick up a trowel again. To Gore, she merely replied coolly, "Well, Gore, it has been many years, as you reminded me the other night. People do change, you know. I have come to enjoy this pursuit quite a lot. Surprised even me, I must confess."

Confession is just what I am waiting for madam, Gore thought to himself, but I do not think I shall get it easily. "Naturally, my dear. One could hardly expect you to remain just as you were, after all, could one? I daresay there are many things about you that have changed."

She nodded heartily. "Right. Oh, my, yes. Why there probably are just dozens of things about me that are fantastically different than they used to be! You are absolutely correct! And then, of course, there undoubtedly are many things that have changed about you and still others that we simply misremember about one another," she added almost breathlessly, rather pleased with her obfuscation.

"Do you think so? Perhaps. But, I must believe that in the important things, those which really matter, do you know, we still are quite as we once were. Do you not agree?"

"No, er, that is to say, um, well, we may be, Gore, and then again, we may not," she pointed out as they walked into the house.

He looked down at her with a peculiar glint in his eyes. "Quite."

They sat sipping lemonade after she had gone to her room to wash and remove her apron.

"Well, Lillie, do you still dream of visiting Italy?"

"Oh, I do not know, Gore. I find that I am enjoying London so much that I have not really given it any thought. Please, have another macaroon."

"You surprise me. You were so intent on it, even learning to speak the language. I was quite impressed."

"Speak the . . . !" Belle choked on her lemonade and a few drops fell onto her bosom.

"Look out, you've dribbled down your, er, front, old girl. Not the done thing, you know." He leaned forward to wipe away the drops.

"*If* you do not mind!" she snapped, taking the linen square from his hand. "And I do wish you would not call me 'old girl,' it makes me feel ancient."

He smiled. "I shall endeavor to remember, but you did write me, did you not, that you were studying Italian?" He knew quite well that Lillie had written no such thing.

She could hardly bluff her way through speaking a foreign language. She would have to brazen it out. "No, Gore, I did not," she replied sweetly and returned his handkerchief. "Whyever did you imagine that I had?"

"My mistake. Now I think of it, I recollect it was Louis Selby's elderly aunt who was learning Greek before a trip to the Peloponnese."

Belle laughed. "Oh, thank you very much."

Gore put his glass on the zebrawood Pembroke table at his side and settled back in his chair. "Do you go to Lord and Lady Tipton's ball on Saturday?"

"Yes. Aunt Eulalie and I."

"Ah. And how is she?"

"Well. Quite well. She has taken me under her wing and introduced me into society," Belle explained.

He decided that, rather than exposing her right away, it might be more enjoyable to see first how she would behave. "Then I shall escort you both. I'll call for you first, and we can go on to Eulalie's house."

Belle managed to tell him how pleased she was with his offer.

FOUR

Belle welcomed her first rainy day in London. She liked the rain, her stay in Newbridge having been the exception to the rule. It watered her garden and gave her the chance to curl up with a cup of tea, some gingerbread and a book. But this morning, when she was wakened by the growl of thunder, she had other plans. She dressed in one of her own older frocks and an apron, and covered her hair with a kerchief, after turning in front of her mirror yet again to admire the new coiffure she had acquired since coming to town. Filbert leapt onto the dressing table and she marveled at the agility of such a large cat. She looked at his reflection in the glass.

"Well, Filbert, today we begin our search for Ethelbert's bracelet. Let's have our breakfast and then we can start with this room. My guess is that it was Virginia's bedroom. Who knows, we may find that he hid it right here." If asked, Belle could not have said when she first began to talk to the cat.

Two hours later, Belle had acquired nothing more than a stray hairpin and the knowledge that the housekeeping staff was unusually diligent. Indeed, she could not conceive how the hairpin had been missed. She sat on a chair by the window and peered out at the rain.

The cat, who had been no help in her effort, now lay staring smugly at her from atop a low armoire, his front paws hanging over the side. Purring loudly, he shifted and settled more comfortably in his spot.

She looked up at him. "Filbert?"

Louder purring.

"I do not suppose you have found something up there?"

The room fairly rumbled.

"You are quite right, I did not look up there. More fool me."

She brought her chair to the side of the armoire and climbed up. The chair was not high enough, however, to allow her to see the top of the cabinet. She reached up blindly and extended an exploratory hand. Filbert batted it away.

"Stop that." She continued her effort. Filbert nipped at the intruding paw.

"Wretch! Oh, this is not working."

Belle climbed down and looked about her. She spotted two large books that might give her sufficient elevation, put them on the chair and carefully stepped back up. The books brought her eye to eye with the cat, who lazily licked her nose.

She managed to look around his large body, which covered a good portion of the cabinet's top, but found nothing.

"Well, if you are anything like your predecessor, you are lying on it! Come on, move!" She gave him a gentle shove, but could not budge him. He shut his eyes. "Filbert!" She pushed again, with greater force this time, and he rose, spitting at her, his mouth wide. The movement startled her and she drew back sharply. Fortunately, just before she toppled over, Belle caught a glimpse of the cabinet's top and saw that it harbored neither dust nor bracelet.

"Oh!" She fell in an undignified, but unharmed, heap on the soft carpet. Filbert jumped down and landed gracefully beside Belle.

"Stupid cat!" His disdainful look clearly questioned who was the stupid one, and he waddled from the room.

By the end of the day, Belle had searched the three other bedrooms and the linen cabinet with no more success than she had had in her own room. Filbert had offered no assistance.

When Belle and Gore arrived at the Singleton house, he renewed his acquaintance with Aunt Eulalie and visited with Uncle Aubrey before they departed. The Tiptons' ball was one of the first major events of the Season, and turned out to be a terrible crush—in short, a resounding success.

Aunt Eulalie was wearing a ball dress of violet silk, its hem decorated in narrow bands of dark green velvet. She wore a small violet toque and the lush Singleton pearls. Belle's coquelicot India muslin with narrow stripes of black had a quilled double flounce banded just above in jet beads, which also trimmed the low, tight corsage. A wreath of silk red and black poppies with jet stamens circled the brown waves of her hair. Cecily and William Rafton also were in attendance, the former stunning in dark green silk with a daringly low corsage.

Eulalie introduced Gore and Belle to several people, then met up with some old friends and took a seat by the side of the room. Gore claimed the first dance, a quadrille, with Belle. After this rigorous exercise, she danced with William Rafton while Gore partnered

Cecily, then stood fanning herself as an acquaintance introduced her to Mr. Charles Goodwin. He bowed and looked at her with cool, grey eyes and a tight smile.

"Mrs. Broadhurst, I understand you are only recently come to town. May I say that London is fortunate to have you, madam, and predict that the Season can only now hope to be a success. May I beg for the next dance?"

Belle blinked. She was unused to such overblown compliments. That Gilbert had appreciated her she had no doubt, but he had not been given to expressing himself so extravagantly. "You are too kind, sir."

By the time they had finished their dance, Belle was disconcerted by his unwavering gaze. Unhappily, she had not yet acquired enough town bronze to graciously refuse his invitation to drive in the park.

"I shall call for you at half-past four on Monday, Mrs. Broadhurst."

"I am looking forward to it, Mr. Goodwin." He nodded and left. Belle sighed.

"That tiresome, was he?" Gore proffered a glass of champagne.

She took it gratefully and sipped. "It would be very rude of me to say that, Gore."

"Perhaps. Are you never rude, Lillie?"

"What an odd question! I should hope that I try not to be."

Right, he thought, you cannot afford to be. "I am happy to hear it." He grinned. "May I take you in when supper is served?"

"Thank you."

He nodded and left to find his next partner. Gore had become quite popular about town, and had received invitations to the best events of the Season. His movements were closely followed by most of the females in attendance, for even if he could not be considered one of the prime catches, he was in demand by most of the women of his acquaintance. The older ones appreciated his maturity and refinement, and the younger ones, despite their mamas' warnings, or perhaps because of them, were drawn to his good looks and war record. Although he never took himself too seriously, Gore had spent so many years away from home, many of them at war, that he took much enjoyment in his popularity.

Gore and Belle danced the first waltz after the supper interval. More than one pair of interested eyes followed the couple as they swept through the graceful patterns of the dance. Her red gown contrasted vividly against the stark black and immaculate white of his formal dress. He smiled down at her.

"Your hair is lovely dressed like that."

Cecily and William whirled by, the former smiling in their direction.

"Thank you." Belle was pleased with the compliment. She liked being in his arms and realized that she had not felt so protected since Gilbert's death. Silly, she told herself, this is just a dance, he is hardly one of Lillie's knights who will ride to my rescue. Still, she could dream, just for these few minutes, for she found that she was more and more enjoying Gore's company.

Indeed, she was enjoying a certain popularity herself, and she danced with several other gentlemen. One, Lord Peter Dunstable, was attentive, but not as cloying or as sober as Mr. Goodwin. A tall, fair man, he was a remarkably good dancer and an avid theatregoer, and they had great fun going through the steps of a Scotch reel.

"Will you come with me to Drury Lane, Mrs. Broadhurst? Kean is performing. We can have a late supper at the Clarendon Hotel afterward."

"That sounds wonderful, Lord Peter." This time, she had no difficulty in sounding enthusiastic.

"Friday, then," he said as he left her.

"So, engaged to attend the theatre with Dunstable, eh?"

She turned in surprise. "Gore, you do tend to come up on one unexpectedly. Are you playing at chaperone?"

He passed her arm through his and they progressed as best they could, that is to say slowly and with some difficulty, about the perimeter of the floor. The evening was warm for early April, due as much to the press of bodies as to the temperature outside, and all the windows were thrown wide. He maneuvered them directly in front of one, somehow dislodging without offense the prior occupants of that prime spot.

"Good gracious, what a crowd," Belle remarked, looking about her. "I have never seen so many people in one room before. Why, carriages were lined up for miles behind us, when we arrived, and the house was nearly full then. Lord and Lady Tipton must have grossly underestimated the number of invitations that would be accepted."

"Not a bit of it, Lillie. Attendance tonight is exactly what they would have wished it to be."

She stared at him. "But, why? People can barely move, there is not a breath of air in here, and all these candles," she looked up at the sparkling chandeliers, "give off so much heat and drip wax onto the dancers."

"Just so. Lillie, in London, a party such as this cannot be considered a success unless it is a crush, just like this. The Tiptons must be ecstatic," he finished dryly.

Belle shook her head in disbelief. "I suppose I am more of a country mouse than I thought, for it does not make any sense to me."

"Nor to me, but there it is." The arm he placed at

her back to protect her from the gesticulations of an exuberant couple was pushed against her for a moment, and she felt the hard muscle under the black superfine of his evening coat. Belle stole a quick glance at him and noticed his strong nose and the long lashes that fringed his eyes. A very nice nose, she decided. She quite liked it. He caught her eye and smiled.

She smiled back. "Have you seen Aunt Eulalie?"

"Yes, just a short while ago. We danced the last waltz."

"It was thoughtful of you to remember her."

"Not at all. I like Eulalie. She always was very kind to me on her visits to Burford, you will remember," he said pointedly.

"I do, yes."

"She dances beautifully, and I told her so. We are engaged for the next country dance."

"Oh, I am so glad." No wonder Lillie is so fond of him, she thought. I really must not mind his teasing me.

"So, you see, Lillie, to answer your question, I have not been chaperoning you for the entire evening. But, you must know I am concerned not only that you enjoy yourself, but also for your welfare."

"My welfare? Honestly, Gore, I am hardly a green girl, you know."

"Hardly," he teased.

The overzealous pair behind them had been joined by others of their set, and the expansion of their numbers resulted in a careless elbow into Gore's back which, in turn, pushed his front against Belle's.

"Oh, I say, I do beg your pardon," the owner of the offending appendage called out offhandedly. "Terrible crush, isn't it?"

Gore looked closely into Belle's eyes and she into his, unsure of what to say.

"No harm done," he replied, stepping back and murmuring an apology to her.

The orchestra began a waltz. "Our dance, Mrs. Broadhurst." Belle looked back at Gore as her new partner led her away.

"Do excuse me, Gore."

"Of course, Lillie." He smiled and bowed as the gentleman twirled her onto the floor.

The next day, Sunday, Belle received flowers from four admirers, among them Lord Peter and Mr. Goodwin. Mr. Goodwin's bouquet was accompanied by a fulsome note, while attached to Lord Peter's posy was a card bearing a lighthearted message. This was a novel experience for her and she was thrilled by the lovely blooms.

Warner chuckled at her reaction. "They are beautiful, ma'am. Shall I arrange them for you?"

"I will help you, for I like to work with flowers. I want you to put some in a vase for your room, also."

"Thank you, ma'am. I shall take a few from each bouquet. That way, when the gentlemen call, they can see what they sent to you."

"You think that they will call here, as well?"

"Yes, very likely."

"Oh, Warner, am I truly such a wantwit? I know so little of how to go on. I thank heaven and Mrs. Broadhurst that I have you to help me. Please, when they come, if they do, I would like you to remain with me."

Warner wanted to hear all about the ball, and they worked together for some time, for the flowers were numerous. Suddenly, there came a loud rumbling from the hallway. The women looked at one another and smiled, then turned expectantly to see Filbert race into the room as if the devil were after him. He shot over to the windows, leapt across a satinwood chair, stopped abruptly, looked over his shoulder at nothing, then tore off in the direction of the front stairs, whence he could be heard taking the steps with breakneck speed.

Belle and Warner grinned. Filbert's cat fits, as they had come to call them, came upon him out of nowhere and dissipated just as quickly. They paused in their work, heads inclined toward the door. "In just a second now . . ." Warner predicted. True to form, Filbert came charging back down the stairs, slid across the marble hall floor, bumping into a pedestal that threatened to drop the vase it held, and came to rest near their feet, where he proceeded to begin his bath in a most leisurely fashion.

"What is that?" Warner asked.

"What?"

"I thought he had something in his mouth when he came in. I think he is lying on it."

They flipped Filbert gently onto his other side, uncovering a small enamel pin.

"You devil!" Warner laughed. "I've been wondering where that had got to. He must have taken it and hidden it somewhere! Give it back, thief!"

"Apparently more like his ancestor than just his appearance, Warner."

"Perhaps not, ma'am. At least Filbert returns his plunder." They both enjoyed a good laugh that Filbert pretended not to notice.

Cecily Rafton called later in the morning to report on the progress of the refurbishments at No. 12 and to discuss the details of the Tipton ball.

"I adore balls," she said, "but I cannot say that I care for such crowds. I so much prefer the outdoors. My idea of the perfect gathering, I am afraid, is a picnic, where one may move about and breathe fresh air. Fortunately, Mr. Rafton agrees, and we make a point of doing that when we are at home in Gloucestershire. Perhaps we could organize such an outing here this Season. Would you come?" Belle assured her that she would. "Good. I shall speak to my husband. First, however, I am come to invite you to dinner on Wednesday." Her eyes twinkled. "But who shall I invite for you? Mr. Goodwin, Lord Peter or your cousin?" she teased. "Actually, I hope you will bring Major Lindley. I find him quite charming, do not you?" She gave Belle a telling glance.

"Mrs. Rafton, I am afraid you are out there. Gore and I have known one another forever."

"All the better, I think. For in such situations, one already knows the other's faults. It can be quite a surprising discovery, otherwise," she grinned. "I had thought you seemed to look at him . . . Well, I will say only that I thought your interest might have been caught."

"I assure you, it was not." Belle flushed.

"My mistake, then," Cecily spoke lightly and with upraised brows. "But I do hope that you will bring him to dinner."

"I am sure he will be pleased to come." She smiled.

Mr. Goodwin did call, as did Lord Peter, bringing with him his younger brother, Holden. None of them stayed beyond the prescribed time, but since their arrivals were nearly simultaneous, the drawing room was still full of deep voices when Gore arrived.

"I do not intrude, I hope. I should hate to dislodge your callers," he drawled softly to Belle after introductions had been made. It was obvious that she was quite enjoying her circle of admirers and, for some reason, this piqued him.

She noticed the glint in his eye and determined that

she would not let him spoil the afternoon. "Not at all, Gore. Did you mean to?"

He raised his brows in mock surprise. "Ah, giving as good as you get, eh?" He chuckled at her and joined in the conversation.

Really, Belle thought, as she smiled at her guests, he can be so exasperating.

Soon, the gentlemen, all but Gore, left, with Mr. Goodwin and Lord Peter confirming their plans with Belle.

"Well, Lillie, you seem to have made quite a success of your first ball. Has it occurred to you that these men may be chasing your considerable fortune and not your charm?"

"How very ungallant, Gore, and you a former officer, to suggest such a thing," she replied dryly. "Do you take me for such a paper skull that I had not considered that they could easily find younger and prettier women to call on? I am well aware that my most singular 'charm,' dear cousin, is my money."

This was true. Despite the physical and mental exhaustion that followed her first society ball, sleep had not come quickly to Belle the previous night. She had been flattered by the attention given her, but she was neither naive nor slow, and recognized that her popularity might be due to her, that is, Lillie's, wealth. Many a man was hanging out for a rich wife; the need or desire to marry well in that regard was not solely the province of women. Even a country widow knew the rules of this game, and because she did, it made her all the more able to play it. She could enjoy the company of gentlemen, so long as she did not lose her head. And lose it she could not, for she was not even the woman they believed her to be!

But then there was Gore. She admired his strength

and his wit, even if he did tease her out of countenance. Still, he never would, or could, have any interest in her. Why, he hardly seemed to notice that she existed. The problem was, she was halfway to loving him, and if by some strange chance he did pursue her, she was not at all certain she would run fast enough to elude him.

"Forgive me, Lillie, I did not mean to sound harsh or insensitive. I am concerned for you, as I said last night. You are no longer my little 'cousin,' after all."

"Oh, Gore, I was not that when you left all those years ago."

He was convinced that she was on the lookout for a rich husband to care for her when these machinations were concluded, and he would make it his business to learn just how well fixed these two men were. They had best be on their guard, for she was a delightful creature—good eyes, trim figure, quick mind. Pity she was such a schemer.

"All right, then, tell me, what other plans have you for today?"

"I thought I might hunt for The Cat's Bracelet."

"Pardon?"

"Did Randolph never tell you of it?" She was gratified, for once, to have some information that he did not.

He pondered a moment. "Yes, yes, I recall it now. Lost somewhere here in the house, was it not? You mean you actually intend to look for the thing?"

"Why not? I have already searched some of the rooms, and it was rather fun. I like puzzles." *God, did Lillie?*

"Yes. Well, enjoy yourself, my dear." (Apparently, Lillie did.) "I shall be at Tattersall's looking at some horses." Leave it to Lillie to tell her about The Bracelet. He suspected that, if she found it, she would never tell

Lillie, but simply take it with her when this ridiculous charade was over. She was even more devious than he had feared.

"Oh, Gore. Cecily and William Rafton have invited us to supper on Wednesday. Shall you come?"

"Delighted. I shall call for you. Seven o'clock?"

Filbert slipped into the room and sat several feet away, staring at Gore.

"What a handsome cat," he said with a wide smile. Somehow, Belle would never have expected him to like cats, but there he was, positively crooning to him! There must be something in the air at Burford. "What do you call him?"

"Filbert."

He laughed, crouching in front of his chair. "Such a ridiculous name for him." He crept slowly toward Filbert, calling to him softly. The cat continued to watch calmly until the man reached him. Then, he turned his back and strolled off, tail high.

"Infernal beast! I don't think he likes me."

"Perhaps it is his way of saying he cannot be had just for the price of a few kind words."

"That is one of the things I like about cats. They do not give their affection or esteem lightly."

Belle considered what Lillie had told her about Filbert's judgment. Did he indeed know something about Gore that Belle did not?

Cecily did not know Lord Peter, although she did know that he was very well-fixed; but she was slightly acquainted with Mr. Goodwin and had provided some background information. He was tolerably well-off, but frequently gambled and lost far too much. Although he was a thoroughly decent man, he was also, not to put too fine a point on it, a crashing bore. Rumor had it that he was looking for a wife. A rich wife.

"Well, there is no polite way for you to cancel the drive, now. But, I urge you, Mrs. Broadhurst, not to fall easy prey to his flattery." The facts, rather the gossip—for no one could have *that* much money—about the Broadhurst fortune had been abroad for some days, and Cecily was as familiar with them as the next person. "Every mama in town knows which way the wind is blowing, so they all keep their daughters clear of Mr. Goodwin."

That gentleman was sufficiently deft with the ribbons that Belle felt no qualms when he maintained a constant barrage of chatter as he drove. After a while, she was only half listening, as she enjoyed the ride through the green expanse of Hyde Park. Numerous other carriages, as well as people on foot, prevented their making much progress, but a drive through the park was about socializing, not about reaching any particular destination.

Her companion droned on, apparently needing little encouragement or response from Belle. When he stopped to exchange pleasantries with acquaintances and to introduce her, she spied Gore farther down the path accompanied by a giggling young woman.

Maryanne Stockdale, in her second Season on the town, was possessed of a beautiful face, a very respectable fortune and a spoiled, petulant nature that was matched only by that of her mother. Gore caught Belle's eye and tipped his hat, smiling. Miss Stockdale promptly reclaimed his attention, and they laughed together at whatever she had said. Their movements shortly brought the two couples abreast and introductions were made all around.

"Major Lindley, I understand that General Sir John

Daily is lecturing on his participation in The Battle of Tolentino. Do you go?"

"I do not, Mr. Goodwin. I find that I have had enough of war. The company of a beautiful woman," he smiled at the vision by his side and Belle wondered if her blond coloring was not just a trifle insipid, "is all I need these days. But, the general is a brave soldier and, I hear, a fine speaker. No doubt you would think him most enlightening. Perhaps you would be good enough to take my cousin. She would find his words both fascinating and inspiring. Would you not, Lillie?" Although he could not be certain, Gore guessed rightly that Belle would be bored to distraction by the talk. More importantly, however, he had learned that, unlike Lord Peter's income Mr. Goodwin's was something less than robust, and he would see to it that she spent as much time in the latter's company as possible. That should put paid to her plans for Dunstable or any other fool with a fortune to let.

Indeed, Lillie would have loved to hear the general's tales, but Belle nearly choked. An evening spent with Mr. Goodwin was fated to be tedious, but listening to war reminiscences was the outside of enough! "Oh, I do not know, Gore, I—"

"Nonsense, Lillie, no need to be shy. I am sure Mr. Goodwin would be happy to escort you." He made it sound as if attending had been her wish!

"Indeed, I would," that gentleman assured her.

"There, you see? And then, I understand that the proceeds of admission are to aid those many servicemen who still find themselves in desperate straits, today," he concluded very soberly.

She could not refuse without rudeness or insensitivity. Thousands of British soldiers had returned home from the war to unemployment and an uninterested government, and they still were in heartbreaking evidence in the streets of London. "I should be happy to accompany you, Mr. Goodwin," she said quietly.

When their carriage resumed its sedate progress with the stream of traffic, she could swear she heard Gore chuckle as he strolled off with Miss Stockdale. A frisky easterly wind tugged at her cottage bonnet. Putting up a hand to hold it in place, Belle looked at the blue sky and the trees and shrubbery, an almost pastoral scene in the midst of the crowded, filthy city. She began to think of ways to murder Gore that might have the least likelihood of attaching her to the crime.

"Humph," said Mr. Goodwin, interrupting her thoughts. "That Maryanne Stockdale looks barely out of the schoolroom. Quite a fortune there, too, if I remember aright. Lindley could do a lot worse."

"Why, Mr. Goodwin, you almost make it sound as if Major Lindley were hanging out for a fortune!" Belle remarked.

"Humph! Would hardly be wonderful if he were, Mrs. Broadhurst. Everyone knows Lindley ain't exactly plump in the pockets."

He sounded almost put out that Gore had gotten to the young lady first. Perhaps, Belle thought with a smile, *Mr. Goodwin realizes he could have done better. If he had chosen to follow Miss Stockdale instead of me, he probably considers he could have had youth and beauty, as well as a great deal of money. Perhaps he would try to cut Gore out. That was a pleasant thought all around, for she would be rid of him and Gore might lose Miss Stockdale.* She wondered if Mr. Goodwin were aware that he had likely given away his own motives! But he recovered himself.

"Of course," he smiled unctuously, *"we* know that fortune isn't everything, do we not?"

She responded with a smile. "Perhaps not, sir, but there is a great deal to be said for the youth and beauty that Miss Stockdale would bring to a match. I, for one, could hardly fault a gentleman for being attracted to such a, well, *wealth* of charms." There, that might do it. Goodwin looked pensive. She could almost hear the wheels turning in his head, as if he were thinking of ways to fasten onto the unsuspecting Stockdale child. Something told her she would not be bothered over-much by Mr. Goodwin in the future.

Gore and his companion walked on. He had not mentioned that he had contributed a substantial sum toward the relief of the soldiers forgotten by their king and Parliament. His interest had assumed a more direct and personal form just a few days ago, when he had stopped to buy a hot pie from a street vendor. Standing nearby was a tall man wearing an eyepatch and looking malnourished, not an uncommon sight, and watching Gore hungrily. When he caught his eye, the man flushed.

"Pardon, sir," he said softly, "but could you spare a penny?"

The warm, delicious pie lost its flavor. "Here," he instructed the vendor, "another pie, if you please. No—two." He handed them to the hungry man and led him away from the street, where the clatter of iron wheels might be less deafening. The recipient accepted the food and devoured the first pie in a trice. He wiped his mouth with the back of a dirty hand.

He cleared his throat. "Sorry, sir, I used to have manners. Thank you."

"Not at all. Let's go into that coffee house and get something to drink."

It had been a long time since anyone had given anything to Timothy Riddell or asked for his company. He gulped his coffee and finished the second pie, flashing a grateful smile at Gore.

Gore set his cup down on the wooden table. "How did you come by that?" Gore asked gently, nodding to the eye patch.

"In His Majesty's service, sir. I was with the Eleventh Foot at Salamanca." There was pride in his voice.

"A filthy mess, that."

"You were there?"

"No, but I heard of it. I am late of the Ninth Regiment."

The man grinned. "And a bit higher up than me, I should think, sir. Captain, were you?"

"Major, actually. Gore Lindley."

"Timothy Riddell, and pleased I am to make your acquaintance, Major Lindley. You're a kind man."

Gore waved away the compliment. "Well, Salamanca was back in . . . 'twelve, was it?" Riddell nodded. "You've been back a while, then. How have you been getting along, since you came home?"

Riddell's face clouded. "Bit of this, bit of that. There's not much work. Government doesn't seem to care, now that we've served our purpose. It's not like those recruitment posters promised. Especially not after you've come home.

"You know, you can count on a war to be a horror, no matter how grand they try to make it sound. But, you expect better once you're back in your own country. We lost so many men—you'd be knowing that, sir—and a lot that ended up like me. And worse. A great deal worse. At least I can fill my belly in one way or another. There's some can't even do that, poor devils." They both fell silent.

"Ever wonder why we did it, sir?"

Gore nodded. "More than once, Riddell." The man

was fairly well-spoken. "What was your occupation before you joined up?"

"Footman, sir. But there are more footmen than
there are jobs these days."

"I have no need of a footman, I am afraid."

The man nodded as if he had already known the answer to an unspoken question. He tried not to look
disappointed. After all, this man owed him nothing. His
belly was full, anyway.

"But, I do need a valet."

"I'm no valet, sir. Have to tell you that," Riddell replied, but there was hope in his words.

"To say the truth, Riddell, I have never employed one
before, so perhaps we could learn together. We might
brush along nicely." He gave a crooked grin.

Riddell looked at Gore and saw that he meant his
words. He gulped. "I would be proud to work for you,
Major, and I'll do right by you. You can count on that.
How soon could I start?"

Gore joked that there probably was no time to be lost
for either of them. Their respective stations all but pro-
hibited friendship, but there would be many a night
before a welcoming fire when the two would share stories of past campaigns and lost friends, and the kind of
desperately sad jokes that only two comrades in arms
could understand and forgive.

FIVE

The late morning sun burned through the last wisps of the fog that had seeped into the square in the early dawn. Filbert jumped into his chair by the window, looked out, blinked and collapsed. An unusually hectic morning had left him quite tired. Rising early, he had patrolled the house. Occasionally, the odd mouse slipped in, and its dispatch was something he dared not rely upon anyone else to accomplish. In truth, it was a responsibility he preferred to keep, having been the sole caretaker of the house for so long. He washed one mitten, eyes shut tight in concentration, then pricked his ears, looked about him, listened and decided he had better wash it again.

Belle might think this place was immaculate, but he knew better. Lap. Lap. The floors in the upper regions were dusty. Of course, people did not eat off of floors, no matter that they claimed they should be clean enough to do so. Filbert, on the other hand, did eat off them, and while he had to concede that the kitchen floor on which his Stoke porcelain bowls were placed was clean enough, the attics were another matter entirely. He rolled onto his back and bent forward to wash the large expanse of his tummy. Stopping in mid-lap, he pricked his ears again and looked into space for a moment, then resumed his task. He wondered if Belle and Warner and the others appreciated him. Did they ever ask themselves who kept this place mouse-free? Probably not. If they did, he expected that they would have kept the attic floors cleaner, so that his clandestine meetings with trespassing rodents, meetings that always resulted in impromptu meals, could be held on a more suitable surface. No, they did not think about it much.

He finished his ablutions, stood, stretched and, purring, began to knead a comfortable spot into the cushion. Servants were servants, but Belle and Warner were the head people and he had expected more from them. Filbert yawned. He had not been best pleased when Lillie left. He had made that quite clear at the time. But, actually, Belle was working out rather well. If she did not see to the attic floors, she had quickly learned his other needs. She knew now which treats he preferred—salmon was best—and, in fact, gave a better tummy rub than Lillie did. He must remember to see to it that Lillie realized this when she returned.

Well, he supposed he would remain here. He had cared for the house for so long that, honestly, he could not imagine living anywhere else. But they did not know that, and he did not intend to tell them. Only, sometimes, he was baffled by it all. Belle was pretending to be Lillie, and he had no idea why. Did she really imagine she could get away with it? It was all too complicated for his cat's mind. He stood up, turned around and settled back contentedly into the same position.

Filbert decided that he would join in their game. After all, game-playing was in the family lines, wasn't it? Besides, he liked Belle now. He burrowed his head deeper into the cushion. The sun felt good. Now Gore was another story. Filbert had a bad feeling about him. He did not quite trust Belle to him, although he could not have said why. He hoped she had noticed that Gore was not high on his list of people. After all, he did not allow just anyone to pet him. Well, it would all come out as it should, and he would help when necessary.

At least there were people in the house again. He had been lonely here before Aunt Eulalie had brought him to Lillie in Burford. And he had liked the country well enough at first. All those mice. His baritone purr began to rumble at the memory, and he stretched his neck toward the warmth of the sunlight. They had really needed him there. The other cats had been fat and lazy. Too many mice to handle, they had whispered to him complacently. Filbert had sniffed in contempt. Hangers-on, he had called them (and had not won many friends when he did) and then he proceeded to show them just how it was done. And there had been Columbine, the most beautiful cat he had ever met—although, until his stay in Burford, he had met few—with soft white fur and a dainty mew. She had flirted with him outrageously.

But, his task complete, it had been time and past to get back to London and to his real responsibility. The one he had assumed, in his turn, like all the other cats in the house in Berkeley Square. Guarding The Bracelet. It had been left alone too long. Suppose other people, *not Broadhurst people,* came to live here? They might just find it, although that possibility was remote, and that would not be right. Maybe it was time, however, that someone did. Or, maybe not. All this thinking was too exhausting for an already overtaxed cat, and Filbert snuggled deeper still and slept.

Glossy boxes tied with pretty ribbons were delivered regularly from Mrs. Niven's shop. Belle could hardly believe that she had ordered all these clothes. Warner drew the tissue from a Bishop's blue walking dress of silk, with a fall of lace at the throat.

"Now, where is the spencer that will go with this?" She lifted the lid of one box after another until she located the sought-for garment. "Ah, here. Yes, this will look quite nice on you, ma'am."

Belle looked at the two commodious clothespresses that stood agape, as if in attempt to disgorge some of their excessive contents. Inside, struggling for space amongst yards of silk, muslin, lutestring, zephyr and kerseymere, were dozens of motionless feet. Could she possibly wear all those shoes? Her eyes moved to the enormous chest of drawers that held more stockings, night shifts, gloves, shawls, scarves, reticules and petticoats than any one female had a right, much less need, to own. She sighed and shook her head a bit, wondering where on earth to put the lavender pelisse she held and if she would even miss it, if it were misplaced.

Warner chuckled. "You know, Mrs. Broadhurst, Mrs. Broadhurst has a wardrobe as large as this back in Burford, and she did not mingle in society nearly as much as you will." They had decided early on that it would be safest for the maid to call her by Lillie's name, but in circumstances like this it had the ring of the ridiculous. "Just leave that for me, I shall find a place for it. All those bonnets, on the other hand," she nodded in the direction of a phalanx of band boxes that stood atop the armoires, "are going to be needing their own address, soon."

Belle sighed again and squeezed onto the bed between a gold zephyrine ball gown and a pair of half boots, previously prized from the armoire to judge their coordination with a slate-colored carriage dress. "Yes, Warner, but that is what I am afraid of."

"What," she teased, "the bonnets?"

"No, silly, the mingling. Everything."

Warner picked up the boots and sat beside her on the bed. "But you have done beautifully, so far. You said yourself how much you enjoyed the ball, and the other day, you went driving with Mr. Goodwin. That went well, did it not?"

Belle brightened. "Oh, yes, the ball was such fun. And I did manage the drive, but only wait until I tell you what Major Lindley did, Warner. No, what I mean is, how shall I continue? I am to go to the theatre with Lord Peter. And Gore and Aunt Eulalie are threatening to take me absolutely everywhere."

Warner did not point out that most ladies would give up their last pair of clocked stockings to be in such a fix, because she knew it would only make her mistress feel ungrateful. "You will go on splendidly," she patted her arm. "Just be Annabelle Makepeace. Lord Peter and Mr. Goodwin have already met her, even if they do not know it, and, apparently, decided they like her."

Filbert, roused from his slumber on the chair by the window, leapt to the bed. He stretched out on the carriage dress, rolled onto his back and, four legs stretched in opposing directions, exposed his tummy and looked at Belle expectantly. "Oh, Filbert, do you need a tummy rub?" she asked unnecessarily and, distractedly, began to scratch.

"Yes, but what of Gore and Lillie's aunt? I do not feel right about deceiving them. Well, I am not really at all sorry about Gore, especially after he tricked me into that engagement with Mr. Goodwin. Oh, he thinks I would be interested—only hear this, Warner—in attending a talk by General Daily about his war experiences, but he knew full well that I do not wish to spend more time in Mr. Goodwin's company. He did it deliberately. I know he did! He thinks it is amusing. And you

know, Warner, once or twice, I have caught him looking
at me in a certain way, and I suspect he knows that I
am not Lillie."

Warner smiled. "I do not think so, ma'am. Truly, he
has given no sign of it."

Belle pulled a face. "No, nor do I, in my saner moments. So far as I can tell, I have passed muster, as it
were. And, if he did know, surely he would expose me."

"Just so. I do not believe you need worry about him
overmuch. As for Mrs. Singleton, you must not let yourself feel too badly. Unless you wish to tell her the truth,
you must simply continue as you have begun. You are
kind to her, and she is spending more time in society,
as she wanted, and enjoying it immensely. I am convinced that she, at least, suspects nothing. When Mrs.
Broadhurst returns, she must deal with the truth and
its repercussions. But, Mrs. Singleton is a woman of the
world and I think, when all is said and done, that she
might just see the humor in it all."

"Yes, Warner, perhaps you are right. Anyway, as you
said, unless I want to make a clean breast of it all—and
Lillie would have a fit if I did—I must cease this point-
less worrying."

The Theatre Royal at Drury Lane was filled as only
Edmund Kean could fill it. He was reprising his role as
Sir Giles Overreach in the dark comedy, *A New Way to
Pay Old Debts*. He had first played the part of the villain-
ous Sir Giles a few years earlier, and his performance
had been so vivid, his character so believably evil, that
many people had been removed in hysterics. Byron was
said to have had a convulsive seizure, and Kean's fellow
actors had been frightened to death by the transforma-
tion of their peer. As Belle and Lord Peter climbed the

double staircase to their box, she was amazed by the
beauty of her surroundings, which blazed with light.

But, when they had reached their seats, she was
shocked by the behavior of those in attendance. The
people in the pit appeared to be interested in nothing
more than behaving in the most raucous manner, and
those in boxes, such as she shared with Lord Peter,
seemed to care only about socializing. Given that the
theatre seated some three thousand people, the noise
could be deafening. Most startling was that it hardly
abated once the performance began! A few minutes
later, however, Mr. Kean had cast his spell over the audience and relative quiet descended, but for his magnificent voice.

"Lord Peter," Belle said, while they dined on one of
M. Jacquier's wonderful French meals at the Clarendon
Hotel, "I cannot tell you when I have enjoyed anything
so much."

Her handsome escort sipped some of his champagne
and smiled. "Mrs. Broadhurst, I, too, had a wonderful
time. Kean is quite something, isn't he?"

"Everything I had heard he was. And more! Why,
even the people in the pit seemed enthralled."

"Yes. Pity he is throwing away his talent. He drinks
excessively, you know."

Belle expressed her dismay, but they soon turned to
happier subjects, including Kean's portrayal of Hamlet,
which Lord Peter had seen a year or two before, and
the evening passed very pleasantly.

The tablecloth had been removed and dessert served.
The cutlery, just washed at the sideboard, was set once
again on the table with dishes of nuts, costly hothouse
pineapples, decanters of wine and two glass tazzas hold-

ing fresh fruit and jellies. Cecily smiled over a low bowl of fresh flowers at her guests.

Gore to her right, Belle to her left, Elwood Drabble, the Rafton lawyer and his wife, Daphne, and Lockwood and Mary Farley, neighbors from No. 1. William sat at the opposite end, and she looked in his direction. The conversation was flowing easily, and the meal had been perfect. Cecily at last felt she could begin to relax and enjoy the evening as much as her guests seemed to be doing.

She turned to her right. "Major, do you plan to make your home in London?"

"I do not, Mrs. Rafton. I have rented some very nice rooms for the Season, but I have just begun to look about for a country house, a modest one I think, to buy or perhaps lease."

"And where shall you look?"

"Oh, in the Burford area. I was raised there with Mrs. Broadhurst, as you may know, and I have a great fondness for it." Gore glanced at Belle. "That way, we would still be just a stone's throw from one another, Lillie. Until you marry again, that is." He smiled. "Actually, my dear, I wondered if you had heard of anything that might be available in the neighborhood."

"I cannot think of a thing," she replied with truth, but somewhat absentmindedly, for his words had made her think of how wonderful it might be to live close to him.

"Can you not? Too bad. I confess, I always liked Harley Wood. That would be perfect, if it were available. The house is small, but quite fine. You remember it."

"Hmm. No, I do not think that I do."

"But you must. It lies just beside that little forest where we used to play so often. You remember climbing that tree to look at the bird's nest. You would have fallen out, if I had not caught you."

This tale was true. Lillie and Gore had gone to the woods where he had promised to show her the little birds in the aerie well above their heads. Lillie had kilted her skirts and climbed fearlessly. When they at last reached their destination, each had crouched back.

"We mustn't frighten them, Lillie, they've never seen people before," Gore had whispered with the infinite wisdom of a twelve-year-old. Lillie did as she was told, but the mother bird chose that moment to return to her babies and first screeched, then flew, at the children. The frightened Lillie started, losing her balance. Had Gore not caught her apron, she would have fallen from the tree, doubtless with considerable injury.

Unfortunately, Gore continued. "And, surely, you remember the poor grass snake we chased." He laughed. "Lillie, you are the only female I have ever met who actually likes snakes."

Belle blanched. Oh, no, not snakes. On the few occasions she had seen one in her garden at home, she had nearly had a fit of apoplexy. If there were the remotest likelihood that her role would require making friends with a snake, she would leave tomorrow.

She decided to ignore that particular story. "Of course I remember the birds. Robins, were they not? How could I forget? I might have broken my neck, but for you."

"Nightingales."

"Pardon?"

"They were nightingales, Lillie, not robins."

"Oh, yes, that's right. How could I have forgotten?"

"How indeed?" His voice was light, but her heart skipped a beat, nonetheless.

"Mrs. Broadhurst, if you are interested in birds, you

must ask Mr. Rafton. To say that he is keen on the subject is a considerable understatement."

While Belle quite liked birds, she thought it was safer to turn the subject. Gore, however, had other ideas.

"Splendid. Perhaps the four of us could go to the country one day. We might take a picnic and observe the birds. Mr. Rafton could enlighten us all."

"What a wonderful idea! I shall speak to him about it, and we can make the necessary arrangements."

Belle had experienced a period of considerable adjustment upon her arrival in London. Whichford was a quiet town, and London, in contrast, was dirty, crowded and, whenever one ventured into the streets or sat close to an open window, deafening. A few days after the Rafton dinner party, Belle and Gore were walking in the Green Park, the din and bustle of the streets blessedly absent and the air fresher.

"Has Mrs. Rafton said anything further about our picnic?"

"Yes, she has, but I am not at all certain that I wish to go with you."

"Oh? How have I offended, dear cousin?" A smile teased at his lips.

"You know perfectly well, Gore. I could not say so the other night at the Raftons, but it was too bad of you to force me into attending that talk with Mr. Goodwin."

" 'Force' you? Was it so bad?"

The event had taken place the previous evening and so was very fresh in her memory. It had been worse than she had imagined. She could not have said who was more boring, Mr. Goodwin or the general. She had listened to war stories for what seemed hours, then had had to listen to her escort's opinions about them all the way home in the carriage. Her head had ached abominably, and all she could think of was that Gore had got her into it. Now all her irritation spilled out at him.

"Bad? You have no idea. Oh, I know Mr. Goodwin means well. He is a nice enough man, I do not even dislike him, but he never stops talking. About nothing. Or about things too dull to discuss. And I would not have had to go, but for your interference." Laughing, and thus infuriating her further, Gore tried to interrupt her, but she kept on. "*You* did not have to go . . ." Her head whirled around as the words he was trying to get in filtered through her ravings.

". . . make peace . . ."

"What?"

"I said 'make peace,' for God's sake!"

"Who?" She knew she sounded like an idiot, but with her heart in her mouth, she did not seem able to say much else.

"Who? You, of course!"

"What?"

This was more enjoyable than he had hoped. "Please stop saying 'what.' I said, let us 'make peace.' "

"I—oh, yes. You are right, we should, ah, make peace. Thought you meant a person. By the name of Makepeace, that is."

"Now why would I do that? I do not even know anyone of that name. Or do I?" He looked at her, his eyes innocently wide. "From back in Burford, do you mean? Or is it someone of your more recent acquaintance? Rather an odd name."

Her voice rose two or three octaves. "No, no. I do not know a soul by that name. Odd, do you say? I do not think so. It is quite an old name, I believe. Probably older than Lindley."

"You seem rather taken with it, in any event."

"No, no," she repeated, her voice even higher and thinner. "Not a bit of it. Why should I be?"

"Why, indeed?"

"Well, as you said, Gore, we should cease this arguing."

Although his role in that circumstance had been only as listener, he gallantly agreed. "I am sorry that I got you into such a scrape," he apologized, eyes hooded.

Dining at his club the past night, Gore had remembered just where Lillie was and what she was doing. Good, he had thought, the more time she spends with fortune hunters—this was an overstatement, but he was not interested in the niceties of the circumstances—the less she will spend chasing after rich men like Lord Peter. It was all working out nicely, so far. Of course, throwing her together with the likes of Mr. Goodwin, in whom he knew she had no interest, and hoping to keep her away from Dunstable, was simply the right thing to do. Wasn't it? He could have no other reason for keeping her unattached. Could he? Well, she was a damn fine-looking woman, and she seemed decent enough—for a fortune hunter. But, he had not given in to the temptation to explore this aberrant thought and he did not bother to consider that his cousin was equally culpable in the connivance.

"But I believed that you would truly enjoy the general."

"Oh, he was a delight," she said dryly and then redirected the conversation, "but we had begun to talk of the picnic. Mrs. Rafton thought perhaps next Friday, if that is convenient for you."

"It is. And I have found you the perfect mount at Tattersall's. The ride should be invigorating."

Belle tripped over her left foot. Ride! She had been on a horse twice in her life, been thrown or fallen both times, and had taken a solemn oath never to attempt it again.

"Did you hurt your ankle? Here, let me help you to that bench." Once seated, Belle's breath came in gasps. "Is it that painful, Lillie?"

She looked at him in a panic. For a moment, she considered claiming it was broken, that would put paid to the possibility of riding surely, but she knew she could not carry it off.

"No. It is not very bad. Just a little twist," she managed between gasps. She knew there was no way out. Even if she could avoid riding in this instance, she was bound, eventually, to find herself in a situation where she could not.

Gore looked at her ashen face, at her wide eyes. She sounded almost disappointed that serious damage had not been done. Could she not ride? Could he be this fortunate? "I am certain you will be recovered by next week. And you will like Thistle, she is a sweet goer."

Belle had no idea what that meant, but she had a feeling it could not be good.

When they returned to Berkeley Square, she not even bothering to limp for effect, they found Cecily was just leaving, having called and found Belle from home.

"Oh, there you are," she greeted them gaily on the doorstep.

"Mrs. Rafton, Lillie tells me that you have the plans for our outing well in hand."

"Yes. Mr. Rafton and I are looking forward to it. I hope this fine weather holds." She related the details of her plans.

"Most agreeable. I was saying to Lillie that we could ride to the picnic spot." He watched Belle carefully from the corner of his eye. She looked pained. "You must forgive my cousin, Mrs. Rafton, she stumbled whilst we were walking in the park. Oh, she is quite fine now," he added cavalierly. "And you must believe that she really is not at all clumsy normally—are you Lillie? Why, you should see her sit a horse."

"I am sorry to hear it. No, not about your riding, but your ankle. You are well now?" Assured that she was, Cecily went on. "I had called to take you driving in my phaeton, but I expect you would rather do it another time." Belle nodded. "I am most pleased to hear you so enjoy riding, Mrs. Broadhurst . . ."

"Oh, she does. Loves it. Born to it, you might say. I've found just the horse for her, too."

"I so love to ride, myself. But, Major Lindley, I do not think riding to the picnic such a good idea. We shall have blankets and cushions and hampers of food. Much better that we take a carriage, don't you agree?"

Gore was crestfallen. He nodded. "Of course, Mrs. Rafton, that is much more sensible." Belle could have kissed her and thought she would faint with relief.

"But, Mrs. Broadhurst, we must ride together often. Riding is one of the great pleasures of my life, too. Let's arrange to go together soon, shall we?"

"I, well, it has been some time since I last rode," that much at least was true, "and—"

"Nonsense, Lillie. One never forgets, you know."

"Why thank you, Gore, for reminding me." Her tone was decidedly acidic and her breathing was becoming more labored again. "Oh, dear, I find that my ankle still aches just a wee bit. Perhaps I should lie down for a while. If you both will excuse me?"

"What am I thinking, keeping you standing here on the step? Please do go inside, Mrs. Broadhurst. Put a cushion under your foot and you will feel better in a trice. Goodbye, my dear."

"I will see you to your door, Mrs. Rafton. Lillie, do

take care of that ankle." His eyes twinkled. "I am concerned for you." Chattering like two birds, he and Cecily strolled off under the cover of Berkeley Square's beautiful plane trees.

"Too kind." Belle stretched a smile around gritted teeth, then stepped inside.

Late that afternoon, Warner found her sitting against a big chintz cushion on the teak garden bench. Most everything had turned healthy shades of green, a sign of the flourishing to come. Belle referred to this small, enclosed spot as her private Eden. Normally, she found it restful to be here, no matter that she could never sit five minutes together without getting up to pull a weed or pinch off a piece of dead branch, but today, the garden might as well have turned to ashes for all the thought she gave to it, or the rest it gave to her. Noting her agitated state, Warner sat beside her on the bench.

"Mrs. Broadhurst, is anything wrong?"

"Oh, Warner, I am in such a fix, and it is all Gore's fault."

"Again? What has he done this time?"

"He has bought a horse for me! Can you imagine? And he expects me to ride it! He has told Mrs. Rafton of Lillie's great riding skills, and now, if she has her way, I shall spend the rest of the Season galloping about the city."

Warner smiled at this hyperbole. "Something tells me you do not ride."

"Warner, if it were only a case of 'not' riding, I might muddle through. The problem is, I *cannot* ride. My previous attempts were unsuccessful, to say the least."

"Oh, dear. I suppose you know that Mrs. Broadhurst rides as if she were part of the horse?"

"Naturally," Belle drawled. "So, you see, even supposing I could manage it, I could not just get on the stupid horse and hope for the best. I must do it beautifully! Hah!"

"I am afraid that I do not ride well enough at all to teach you."

"Good of you to offer, Warner, but this calls for more drastic measures."

"What are you going to do?" the maid asked with some trepidation.

"I am going to enlist Mrs. Rafton's help."

"You are going to tell her the truth? Oh my, do you think you should?"

"I have no choice, Warner. I cannot continue this masquerade without her help. She is such a kind person and we have become friends, so I must believe that she will help. The sooner it is done, the better, to paraphrase the Bard. Please go and ask if she will be at home tomorrow, so that I might call to discuss a matter on which I require her advice."

Warner shook her head with apprehension, but bustled off in the direction of No. 12.

Cecily replied that she would be happy to see Mrs. Broadhurst, but that she would come to her, given that the workmen still were wreaking havoc at No. 12. They now sat in the morning room while Warner passed cups of tea and cakes to both ladies.

Belle began. "I have something to tell you, something, well, rather unusual. You will, no doubt, be quite surprised, Mrs. Raf—Cecily . . ."

Her guest smiled broadly. "Yes, please let it be Cecily. And I may call you Lillie?"

"Actually, that would not be entirely correct . . ."

Cecily's face clouded. "I beg your pardon?"

Belle touched her hand. "I am sorry. That sounded very rude, and I did not mean it to." She smiled gently. "Warner, do pour yourself some tea and stay." She looked back to her visitor. "Warner knows all. I need her for moral support, and she can also help to explain what I have to tell you."

Cecily was perplexed.

"Cecily, I did not mean that it would be improper for you to address me by my given name, for of course it would be perfectly fine and I want you to do so. It is only that my name is not Lillie."

"Oh, well, my name is not Cecily." She looked at their puzzled faces. "It is Susan, after my maternal grandmother; Eloise, after my paternal grandmother; Cecily, after I do not know whom; but I have always been called just Cecily . . ."

"None of my names is Lillie."

"Oh!"

"And my last name is not Broadhurst."

There was a brief pause. "I am afraid I am confused."

"Well, of course you are. Only listen. My name is Annabelle Makepeace. I am not Lillie Broadhurst."

Cecily blinked, opened her mouth, closed it, and opened it again to little purpose. "But—"

"I know."

"Well, er, Mrs., ah, Makepeace was it?"

"Belle."

"Belle." She turned wide eyes toward Warner. "And you are?"

The abigail smiled. "I am still Warner, ma'am. I promise you." Well, that was something, at least.

Belle continued. "You see, Mrs. Broadhurst and I met quite by chance at an inn. We were stranded by a dreadful storm . . ." For several minutes, she narrated her strange tale, helped now and then by explanatory contributions from Warner. Cecily listened, contributing hardly a word.

"And you say no one knows of this?"

"Only we three. And Lillie, naturally."

Cecily grinned impishly. "I do love secrets."

Belle laughed with relief. "Oh, Cecily, then you are not angry?"

She shook a playful but admonishing finger. "I suppose I should be, but I am not. I think you and Lillie—I feel that I may call her that—" she twinkled, "very daring, although," she added thoughtfully, "I suppose you are all," her gaze extended to Warner, "quite mad. Still, this will be such a lark."

"Lark? Good heavens, anything but, I promise you. But, you are right about one thing, we must be mad. Oh, it feels so good to have told someone."

Cecily accepted another piece of cake and allowed Warner to refill her cup. "But, why *did* you decide to tell me?"

"For a selfish reason, I must confess. Because I need your help. Not that I have the smallest right to ask it of you."

"You do? How grand! I should love to help. How?"

"Thank heaven. Cecily, I do not know how to ride."

"Dear, dear. Had a sheltered life, did you?" It was beyond her comprehension that there might exist people who had not spent their childhoods atop a horse.

"I have tried, in the distant past, but failed miserably on both occasions." She provided the necessary details.

"Tsk, tsk, that is bad."

"But not beyond hope, surely. Oh, Cecily, you can see how desperate my situation is! Say you can help. Say you will. Otherwise, I must just pray for rain for the rest of the Season!"

"Of course I shall. It will not be easy," she warned, "but I daresay you already know that. Now, let me think. There is no time to waste." She pondered for a few moments, and Belle tried to loosen the grip her hands had on the chair arms.

"Yes, right then. The first thing we must do is visit Mrs. Niven. We can leave now," she said, rising.

"Mrs. Niven! Cecily, surely even you must see that this is no time to go shopping. A new gown will not answer my problem!"

Her friend's tone was lofty. "Well, yes it will, unless you plan to ride in that lovely lawn morning gown. You need a riding dress, silly!"

"Oh! Good God, what next?"

Cecily laughed. "Come, Lillie—er, Belle. Oh my, what am I to call you now?"

"You must keep to the method Warner and I have worked out. Never, ever call me Belle, even when we are alone. That way, you cannot go amiss." Warner brought Belle's spencer, bonnet and reticule.

"All right—Lillie. Ha, ha! This is going to be such fun." The three of them stepped into the warm sunlight. "William is the soul of discretion, but, unfortunately, honest to a fault. So, I will wait to tell him until I think the time is right. With your permission, of course." Belle agreed. "Now, let us get your riding habit. You know, I think I could use a new evening dress as well . . ."

And this part of the endeavor was deceptively easy. Mrs. Niven miraculously had a riding habit all but finished for a client who had, fortuitously for Belle, broken a wrist, and the garment required only a few alterations. Riding lessons were to occur in the very early morning in Hyde Park. They would use one of the more secluded roads to the north or west of Rotten Row, where they were likely to encounter the fewest people, until Belle had mastered the rudimentaries.

* * *

The Magic Lantern display ended and the last of the beautiful painted slides were returned to their velvet-lined boxes. The conversation of the small group seated about the room began to resume its normal pitch. Belle was flanked by Lord Peter and Aunt Eulalie, and, heads together, they were in animated discussion about the images.

"You young people take such marvels as this quite in stride, but I tell you, I remember when we did not have such sophisticated amusements. The world is advancing so fast." She shook her head in wonder.

Belle agreed. "The pictures were marvelous. I had never seen a Magic Lantern show before, had you, Lord Peter?" She smiled at him prettily. That gentleman allowed as how he had, but judged this display to be among the best he had seen.

Gore, several chairs away, watched her closely. She looked lovely. He liked the way her maid had framed her face in curls, and that peach blossom mull dress set off her coloring beautifully. He realized that this was not the first time he had noticed Belle in this way, but it was the first time he had actually acknowledged it to himself, and the realization startled him. He rose and, looking down, extended his arm.

"Miss Booth, shall we take a turn about the room?"

Miss Caroline Booth was one of the handsomest women he had ever seen. In truth, she was one of the handsomest women that anyone had seen for many a London Season. Her red hair was like an aureole against her perfect porcelain features, and she was blessed with grace, a happy disposition, fine humor and not a little intelligence. But the Booth fortune came originally from trade, and the smell of it still rankled in the nose of more than one of society's discerning doyennes. Her doting parents had spared neither ex-

pense nor effort in her "education." They had bred
her up to be a lady and to find a husband who would
appreciate their darling girl, no matter that he might
have no money of his own, but the *ton*'s cats barred her
from certain of the most elite drawing rooms and entertainments. Nor had the coveted Almack's vouchers
been bestowed, and wouldn't *that* have cowed a lesser
lady. Not Miss Caroline Booth, however. Most people,
the only ones she cared about at least, liked Caroline.
A sense of the absurd and a readiness to laugh, even at
herself, made her vastly popular with both the men and
women of her acquaintance.

She and Gore strolled, admiring paintings and gossiping harmlessly. Caroline glanced up at her escort.
She enjoyed Major Lindley's company, had enjoyed it
two nights ago at the theatre, but her heart was not yet
given. And lucky for me, she laughed to herself, for
Major Lindley's heart does not appear to be his for the
giving—not to me, at any rate.

"Miss Booth, you look enchanting this evening."

"Thank you, Major." It was not in her nature to fish
for compliments, but she decided to tease him. "But, I
am surprised that you noticed."

"I beg your pardon?"

Caroline Booth laughed lightly. "Come, Major, your
eyes may appreciate beauty, but I assure you, they were
not appreciating mine, for I found they were elsewhere
more than once." She inclined her head discreetly in
Belle's direction and watched for his reaction.

He flushed. "Miss Booth, I apologize if I have offended in some way, but I promise you that I . . ."

She patted his arm. "It is quite all right, you know. I
like Mrs. Broadhurst. She is charming, and I am not in
the least offended." She smiled sweetly at his befuddle-
ment, and abruptly changed the subject. "I do hope

that supper will be served soon, I must confess I am very sharp set. Ah, yes, I see people are starting into the dining room. Come, Major, I want to see if the Ferrars' suppers are as good as Sally Althorp told me, and I think you might be the better for a glass of wine." She patted his arm and led him gently into the next room.

Everything went so well that morning in Hyde Park. Until the squirrels arrived.

Belle shifted in the saddle, eased her leg to a more comfortable position around the horn, trying to sit up straighter, then carefully rearranged the skirt of her Levantine silk riding habit. She was examining her glove for a spot she had noticed earlier, when Cecily began to lose patience.

"Ahem!"

"Yes?"

"Lillie, if we wanted to stay put, we could have remained at *home*. You have been rearranging yourself *again* these past five minutes. I must say, however, your habit is no end becoming. That claret color is just right for you, and the braiding on the sleeves is very *au courant.*" The sad fact was that Cecily Rafton could no more stop thinking about clothes, even at the most inappropriate of times, than she could cease breathing. But, at length, she recalled herself. "Well, that is beside the point," as if Belle had initiated the fashion talk. "Stop dawdling!"

"Dawdling? I am uncomfortable, that is all. Whoever it was deemed that women must ride sidesaddle—and I am convinced it must have been a man—should be made to sit in one for the rest of his days! They are a torture! My right leg is stiff from keeping it in this ridiculous position, and I never feel as if I am properly balanced . . ."

"Yes, yes, I know, for you have already said so a hundred times! I dislike them myself and often ride astride when we are at home in Gloucestershire—wouldn't the tabbies have fun with *that*, if they knew?" She grinned. "But, here, we must make the best of it, Lillie." This last was stated rather firmly, for it was clear that her student was stalling and sympathy would not help matters. "Let's go."

"No need to cut up stiff, Cecily," Belle retorted in aggrieved tones, "I just want to be sure I do not fall off."

Her friend contained a smile. "Lillie, you are doing quite well. And you have not fallen off yet—don't even think of it! Come on!" She urged her horse into a trot.

"Oh, very well."

Truth to say, Belle had begun to enjoy riding. She had not fallen or otherwise disgraced herself, and was starting to think that she might just be able to become a reasonably adept horsewoman. Not that it had been easy. Oh, no. Those first mornings had been difficult. In the beginning she had been afraid to let Comet do more than walk, a pace which the horse felt beneath her dignity. In fact, in the beginning, she had been all for forgetting the whole idea, but Cecily and Warner had prevailed. Warner had pointed out that she, Belle, had been right and probably could not survive the Season without displaying her equestrianism.

Cecily had put her case less practically, if not more typically. "Lillie, if God had not meant us to ride, he would not have made riding dresses." There being no logical reply to either woman's argument, she had relented, but she had regretted it more than once. First, there was the height.

"Oh, Cecily, I had forgotten how high off the ground it is to be on a horse."

"Isn't it grand? So nice to be able to see everything from this vantage point," was the only reply her teacher had made.

" 'Grand.' Definitely. Just as I would have described it," Belle had growled.

Then, there was the horse. When Cecily had introduced them, Belle had laughed. She was a huge mare with a noble head which she pushed up against Belle, nearly knocking her over, then looked at her dubiously.

"Come, Cecily, surely you could have found a bigger beast," she asked sarcastically, then demanded, "you do not expect me to ride *her* do you? She's gigantic! I thought mares were smaller than this!"

"She is a beauty. And, Lillie, you will love her, I promise you. She is most biddable and easy going. You will see."

"Easy going? Cecily, someone named her Comet for a reason, you know. I may be wrong, but my guess is that she moves rather quickly, given the opportunity."

Cecily laughed at her. "Considering all the carrots you have fed her, I am astonished that she can move at all! Come, do not be such a goose. She is a darling, honestly."

" 'Darling,' certainly," Belle could be heard muttering, as she was boosted into the saddle. Cecily handed her a crop. "I do not need that."

"Yes, you do."

"Cecily, if you think I intend to give this creature an excuse, any excuse at all, to move quickly, you are quite out."

But, Comet had proceeded gamely, if grudgingly, until Belle became more confident. Two days ago, when

Cecily had said they would progress to trotting, Belle had resisted.

"Cecily, I do not think that is a very good idea."

"What? Lillie, if all we are going to do is walk, we could do without the horses, you know."

It was the combination of growing confidence and enjoyment, and the grudging admission that, after all, she was right, that made Belle agree. She drew abreast now of Cecily and grinned at her. "This *is* fun, isn't it?"

Cecily threw back her head and laughed. "Let's canter. Follow me." And she was off.

In for a penny, Belle thought, and let Comet match her pace with Tartan's. Leave it to Cecily to name her horse after a piece of clothing. Really, she thought, this was *definitely* fun. The morning was already warm, and she liked the feel of the breeze on her face.

"Good girl, Comet, wonderful girl."

Cecily looked back and laughed. "That's it, Lillie! A little faster, now." She touched her crop to Tartan's side.

The wind tugged at Belle's hat and billowed her skirt, as she picked up speed. They continued down the road for some moments, leaving a couple of more sedate riders in their wake. Soon, Cecily reined in Tartan and Belle pulled up easily beside her.

"Oh, Cecily, that was so exhilarating! I can see now why you love it so." She was out of breath.

"Yes, it is like nothing else, is it? Lillie, you are coming along splendidly. Really, all you need now is practice."

Belle was gratified. "Only because I have had such a good teacher. Thank you, Cecily," she said warmly. "But, I think I have had enough for today. I do not want to press my luck. Shall we go back?" She turned Comet and looked back at her friend to see if she was in agreement.

"All right. I am famished, anyway. You will stay to breakfast?"

Belle had no opportunity to reply. Two chattering red squirrels, one madly chasing the other, rocketed from beneath the hedge and raced across Comet's path, too close for the horse's liking. The mare reared up. Belle, still looking back at Cecily, was caught off balance and thrown indecorously into the undergrowth, landing hard on her bottom.

"Oh, Lillie!" Cecily dismounted quickly and rushed to her side. "Are you hurt?"

Belle pushed her bonnet off her face and struggled to a somewhat more dignified sitting position. "What happened?"

"Some squirrels startled Comet."

"I shall never understand horses. This great beast is a thousand times bigger, but she is frightened by a couple of squirrels."

"Not 'frightened' precisely, Lillie. Horses get startled by things that, for them, appear out of nowhere."

"Fancy that. Well, I am not hurt, in any event."

"Good. Because tomorrow, I thought we might try a real gallop, and next week, we might attempt jumping over one or two of these low hedges." She gestured behind her. "Although, of course, we are not supposed to."

Belle glared at her. "Are you out of your mind?"

Cecily laughed and Belle joined her. "All right, come on, help me up. If I do not get back on this stupid creature now, I guess I never shall. Actually," she confided as they went slowly back to the mews, "that was not as bad as I recalled. Of course, I could have landed on a less forgiving surface, but, Cecily, I am not frightened. Isn't that marvelous?"

SIX

The fine weather had indeed held for the picnic. The small party spread blankets and cushions in a meadow near the shade of beeches and fruit trees just coming into flower. A tiny pond, partly fringed with yellow gorse, reflected the blue sky and the air was clean and sweet-smelling. Bees swung among wildflowers, softly buzzing, and birdsong reverberated from the trees.

"This is perfect," Belle remarked. "We are only thirty minutes from the city, but it is as if we are in another country." Gore agreed.

"Yes, isn't it odd that we should all pile together in London, practically living in one another's pockets," William began.

"But, dearest, London is the greatest city in the world!" Cecily exclaimed. "Why, it has everything—"

"Crowds!" William interjected.

"Dirt!" Belle added.

"Noise!" Gore chorused. "I have seen some battle-fields with fewer people and less commotion!"

"Shops!" Cecily put in gaily. They all laughed and settled into comfortable repose against the cushions.

Cecily took up the thread once again. "I cannot honestly argue with any of you. London is, indeed, all those things. But it *does* have many redeeming qualities. Still,

I confess I am happy to be there only a few months of the year, and the rest at Abbey Chase." She looked around. "It is even more beautiful there than here." She nodded to Belle and Gore. "You must both come to us after the Season." William seconded the invitation, and they accepted.

"And then, William says the birds are better there." She smiled and took her husband's hand. "Don't you, William?"

"I do and they are." He grinned. "Not that I expect anyone else to share my enthusiasm."

"Not a bit of it, Rafton. I can't say I share your fervor, exactly, but I have always taken an interest in birds. Isn't that so, Lillie?"

"Since we both were just out of leading strings, sir," Belle assured William.

"What do you think we might see today?" Gore gestured toward the trees.

William needed little encouragement. "Ah, come with me, Lindley. There is nothing exotic here, of course, but I think I spied a rook . . ." His voice was fading as the two gentlemen began to stroll toward the wood. "Oh, you will excuse us, ladies?" he asked as an afterthought.

"Of course, William. Enjoy yourselves." Cecily smiled and waved them off, Belle nodding agreement.

The men sauntered off, chatting amiably. Cecily lazily poured ale into two cups. She stole a glance up at Belle. "Nice to see them getting on so well. Devilish handsome, isn't he?"

Belle was equally casual. "William? Why, yes, so he is, Cecily, he is very—"

"Not William, you chucklehead, although *I* think he is splendid. No, I was speaking of Major Lindley. *As well you know,*" she added pointedly.

"Gore? Oh, yes, I suppose he is."

"You *suppose*? My dear, if you cannot be sure of it, you are either blind or dead. And you are neither. He is also intelligent and well mannered, and he has a good sense of humor. I grant you, he evidently has only a modest income, but people have lived on less. So, tell me, how do you resist him? I mean, being together all the time, the way you are."

Belle leaned forward to accept the ale, then leaned back against the cushion and capitulated. "I know. *I know.* I find myself thinking of him more and more. It is getting so that I compare every other gentleman I meet to Gore. And each of them falls short of the mark. It is very frustrating, I assure you."

"Hmm. Well, but need it be? Sometimes, oh, I cannot quite put my finger on it, but sometimes he seems to regard you with something other than cousinly interest."

"Actually, I have had the same impression once or twice. That is, when I have not been wondering if those deep looks mean that he suspects I am an imposter. I thought I must have windmills in my head, but if you . . . No, we must be mistaken. Lillie told me their relationship was nothing like that."

"People change."

"I know, but . . . Well, if it *were* true, very like he is just after Lillie's money, not me. As you said, he has just a competent income."

"Not a very high opinion of yourself have you?" Belle made a face. "Never mind. Did Lillie tell you anything about Gore that would lead you to suspect him of such behavior?"

"No, not at all. She spoke of him only in the very highest of terms."

"Well then?"

" 'People change,' Cecily."

"Ha! Touché! Come, Lillie, don't be so hard on him. Or you. Concede the possibility, at least."

"All right, Cecily, I concede." Belle laughed softly.

"And?"

"And what? Cecily, I can do nothing about it. Could let *him* do nothing about it. Remember my circumstances. He does not know who I really am, and I am convinced he would be furious were he to find out."

"To clarify, Lillie, he knows rather well who you are."

Belle's eyes widened.

"Think, my dear. He has not seen Lillie in *years.* The woman he sees now, the woman he has come to know again, is *you.* It is only your real name, then, he does not know."

Belle considered. "A minor detail," she said dryly. "And that is rather an oversimplification, but I do see your point. Still, if you are right, and assuming he does have any romantic interest in me, what can I do about it? If I tell him who I am, surely he will hate me. And if I do not, well, that alternative cannot even be considered."

William and Gore could be heard returning, their deep voices floating in snatches across the meadow.

Cecily had a very satisfied smile on her face. "We shall contrive, I know we shall. You were not gone very long," she called to the men.

They laughed and sat down on the blankets. "We decided we needed sustenance. After we eat, we can all go back," Gore explained.

"What have we got in those hampers, Cecily, for my stomach thinks my throat's been cut!" William added. "A haunch of venison for your lord and master, madam!"

"Ho! Who might that be, sir?" She explored the hamper's contents and produced a chicken leg. "I am afraid this will have to do you, *my lord!*" She chuckled.

"Ah, well, if that is the best you can produce." He sunk his teeth into the meat and laughed. "And dashed good it is!"

On the way home, they began to talk of the *soirée* they all were attending later that week, Belle with Lord Peter, and Gore with Maryanne Stockdale. Then Gore invited Belle to ride in Hyde Park. Shooting a surreptitious glance at Cecily, she smiled sweetly. "Yes, I would like that."

He was taken aback. "You, er, would?"

She nodded eagerly.

"Oh. Well. Uh, that is fine then."

"You see, I have practiced a bit with Cecily. I mentioned to you that it has been some time since I last rode. Just as I had suspected, I was quite rusty, so I am glad it was just she and I trundling along until I got my seat back."

"But, Lillie, you always loved to ride. How was it that you had got away from it?"

"Did I not tell you?" He shook his head. "Well, a few years ago, I had a nasty spill. Didn't actually hurt myself, well, not much, thank heaven. But, as it happened, I landed very close to a stone wall—just missed hitting my head on it, as a matter of fact. I never would have thought it, but that put quite a scare into me. And so, you must humor me, Gore, for I am not the hay-go-mad rider I once was. These days, I am a much less reckless horsewoman. Why, I daresay you could even call me dull!"

There! She and Cecily had cooked up this tale between them. While Cecily's tutelage had given Belle the basics and confidence she needed to ride capably, only time and practice could make her the rider Gore no doubt remembered Lillie to be—if, indeed, she could ever become so proficient. This way, she had a ready excuse for not living up to his expectations, and, being a gentleman, he could hardly press her to do more. It worked.

"You astonish me, Lillie, I would never have believed that anything could have frightened you away from the saddle. Don't worry, we shall go easy. At first. I know you shall have your old courage back soon."

That would have to be good enough.

Before Percival Stockdale had wed Hermione Godfrey, later mother to Maryanne, he had looked long and hard for a lady who would do justice to his name and quite substantial fortune. This process should not have been difficult, for he was possessed of a very handsome income, a sizeable estate in Surrey, houses in London and Bath, and he was not unpleasant to look upon. These charms should have ensured that Percival wed within a twelvemonth of his arrival on the marriage mart. But, what he lacked in address—and, to be truthful, he had none—he more than made up for with an arrogant disposition and insufferable pride instilled in him by parents consumed with said fortune and long family lines. Many a miss presented herself enthusiastically for his consideration, but all ultimately were rejected, and those few who were given any consideration soon ran quickly in the other direction, driven off either by his mean spirit or the unreasonable demands of his family.

When Hermione Godfrey entered the lists, things took a decidedly positive turn. She, too, had seen more than a Season on the town, but her income, only respectable—less perspicacious investing than the Stockdales'—could never hope to offset her snobbery—her family was as old as Percival's—much less a temper that on her better days could only be described as unpleasant—for no known reason. Percival and Hermione discovered they were soul mates after their first dance. But, despite their son's lack of success with the ladies and despite her lineage, his family remained adamant that he marry someone of at least equal wealth.

"Just how do you suppose this family built the fortune it has today, I ask you," his father had demanded, in a rage.

"But, Father, we have enough money for several families already," cried the son. "Why can I not marry where I choose?"

"Because you'll damned well do as you are told, my boy," screamed his father, whilst his mother inhaled deeply from her vinaigrette, "that is why. One *never* has enough money. I thought I had taught you that. One adds to the fortune which has been passed down to one. If I left matters to you, you would simply *spend* it! Good God! Have you learned nothing?" His face was scarlet with fury. *"That* woman will not do. Do you understand me? *She will not do!"*

Percival understood quite well. And, to his family's relief, he tried for the remainder of that Season to find the woman they would have him wed. Not surprisingly, she never appeared. The months wore on, and their removal from town evolved from talk to impending actuality. The house in Bath was readied for their arrival and Percival's will deepened, eventually asserting itself in a splendid show of defiance which, once given vent, would never again be gainsaid.

The angry scene with his parents and his aunts and uncles was more than would have been believed had it been presented upon the stage. When it ended—after his mother and his oldest aunt had fainted at least twice and had been ministered to with burned feathers and sal volatile, after his father had bellowed fit to raise the dead, face purple and he approaching apoplexy with the knowledge that the entail prevented his disinheriting his ungrateful, stupid, *only* son, after that thankless child threatened to take his inheritance and remove to the Continent, explaining in a bloodless manner that would have made the most coldhearted blush, that he cared nothing for them or their wishes, and he would marry Hermione—after all that, silence finally fell in the drawing room in Mayfair. His family's shock was not due to Percival's having at last stood up for what he wanted, although that alone was cause enough for rage, it was their sudden consciousness of the thankless, inconsiderate monster they had all had a hand in creating.

Hermione did not care that she was never really welcomed as their son's and nephew's wife, for the couple was quite content to do without the ravages of extended kinship. They moved in their own top-lofty circle which, perforce, was a small but select one, and ruled it with an iron grip. And, contrary to his father's dire predictions, Percival's wise investing increased their fortune far beyond anyone's expectations.

It was into this environment that Maryanne was born some years later. If her life had been a novel or a melodrama, she would have emerged as a changeling, a sweet, altruistic child who grew into a woman caring nothing for money, position or society; but Fate can be less capricious than it is often perceived to be. Maryanne was her parents' child and her grandparents' child and her great-aunts' and -uncles' child, and they all doted on her, making her disposition and expectations

considerably worse than they might otherwise have
been.

A pity, for she was in appearance all that was good.
Very tall and straight, she had enormous brown, long-
lashed eyes, full lips and a figure which did justice to
anything she might choose to wear. She had a charming
singing voice, was skilled on the pianoforte, rode like
Diana and danced like Terpsichore. Her friends envied
her, and she was the queen of her set, deciding where
they would go, what they would do and, most importantly, with whom. What more could a young lady want?

Unhappily, while she had any number of gentlemen
who hung about her, Maryanne, like her parents before
her, had been on the town just a bit too long. Few of
the gentlemen had been daring, or foolish, enough to
offer for her, and those who did were never considered
to be good enough for anyone in the Stockdale family,
memory and empathy not being amongst her parents'
strong suits. In truth, Maryanne was in danger of becoming just the tiniest bit shopworn, but this fact had
not yet evolved into words on anyone's lips, had not
even formed into a coherent thought in their minds.
In the meantime, Maryanne ruled all who came in her
path, made certain that she always had her way and,
generally, enjoyed her second Season in London. And
so, her fury at the prospect of a possible adversary was
perfectly understandable.

"She is old! *And* not even pretty! Can you credit it,
Mama? I cannot imagine what a gentleman like Major
Lindley could see in such a creature! *I* think his attention is far beyond what is required to show to one who
is practically a cousin!" Maryanne Stockdale stamped
her foot—a rather large foot, as it happened, this being
one of her few physical flaws—for emphasis.

Mrs. Stockdale sniffed. "Cousins do marry sometimes, dear," she explained. Maryanne glared. "Not that I am suggesting he intends to offer for her," she added hurriedly. "Only that it is *done*, you know. And then, they are not actually related, after all. Although, if it were done, I cannot think why he would choose someone so, so common."

Mrs. Stockdale had previously informed her daughter that she was not to entertain any notions of marriage in *that* quarter. She was very popular among the gentlemen, although for some reason that eluded both of them, had not yet received any really respectable offers. Major Lindley might be all that was charming, but he was definitely *not* an eligible *parti*. Not for *her* daughter.

"Really, Mama, do you think me so needle-witted? I do not wish to *marry* Major Lindley. I merely wish him to wish to marry *me*. Mama," she had explained slowly as if to someone hopelessly obtuse, as, indeed, she felt her mother to be, "Major Lindley is handsome and clever. He is a marvelous dancer, rides to the inch and, if Helen Ludden's brother is to be believed, could go more than a few rounds in the ring with Tom Cribb. In short, Mama, he would be a prime catch, were it not for his modest income. Nevertheless, for all the reasons I have just given you, most every female, even if she would never marry him, wants to be the object of his desire. So do I, dear Mama. But *I* intend to be successful, as I have informed all my friends. Once he comes up to scratch, and he *will*, I shall send him on his way with a flea in his ear. I shall not let that Broadhurst woman cut me out! Never!" The foot came down again to underscore her point.

Once Mrs. Stockdale was convinced that her darling girl had no intention of throwing away all that she and her father had bred her up to be, she saw no reason to stand in the way of what her child wanted.

"Well, Maryanne, there are ways of dealing with people like Lillie Broadhurst. Let's just put our heads together, shall we? I have more connections in this town than an upstart such as she could ever hope to gain in a hundred Seasons. Shall we ruin her reputation, or just send her packing back to . . . Burford, was it?" The Stockdale money and the Stockdale name—it was ancient—were good for more than an invitation to the Queen's drawing room, after all. "Now, tell me, just what do we actually *know* about this person?"

"Oh, Mama, I knew that I could count on you." Maryanne was her mother's daughter. All would be well, she was assured of that. She enveloped her mother in a hug, and they sat together on the sofa to plot Belle's social demise.

"What have you got there? Come on, Filbert, let me see." Belle was on her hands and knees half under a table, head next to the cat's as he pawed at something, something she could not see, between the drapery and the wall. From behind them, all that Gore could see was two bottoms wriggling as they worked, one upholstered with fur and finished with a plume, the other covered with sprigged blue lawn. On the whole, he decided that he preferred the one without the tail.

"Ahem."

"What? Ouch!"

Belle struggled up, rubbing her head, which had struck the table, further mussing her cap, and glared at her guest. "I might have known it was you."

"What a warm welcome, Lillie." He grinned. "Here, let me." He stepped forward and straightened her frilled cap. "That's better. You look quite charming in that."

"Thank you, I think," she replied suspiciously.

"Can't you accept a compliment?"

"Oh, well, I never can be sure when you say things that they *are* compliments." She busied herself setting her skirts to rights.

Gore realized that this was true. He did always seem to be teasing her or picking at her about something. No way to treat a lady, he chided himself, especially not one as pretty and nice as she. Oh ho! There you go swallowing the hook, just as she wants you to. If you're not careful, you will be taken in just like that birdbrain Dunstable. Still, he had noticed of late that his thoughts of Lillie were focused less on who she was not, and a great deal more on who she seemed to be.

To his embarrassment, Caroline Booth had pointed that out to him quite clearly. Of course, he had taken great pains for the remainder of that evening to pay particular attention to Miss Booth. She had even agreed to go with him to the opera. The odd part was, she had seemed to find the whole thing amusing. Damn fine woman, Miss Booth. Understanding, kind, good deal of fun, too.

Well, he was not about to hitch his wagon to Annabelle Makepeace's star, that much was certain. Even if he was not able to keep her from invading his thoughts—and she was doing that quite a lot lately, he found. Well, he did find her quite attractive—not that she was beautiful, mind you, because she wasn't, not at all in the way of Miss Booth or Miss Stockdale, no. But he found her quite nice to look at, easy on the eyes, as it were. The fact was, despite their being at daggers drawn twenty minutes out of every hour, he had come to enjoy their time together and found her easy, yes, comfortable, to be with.

Still, he was not about to be taken in by her. But

wasn't he already? He could have exposed her at any time, told her that he knew who she was, shamed her for all the *ton* to see, but he had not. Why? He truly could not have said. In the beginning, he had wanted to see just how far she would take the whole thing, just what she would do. But now? Oh, devil take her, he decided. She is not harming me, after all. Nor Lillie. My mad cousin is cavorting somewhere in Italy with little care for what happens here in London, so why am I worrying? It could do no harm to be nice to the woman.

"You have the right of it, Lillie, I suppose I do tease you horribly, don't I? I promise to do better. Pax?"

Belle looked at him askance. She wanted to believe him. She wanted to look in those eyes and see admiration, not teasing or suspicion. She wanted . . . too much, and she knew it. Well she would take what he offered and be glad of it.

"Pax."

"Now, tell me, what were you doing on the floor?"

Given the way he had scoffed at her previously stated intention to hunt for The Bracelet, she was not sure if she should tell him, but in the interest of better relations, she decided to give him the benefit of the doubt.

"I saw Filbert worrying at that bit of wall near the table and thought he might have found The Bracelet."

"I take it he had not?"

"No. Heaven only knows what he was at, he does do the strangest things at times, but it was not The Bracelet." Good. Evidently, he was not going to make any rude remarks.

"I suppose you must continue the hunt, then." No point in ruffling her feathers, especially after he had just declared a peace. He would just have to believe that she would give it to Lillie if she did find it. And, of course, she had no hope of doing so. Many had tried before her and all had failed. There was no reason to expect her to be any more successful. "I cannot stay. I only came to ask if you would like to ride with me on Monday."

"I would. I have a charming new habit, and hope to cut a dash with that, even if my riding skills are not what they should be." She felt the need to remind him of her reduced ability.

"I shall look forward to the ride and to the new dress, Lillie. Well, I'll be off, then. I shall see you at the *soirée* on Saturday?"

The *soirée* was not, happily to Belle's way of thinking, the crush that so many other entertainments had been. The orchestra played a program which leaned heavily toward reels and country dances, and few sat out the opportunity to demonstrate his or her skills on the dance floor. Belle was fanning herself after a particularly strenuous reel while her partner fetched her a cold drink. Flushed and smiling, she raised sparkling eyes to Gore, as he came up beside her.

"Having fun, Lillie? You remember Miss Stockdale?"

"Yes on both counts, Gore. Good evening, Miss Stockdale. Isn't this a wonderful party?"

"This? Oh, I suppose one might consider it acceptable." Miss Stockdale was waiting to waltz with Major Lindley, who excused himself to find refreshment for them both. "I find these country dances rather . . . tedious, but I suspect that you quite enjoy them."

Belle raised fine brows and smiled. "I must admit that I do."

"Yes. Well, perhaps it is what you are used to. I understand there is little fine entertainment in the country. You are from . . . Bradford was it?"

"Burford."

"And so I expect your taste is less refined. Here in London, we are used to better. All this jumping about is fatiguing and rather common, I think." Miss Stockdale smirked. "So suitable for the country."

"To say the truth, I like 'jumping about.' It is good exercise, something I find myself getting little of in London, and it is a great deal of fun, besides."

"Really? To say nothing of what it does for one's coiffure. Your hair is quite mussed." Miss Stockdale smiled spitefully. "Perhaps you were not aware of it. Or, perhaps, it is worn that way in, uh, Burnside."

Belle put a hand up to her hair, which seemed to have survived the last reel quite well. Still, going to "fix" it was as good an excuse as any to get away from the unpleasant Miss Stockdale. She continued to smile, determined that this creature would not get the better of her. *"Burford.* If you will excuse me, I shall go to the retiring room and see to the damage, Miss Stockdale."

"What a good idea," the younger woman purred.

Belle was not aware that Maryanne had placed one large foot on the hem of her flounce until she felt the tug on her dress and heard the sound of silk ripping. She looked back and down, dismayed to find that a large section of flounce had been torn from her gown.

"Oh, how clumsy." Miss Stockdale tittered.

Belle looked around at her and glared. She was not certain if the woman was apologizing or berating her for being so oafish as to leave the edge of the flounce under her large foot. She wanted very much to mention just how huge a foot it was, but managed to refrain.

"Such an interesting dress, too. Did you get it in Bagley?"

"Burford. And I had it made here in London."

Maryanne's brows raised in doubt. "I could recommend you to another dressmaker, if you like."

Belle knew quite well what the woman was implying, and she also knew that her dress was all the crack, but she was not about to get into a set-to. "Thank you, I am very satisfied with the woman I have."

Maryanne giggled.

"Excuse me."

Gore returned to find Belle gone and Miss Stockdale looking quite pleased with herself. He handed her a cup of punch. "Where is Mrs. Broadhurst?"

"Oh, I do not know. Gone to see to her hair, I think. Some women are obsessed with their appearances. Come, Major, I see someone I want you to meet. And I do so hope that the orchestra will soon play a waltz, do not you?" As they walked, she caught her mother's eye from across the room. That lady nodded almost imperceptibly and smiled. Maryanne gave a smug wink and tightened her grip on her escort's arm.

The waltz was played a short while later, and Miss Stockdale did swirl through it in Gore's arms. To her chagrin, however, she watched Belle dance by in the arms of Lord Peter. When Belle turned, she saw that her flounce had been hastily, and not very expertly, pinned, doubtless by the maid in attendance in the re-tiring room. We shall see about that, Maryanne decided.

When the dance ended, Gore, Maryanne still on his arm, worked his way around to Belle, who with Lord Peter, had been joined by Cecily and William. The four were laughing.

"Honestly, Lillie, I cannot take you anywhere! That beautiful dress is ruined!" Her words were belied by her grin, but Belle had explained all and she was very put out.

"Calm yourself, my love," William said, "it is only a dress, after all."

"Only a dress? William!"

They all laughed the harder. Gore, who had not seen the tear, asked to know the joke.

Belle reached behind her and drew the mangled fabric toward the front, exposing the damage.

"Oh, dear, what happened?"

"Someone trod on it, silly. I am really not sure who." She glanced slyly at Maryanne.

"Well," he replied, "must have been a big chap. Judging by the size of the tear, fellow must have had uncommonly big feet."

Belle and Cecily dissolved into renewed laughter. "Oh, yes, Gore, I am sure this person must have had *enormous* feet."

Maryanne was not amused. She excused herself to Gore and went to work. Within minutes, she and her mother had hissed into the ears of several acquaintances. "Only see Mrs. Broadhurst's dress. Can you believe that she would parade in society with a torn flounce? Did she think that we would not notice the pins? Breeding does tell, does it not? Evidently, she holds the *ton* in so little regard that she cannot be bothered to make herself presentable."

Eyebrows shot up and whispers began to whisk around the room. At last, something for society's spiteful creatures, male and female, to sink their teeth into. The evening had been quite a bore for them up until now. Before long, people were giving sidelong glances to Belle and snickering or expressing shock at the insult she had perpetrated on them. She was, after all, just a nobody from the country. Just because she had a large fortune, she had been invited everywhere, and so was apparently thinking she was considered one of them. Such behavior simply was not to be tolerated. The evening was drawing to a close, so they did not have sufficient opportunity to visit their displeasure on her. That was why Belle thought the whole silly matter would be forgotten in a day or two. But she was quite wrong.

Once again, everything was proceeding nicely in Hyde Park. Until Maryanne Stockdale arrived. Gore could not really be blamed for his part in the affair, for he was an unwitting accomplice. How could he have known that merely mentioning to Miss Stockdale his plans to ride with Lillie on Monday, and that it would be Lillie's first occasion to ride in some time, would set her mind to plotting?

True to his word, Gore did not goad Belle into doing anything daring. He seemed happy to proceed at a fairly leisurely pace and chatted easily with her. He even remembered to admire her riding dress. Thistle was as agreeable a mount as Gore had promised, and Belle quickly felt even more confident atop her than she had riding Comet. They cantered along Rotten Row, waving to acquaintances and stopping once or twice to talk with friends. Belle was enjoying herself enormously and sensed that Gore was, as well. She was so happy that she suggested they ride together on a regular basis. Seeing an opportunity to spend more time with her, which she intended to provide when she made the offer, he gladly agreed.

They were trotting single file, Belle in front, along a fairly narrow section of the path, when they heard hoofbeats pounding up fast behind them. Before they could react, six horses thundered up, riders laughing and cheering, and one voice in particular calling Gore's name. The path was too narrow to accommodate all of them comfortably, but Gore was able, if rather uncomfortably, to make way for those who pushed in beside him. Those who could not fit rushed rudely on, stopping loudly and with much more commotion than necessary when they got abreast of Belle. Since Gore's view of her was blocked by those riders who had come to rest near him, he only heard her cry followed by a loud noise.

Dismounting, he ran to where she had fallen. While she was no more injured than she had been on the first occasion, this circumstance was much worse. For, when she had toppled from the frightened Thistle, the skirt of her habit had caught on a hedge, leaving her legs quite exposed as she lay on the ground. When Gore reached her, she was trying with little success to cover herself as the other riders stood aside and either laughed uproariously or professed to being scandalized. Seeing Gore draw near, Maryanne Stockdale disentangled herself from the group and made as if she were trying to help.

"Oh, Mrs. Broadhurst, are you all right? Are you hurt? Here, let me help you."

Gore knelt by her side, untangled the torn skirt and covered what he was quite pleased to discover was a pair of shapely legs. "Lillie, my God, are you hurt? Lillie!"

Belle looked up at him and beyond to the now-tittering riders, none of whom, save for Maryanne, had dismounted to help her. She could feel her face burning and tested her arms and legs gingerly to be sure they still were properly connected.

"No, I am not, thank you, Gore." She did not thank Miss Stockdale. She knew better. "My bonnet?"

Gore and Maryanne looked around them. Maryanne found it.

"Here it is, Mrs. Broadhurst." She held aloft the trampled remains of a once-lovely hat. "I am very much afraid that it is ruined." She smiled sweetly. "And your hair, well . . ."

Suddenly, Belle found the humor in the situation and began to giggle, then to laugh. "Oh, Gore," she managed to say through the laughter, "my poor dress and my bonnet, too!"

Gore found himself so relieved that she seemed unharmed that he chuckled, but not for long. He was too concerned that she might have incurred an injury not yet discovered, and he wanted to get her home. By now, a few other riders had joined the audience and were busily buzzing amongst themselves.

"Skirts up above her head, you say?"

" 'Pon my word, some women have no dignity."

"Evidently can't control her horse."

Gore was too worried to hear them, and Belle tried not to listen.

"Yes, Mrs. Broadhurst, it appears that you have ruined another costume. If you keep up this pace, you will go through your whole wardrobe in no time," Maryanne commented snidely.

"Now is not the time for jokes, Miss Stockdale," Gore said. "You meant well, I am sure, trying to tease her out of her upset, but there is no humor in this situation."

Belle glared at him. Humor? She'd kill him. Was he so blinded by Miss Stockdale's beauty that he could not understand what was going on? Had he not seen how the creature had startled Thistle into throwing her? Could he not hear the others?

"Pay them no mind, Lillie," he replied when she pointed out that she was again grist for the society mill. "They're young, most of 'em, and foolish. Not worth bothering with."

Maryanne smiled sweetly.

"That is true, I *was* just trying to make poor Mrs. Broadhurst feel better. But, of course, Major, you have the right of it, there is nothing to laugh at here. Stop it all of you!" she shouted to her circle of friends. "Why, Mrs. Broadhurst could have broken something. I have heard that, at her age, bones can be very brittle."

Gore had stopped listening, however. He assisted Belle to her feet, then carried her to Orion, calling to one of the men to bring Thistle along.

"What are you doing?" Belle asked him in horror.

"I am taking you home, where we can be sure that you are not hurt. You will ride with me."

"I will not!"

"You will." He placed her gently on Orion's back and climbed up behind her. "Here, lean back against me."

Maryanne stood alongside Orion and handed Gore the crop that had fallen when he'd dismounted so hurriedly. "Yes, do take care of her, Major. I cannot imagine how such a thing could have happened. You evidently had no control over your animal. Did you learn to ride like that in Boxford? I could give you lessons, if you like," she inquired sweetly.

"Burford," was all Belle managed through grinding teeth, before Gore turned his horse for Berkeley Square.

SEVEN

Once they had returned home, Belle was, at last, able to convince Gore that she was undamaged, but on the following afternoon, she did not have the same success with Eulalie who expressed great concern for her reputation. Though the older woman tried to explain the facts of town life to her, Belle would not listen.

"The fault was not even mine, you know, either time. I would like to say they were accidents, but I believe the incidents to have been intentional. And, honestly, Aunt, the *ton* are merely a lot of top-lofty folks who like nothing more than a touch of scandal, even if the behavior is nothing out of the common way. Why, just the other day, someone told me that a gentleman had actually paid all his tradesmen's bills—can you imagine, Aunt?" she queried with a sarcastic chuckle. "Apparently, they were quite sizeable—Lord only knows how long the poor shopkeepers had to wait in the first place—and set himself back so much that Lord Alvanley was outraged and said the man had ruined himself by paying his bills! So, if people were not shocked by his lordship's judgment, surely they will not think twice about my poor dress."

Eulalie shook her head at this naivete. "Lillie, you have got it entirely backward, my dear. Society never would speak ill of Alvanley—because he is one of them and has a sharp wit, besides. And that fellow who paid the bills probably soon enough came round to his way of thinking, if only so that his peers would not believe him a complete fool. No, no, Lillie, society seldom turns on its own—it takes a far greater transgression than uttering an empty-headed *bon mot* as Alvanley did, to incur their wrath. He *amused* them. That is very important to people who have little to do, less to laugh at and absolutely nothing to think about.

"You, Lillie, are not really one of them. You are gently bred, come of very good, even old, stock and have piles of money. In the normal way of things, that would be sufficient for any self-respecting, self-righteous society. But you are in London now, my dear, and a very provincial society it is. Furthermore, you are here for the first time. These people, the ones at the so-called pinnacle, who think they matter, have spent the Seasons here forever. They hunt together in the country, they have attended the same schools, their families have intermarried—oh, there are a dozen very foolish reasons why they would turn on you at the drop of a pin. You must take care." She narrowed her eyes. "But tell me what you meant when you said that these events were not accidents."

Belle complied. Eulalie listened quietly, shaking her head again. "Oh, my, this could be bad."

"Aunt!"

"I am deadly serious, Lillie. I know it sounds insane. It *is* insane. But it is true all the same. What makes it worse is Hermione Stockdale's hand in this. You have no idea what a witch she is. Well, I have a great deal of work to do."

"What do you mean, Aunt Eulalie?"

"Damage repair, my dear. And the sooner I start, the better."

"But, Aunt Eulalie, I do not care what they think about me. Or what they say."

The older woman sighed in exasperation. "You will, my dear, I promise you. Invitations could dwindle, they might even disappear."

If Belle had been warned of this outcome a few weeks earlier, she would not have minded much. Since then, she had learned how much fun a London Season could be, and she would be sorry to be deprived of it. Still, she had made quite a few friends. They, certainly, would not reject her, she pointed out to Eulalie.

"Don't be too sure. Some people are easily intimidated or led. You could have quite an unpleasant surprise."

"Well, then, they would not really have been my friends, would they? I know that Cecily and William would stay by me. I suppose I could survive without the rest," she said with bravado, "I will not care about them."

"Unfortunately, one needs more than bosom beaux to be successful—or even to enjoy society. One must be accepted by the *ton*. Some, like Lady Castlereagh, will not shun you, if for no other reason than that she is my friend, and that her own behavior has set the tongues wagging more than once. But, when you receive the cut direct at a ball by the likes of Sally Jersey, you will know what it means to be outcast. Oh, Lillie, I do not mean to frighten you. I just want you to be prepared for what could happen. I have seen it, and it is most unpleasant and cruel."

Poor Eulalie called in every favor, every debt, every consideration she could think of, but she had been too long out of the mainstream of society to carry the weight she once did. And even those of her set who had remained in circulation and who were willing to accommodate her, found their opinions too often were

considered those of old ladies and men, who had little
sway with the younger generation. If they had not exactly
retired from town life, their social leverage had long ago
passed into desuetude along with their face patches and
powdered wigs, a fact they had, until now, been too smug
to notice. That this came as a surprise to many of them
would be understating the case. Eulalie had to report
that she could do little to help with Belle's predicament.

A few days later, Belle was walking with Lord Peter and
came upon a small crowd of about a dozen people gathered outside a print-shop window. As they drew near to
learn what the attraction was, they could hear laughter.

Lord Peter chuckled. "I suspect it's a cartoon, Mrs.
Broadhurst. Let's see who Cruikshank is lampooning
this time," he said, referring to the most famous cartoonist of the day.

He drew her closer to the shop. Belle stood on her
toes to see above the heads of those in front. The window was filled with satirical sketches. There was the Regent disporting himself with yet another female. Close
by was a drawing of the Prime Minister. Attached to
Liverpool's head and limbs were long puppet strings
grasped by an over-sized Castlereagh hovering over him.

But the onlookers did not seem to be laughing at these
irreverent representations. When the man in front of
Belle leaned toward the gentleman to his left, she and
Lord Peter could finally see the object of their derision.
There, in pride of place in the center of the window,
stood an easel holding a large cartoon. Belle gasped.
The caricature depicted a woman lying on the ground
amidst trees, shrubbery, horses and riders. The skirt of
her habit was well-above her knees and her limbs were
positioned in a most unladylike fashion, exposing gar-
ters and torn stockings. The woman was leaning back
on her elbows, eyes wide, mouth agape, her face a picture

of outrage and stupidity. A bubble beside her head contained the words, "Stupid Horse!!" Beneath the figure, in large, heavy black script were the words "The Provincial Lily." Belle felt her face flame. Since none of the crowd knew who she was and the image actually was nothing like her in appearance, she was unrecognized. She had told Lord Peter of the incident, however, so he immediately grasped the connection.

"Mrs. Broadhurst, come," he said gently.

"This one's even better," a man in the crowd said. Belle looked back to where he was pointing and felt tears welling up in her eyes. The second cartoon showed Belle dancing at the *soirée*, a huge, gaping hole where a portion of the back flounce of her gown should have been. A banner hung askew above the dance floor with the words "The Provincial Lily Goes Dancing." She was depicted as blithely dancing, a foolish smile on her face, as the other guests stood back and pointed, showing shock or great amusement. This time, she was uttering the words, "Blimey, Don't These London Toffs Know Nothin' About Fashion?"

Lord Peter whispered in her ear. "Mrs. Broadhurst, don't let them see you cry. They'll know, if you do."

She allowed herself to be led away. Lord Peter soon had her back in Berkeley Square, where he and Warner ministered to her with tea and soothing words.

"I am going to fetch Mrs. Rafton," Warner whispered to him.

"No, best you stay with her, Warner. I shall go. Which house is it?"

Warner brought Belle up to her bedroom and had her lie on the chaise by the window. A few minutes later, Lord Peter returned alone.

"Mrs. Rafton is out, I am afraid. I will not go up, of

course, Warner, but I don't want to just leave. Is there someone else I should go for? Her aunt? Her cousin?"

Warner did not think they should distress Eulalie, who would learn of the fuss soon enough, and she had heard Lillie mention that Gore was from town for a day or two. Distressed, Lord Peter paced the drawing room, feeling helpless. He knew he could not visit a lady in her bedchamber, but could not bring himself to go without doing something he felt to be productive. This was worse than any farce he had seen at the theatre, for it involved real people with real feelings. He and Warner had talked with Belle on their return to the house, and there had been much patting of hands from both of them as they counseled her to ignore the cartoons.

"They're vicious and stupid, I know, Mrs. Broadhurst, but you'll see, you'll be, that is, *they'll* be just a nine-days' wonder," Warner offered soothingly.

"That's right. In a few days, they will move on to skewer someone else," Lord Peter added.

Through it all, Belle had sat quietly, not even crying. She wanted to run away and never look back. To forget she ever had been in London. This must be her payment for perpetrating such a fraud in the first place. Those who had not heard what had transpired at the *soirée* or in the park—and, in truth, few had—could not help but receive the intelligence now. If they were not vicious enough to know what to laugh at on their own, society needed only someone like a caricaturist to tell them.

Aunt Eulalie had been right. The *ton* would have a feeding frenzy. And what of Lillie? She would come home to find herself the laughingstock of London! Belle's head was beating like the hammers of hell, though Warner had laid a cloth dampened with lavender water on her brow as Lord Peter paced like an expectant father in the drawing room. He had not been there long when a sharp tattoo on the front door ushered in Cecily Rafton.

"Thomasina, is Mrs. Broadhurst in? I must see her at once." Cecily sounded flustered.

The maid, who knew that something was amiss, let her into the hall and went to see if her mistress was receiving. Lord Peter came out of the drawing room.

"Mrs. Rafton, I am very relieved to see you. I am afraid there is a terrible—"

"I know. I am just come from shopping. Do you mean Lillie has heard?"

He nodded. "She has seen them."

"Oh, dear, I had hoped to soften the news first. People are already buying those filthy cartoons. Poor Lillie. Where is she?"

"She is upstairs with Warner." He explained what had happened.

"Oh, no. I had better go to her."

"Good. I called looking for you before. Please try to convince her that she must not refine upon this too much."

"You mean lie to her, Lord Peter?" Her tone was bitter. "She is not a fool."

"I know. Damn shame. Beg your pardon. Nice woman, Mrs. Broadhurst. Someone has really put the cat among the pigeons. She's going to have the devil of a time for a while."

"We must hope that it is only for a while, sir, and that she is not permanently tainted by this. The Provincial Lily, indeed! I think I know who is responsible for this, and if I get my hands on her . . ."

"Who?" When Belle had related the incidents to Lord Peter, as Aunt Eulalie had instructed, she had made light of them and had brought no one to book for causing them.

"I cannot say, Lord Peter. I must go to Lillie. Pray excuse me."

"Of course. I shall be off, too. Please convey my kind thoughts to Mrs. Broadhurst, and tell her I shall call tomorrow."

Cecily rapped softly on the door, entered and crossed to where Belle lay.

"Oh, my dear, I am so sorry."

"Cecily!" Belle put her head on her friend's shoulder and wept. Warner nodded, satisfied that the release was finally come, and sat on the edge of the bed. Filbert sat to one side, observing the proceedings.

"I know, Lillie, I know," she soothed. "You do realize who must have done this, don't you?"

Belle looked up, her red, wet face furious. "Who else but Maryanne Stockdale? Oh, Cecily, I should like to strangle her. Why is she doing this? Weren't things already bad enough?"

"No, not nearly bad enough for the likes of her, apparently. It was not sufficient that the people in our circle should know of what occurred in the park and at the ball. She wanted to be certain that all of society knows of it . . . Oh! I am sorry!"

"Don't be, I know well what this will do to my reputation. Aunt Eulalie explained it to me, but I would not believe her. And what of Lillie's reputation? She wanted only to travel to Italy for a bit of adventure. Now I have fixed it so that she can never show her face in London!"

"That is not fair, Lillie, and you know it. Lillie is not here—oh, my, these names can be so confusing—but if she were, she would never blame you. Would she, Warner?"

"No, ma'am, she would not," the abigail replied assuredly. "Mrs. Broadhurst would never treat a friend in such a manner."

"There, you see?"

"I should never have been so presumptuous as to take on the identity of someone above me. God, I want to leave here."

"Oh, stuff!"

"Remember, although she is not here, Lillie cannot be held entirely blameless. Yes, that is right," she replied to Belle's raised brows. "She took the same chance you did. She must have been aware that things could go awry. And you are not being fair to yourself, either. Both incidents were contrived by a spiteful creature. You were her unwitting prey. Oh, I've done it again, haven't I? But, honestly, Lillie, it is but the truth. Those things could have happened to anyone."

"Perhaps only to some green girl from the country, Cecily. Whatever possessed me to return to the dance with a torn gown? And then, Lillie would have been better able to control her horse. She would not have fallen off."

Warner spoke. "Madam, if I may?" Belle nodded. "As you know, I have not been with Mrs. Broadhurst—that is, the *real* Mrs. Broadhurst," she smiled, "for a very long time. However, between those months and the stories that she told me, I feel I know her quite well, and I shall tell you a thing or two that you may not know. Indeed," she smiled again, "I think you do not, else you would not be so blue-deviled now.

"First, I must say that I am not telling tales out of school, as it were, for Mrs. Broadhurst would be the first to tease herself. One reason that she did not look forward to coming to London was that she knew what high sticklers the *ton* could be, and she is not like that herself, at all. She despises pretension and snobbery. You returned to the dance after your gown was mended because you were enjoying yourself and could not see why such a mishap should spoil your fun—it was not such a very large rent, after all. She would have done the same thing, I promise you. The fact is, if the tear had been worse, she probably would have removed the entire flounce and *still* stood up for the next dance.

"And, as for being thrown, why Mrs. Broadhurst has fallen more than once herself." Belle looked amazed. "Yes, it is true." Warner was lying through her teeth, Lillie had never been thrown in her life, but desperate times call for desperate measures, she thought. "And I can promise you one more thing," she stated with conviction, for this time she was telling the truth, "Mrs. Broadhurst would never," she looked pointedly at Belle, "let someone the likes of Maryanne Stockdale get away with what she has done, nor let such a one spoil her Season in London."

There was silence for some moments as her listeners digested this information. Belle blew her nose and pushed some strands of hair behind an ear.

"Lillie fell? Honestly?"

Warner raised a hand in oath and nodded. Wryly she realized that, rather than hoping her intentions, not her words, would be remembered come judgment day, she was praying that, in this life, Lillie never heard what she had said about her riding abilities.

"Well, but she was never publicly lampooned by a cartoonist," Belle pointed out doubtfully.

"True, but do you think that she would run away?"

"No, I do not."

"Hah! There!" This from Cecily.

"Well, intentions are all well and good, you two, but I must still determine how to rout that creature," Belle said, her brow furrowed.

"Never fear, we shall think of something. Shall we not, Warner?"

Pleased to be included in the plan, Warner grinned. "We shall indeed, ma'am."

They pondered the problem for some time over tea. Lord Peter would not have recognized the lady he had left just an hour before, for the Belle who entered into the discussion was animated and determined. At length, after having several of her ideas for exacting retribution on the clever Miss Stockdale rejected—"Really, Cecily, we cannot have her set upon by footpads! Not that I should not like to"—Cecily sat up straight in her chair.

"I have it. Mrs. Niven!"

Belle laughed. "Dear Cecily, I know better now than to tax you with that, but whatever can our dressmaker have to do with any of this?"

Her friend grinned broadly. "You shall see." Belle and Warner exchanged doubtful glances. "You shall both see." She laughed.

And so they would, but before that, there was much more to be borne.

First, the lilies began to arrive. Great quantities of them. From "anonymous admirers" and "secret friends," all addressed to "The Provincial Lily in Berkeley Square." "Humph," said Belle, as Thomasina brought in yet another bouquet, "heaven save me from friends and admirers such as these. And to think that I used to like lilies. Take them to the kitchen, Thomasina. I am certain you can find a place for them down there."

Gore, who had not pursued his quest for a wife very assiduously, now decided it was time he did. Dallying with the likes of Maryanne Stockdale was all well and good, but it was not likely to put him in the way of a wife. For one thing, he did not believe for an instant that she would consider him to be suitable matrimonial material, and for another, and much more important reason, she was not at all what he was looking for. She was too shallow, too silly—too young.

He smiled at himself. He had indeed returned from the army an older man in more ways than one. Time was, the attentions of a Maryanne Stockdale would have done more than flatter, they might have caught him, as well. Thank God, he had put all those years and all that space between him and young misses, for he knew now that marriage to someone like her would have driven him to distraction—or murder—inside a twelvemonth. Fortunately, he had not been all that particular in his attentions to her. Rather, he was more frequently one of a group of gentlemen than her sole escort.

It had been easier to simply enjoy the Season, the company of pretty women who doted on his looks and charm, demanding nothing more than his appearance, a ready wit and the desire to flatter. But all that had recently failed to satisfy. He felt a remote, at first indefinable, restlessness that he had not experienced since he had waited on the battlefield for the onset of fighting, an anxiety that asserted itself more and more strongly as time passed and the Season waned. It took him some time to realize this, still longer to put a name to it, but when he did, he knew that it could not be eradicated by attending more routs and balls filled with vapid, empty conversation. And not with Maryanne Stockdale. His attraction to her had been only to her beauty and gaiety after all those years in the army. However, he was beginning to think that she had chosen to interpret his attentions as much more serious than they were, that she might expect them to lead to something. He sought a woman, a *woman,* of more substance; one who could stimulate his mind as well as his senses.

He had first seen the cartoons of The Provincial Lily

at his club and had immediately identified Belle as their subject. Indeed, it had taken a remarkably short period of time for the victim's identity to reach everyone's ear. He knew a pang of guilt as the other members laughed at the sketches, wondering how many times he had reacted in just that way when someone else had been mocked in the press.

One fellow with whom he was slightly acquainted asked if his cousin really was such a bumpkin. Gore wanted to plant him a facer, but, instead, settled for pointing out that anyone who slurped his soup and whose waistcoat hung nearly to his knees, so many fobs and whip points—which by the way he had no business sporting, since he had no notion how to handle a team— did it support; someone who was, in fact, a man-milliner, certainly had no business to question another's style.

The man had been not a little put out by this tirade. As Gore strode from his club in high dudgeon, he wondered why he had reacted so strongly. At first, he decided that he would have behaved as he had on behalf of any friend and, certainly, on behalf of the real Lillie, who was so dear to him. Then, he realized that he had not thought of Belle as Lillie for some time, but, rather, as a person wholly distinct from his cousin. Well, I should hope so, he told himself, for you could not be so cloth-headed as to fall in love with Lillie. He stopped abruptly in the middle of the pavement, earning a disgusted "Well, really!" from the two gentlemen who, perforce, nearly walked into him.

In love? He stared blankly at a passing barouche. Was he? Could he be in love with her? Her smile danced before his eyes, and he felt her in his arms as they waltzed. He pondered. She was witty and kind, and she certainly had pluck. He would swear that she had not known how to ride, but she had contrived to learn—God knew how!—and had acquitted herself well, really, until that unfortunate toss. Too, he had admired the way she had laughed at herself—he prized that gift in anyone. Still, that day, he had been so afraid she might have been injured that he had held her much closer than necessary as he returned her home. And she had not objected. Could that mean . . . ? Probably not. Gore gave a crooked smile, returned by a passing maid, whom he did not even see, and said in a soft voice, "Damn it, I love her. Whoever she is."

He proceeded on his way to Berkeley Square, eager to see Belle and console and protect her in her time of need. Once inside, he was nearly suffocated by the cloying scent of dozens of lilies. Finding her in the morning room, he accepted a cup of tea and remarked on the flowers.

"Someone's idea of humor," she explained dryly. "Hilarious, ain't it?"

He smiled and expressed his sympathy for the torment she must have been enduring. "I had thought to find you distraught, you know, Lillie. But, you look quite the other."

She laughed lightly. "You sound disappointed, Gore."

Gore was almost miffed to find her in such good spirits. As he had covered the distance from St. James's Street to Berkeley Square, he had envisioned her in his arms, weeping as he consoled her with promises of retaliation against the scurrilous attack. But, there would be other opportunities to hold her in his arms. He would see to that. Quickly, he berated himself for being so selfish and hastened to assure her that he was happy to see she was not in the mopes. Maryanne Stockdale's possible connivance did not occur to him, and he resolved to follow Belle's lead and make the best of the matter.

"I thank you. To say the truth, had you seen me yesterday, I should have fulfilled your direst expectations." Her face hardened a moment, then brightened again. "But, you see, I am determined not to let such childish mischief get the better of me." She did not mention the plan of revenge that she, Cecily and Warner were hatching.

"I am glad to know it. Quite the best tactic, I am sure. Just keep your head up, my dear, they will move on to some other poor soul soon enough."

"Yes, so I have been advised."

"I do wonder, though, how your mishaps should have been considered of significant consequence to the artist. No offense intended, of course." He grinned.

"None taken, I promise you! I cannot say how it should have come to his notice." Since she had no proof of Miss Stockdale's involvement, she would not implicate her. It might make Belle sound petty or crazy, particularly as she knew Gore had been the young woman's escort on a couple of occasions.

"More tea?"

He nodded. "Do you still plan to have your dinner party on Thursday?" This event had been planned some time ago, and he wondered if all the tongue-wagging would put her off.

"I do. As I said, I cannot give in to gossip. As well, if I were to cancel now, how would it look? No, I must go on as I have been and hope that it all goes off as it should. And I have been so looking forward to it. You are still coming, are you not?" she teased.

Gore assured her that he was and presently departed. He did not think to mention, and Belle had not thought to ask, who he was bringing with him on Thursday. It was Maryanne Stockdale. While he now found that young woman's beauty insipid and her companionship

quite dull, there was no way that he could politely un-
invite her. He was determined, however, that he would
not be spending any time with her in the future.

Several days later, Belle was driving in the park with
Lord Peter. She had vowed not to let the recent events
force her into hiding, but it had not been easy. Just the
day before, when she had ventured out to the Burlington
Arcade to purchase a present for Warner's birthday, she
had seen more than one person chuckling at her. Well,
she told herself, you knew this would be difficult. Ignore
them. They will go away. And they did. Unfortunately,
they were always replaced by others with the same bad
sense of humor.

She sighed and tried to enjoy the beautiful day and
the company of Lord Peter who had been so supportive
of her. Soon, they saw the Regent tooling down the
path, the Life Guards escorting him. Everyone's eyes
were on their prince and his magnificent yellow carriage. Vehicles halted so as not to impede his progress,
and all bowed their heads as he passed. He slowed once
or twice to exchange a word with a particular friend
but, otherwise, deigned only to nod at his subjects.

When his vehicle had passed Belle and Lord Peter, it
shortly pulled up so that he could speak with a gentleman and lady of his acquaintance. He leaned down to
lend his ear to the man, who was pointing at Belle. The
prince followed the direction, caught sight of her and
said something to his friends. They all laughed aloud.
Soon, many of the others within hearing distance were
laughing, too. Evidently, the Regent had seen the vicious
caricatures and been amused by them. No doubt he was
pleased to see someone else lampooned for a change.
Belle kept her head high and tried to maintain a placid
expression. In a low voice, she begged her escort to take
her home.

Lord Peter looked furious. "I would dearly love to do so, Lillie. But, as you can see, we are mired in this bloody traffic. Your pardon. We could not leave in any event, until he does." He tilted his head to his prince. "The buffoon. He is just laughing because society is enjoying a cartoon about someone other than him for once! You might think he would have more sensitivity, would you not? Besides, if we did leave now, these fools would know that they had succeeded. You don't want that, Lillie, nor do I. I know this must be deuced hard for you, but your real friends will not desert you."

She smiled in gratitude. "Yes, I know, you have all been very kind. And you are quite right, I should not run. Oh, look, the carriages are beginning to move. Is that Mr. Goodwin?"

Belle nodded and smiled as he came abreast of their carriage, but Mr. Goodwin only nodded and gave a reluctant, "Good day, Mrs. Broadhurst. Lord Peter," and moved on as quickly as the traffic would allow.

She and Lord Peter exchanged glances, and Belle giggled. "So, it has come to this! That cartoonist has done for me what I have been unable to do for myself, it seems!"

"That's the spirit!"

"Not to worry, madam, Fortnum's has delivered all the provisions we need for the main courses, and Gunter's will be bringing the cakes and ices later this afternoon. Everything is on schedule, so don't you give the meal a thought."

Belle knew that the meal would be splendid, for Mrs. Butter was an excellent cook, but the food actually was the least of her concerns. She had lain awake most of the previous night, drifting off to sleep now and again only to wake from nightmares, the worst of which had her guests laughing and handing copies of the cartoons around the dinner table. She had finally risen before the servants, gone over the menu again and selected and discarded no less than three gowns to wear that evening. Warner tapped at her door at seven o'clock with her morning coffee.

"Good heavens, you are up with the birds this morning! Couldn't sleep, eh?" she asked sympathetically.

"Not a bit. I'll probably nod off in the middle of dinner and end up with my face in the soup!"

Warner helped her to dress in a plain morning gown and combed her hair back simply, then covered it with a cap.

"No sense in troubling too much with anything now, ma'am. You're too fidgety to sit still for me, and we shall only have to do it all again this evening, anyway, when you dress for dinner."

The maid thought it best to pretend, as much as possible, that this was a day like any other, for she could see that Belle was already in a state of high anxiety.

"Well," she gave a sidelong glance to the dresses spread out on the bed, "you haven't decided what to wear, then?"

"I cannot decide. Whatever it is, we must be sure that there is not a loose stitch anywhere. The last thing I need is to come apart tonight of all nights!"

Warner was not offended by the suggestion that she might send her mistress off in clothes that were less than perfect, for she knew what prompted Belle's concern.

"Never fear, I shall see to it." She smiled.

"Oh, Warner, I am sorry. Of course you will. You always do."

"Mrs. Broadhurst, drink your coffee and eat your toast. You will feel much more the thing if you do."

As Belle munched on her breakfast, they discussed what she should wear. Warner recommended a gown of rich yellow silk with a diaphanous overdress in a lighter shade of the same color. The sleeves consisted of thin bands of tiny, soft green leaves, that also bordered the narrow corsage.

"The very thing, Warner." As she drank the last of her coffee, Belle laughed. "You will notice, please, that this gown was not even amongst those I had considered. Your taste is unerring, as it always is."

"Thank you, ma'am. Now, why don't you rest a while? You might be able to sleep a bit."

"I cannot, I promise you. I do not suppose it is tomorrow yet, is it?" Warner laughed and Belle joined in. "No, I did not think so. I am going to see Mrs. Butter again about the preparations for dinner."

"But, Mrs. Broadhurst, you have been over and over the plans. It will go quite smoothly without your *help*, you know," she teased. "And Mrs. Butter may not thank you for invading her kitchen at such a time."

"Mrs. Butter will have to humor me," Belle replied, heading for the door.

Now, as she climbed the stairs from the kitchen, she sent up a silent prayer—only let people come; please do not let them cut me, and the rest will take care of itself. She proceeded to the library to see to a task she had been putting off for several days. She opened the draperies to let in the sun and sat at the desk. After some minutes spent settling herself comfortably in her chair and trimming her pen, she drew a sheet of paper from the drawer and began to write: Dear *Lillith* . . . (The name was heavily underscored)

From the *two* letters I have received, it sounds as if your adventure is going well, and that Italy is all you had wanted it to be! I hope that you are keeping the journal that we spoke of, so that I can know all the details of your journey when you return. I am sending this to the hotel in Tuscany that your letter said you would be using as a base for the rest of your travel, so I hope that it reaches you.

Life here in London also has been most interesting. There has been the odd incident for which I was, shall I say, *unprepared,* and I might note that I have learned one or two things that I did not previously *know,* but those details I shall regale you with when you are come home. Suffice it to say, for the present, that your cousin, Major Lindley, is all that is charming and that *I was more than a little surprised to make his acquaintance, Lillie!!* Truly, he is all that you said—intelligent, handsome, witty and quite good fun. Aunt Eulalie and Uncle Aubrey have been wonderfully kind, and I have made great friends with our neighbors, Cecily and William Rafton. You will like them, I am sure.

And, now, I come to the primary purpose of my letter, which is to give you news I feel you should have before you return . . .

Belle went on to recount the recent episodes which had caused her so much grief. She felt that Lillie had a right to know what was being said of "her" about town, so that she could be prepared for any lingering repercussions when she came home. As well, she would be very glad of any advice that her friend could offer on the matter. She walked to the window embrasure and watched a carriage clatter past in the street. What would Lillie think? Would she be furious with her for being so gauche? No, probably not. Lillie was too kind and too much of the madcap herself to criticize.

She turned back to seal the letter and was surprised to find Filbert sitting on the desk, watching her, for she had left him in the kitchen cadging scraps from Mrs. Butter, and she had shut the library door behind her. "How did you get in here?" He gazed steadily at her. "How . . . ? Listen to me. If the gossips could hear me talking to my cat, they would have some real sport. Oh, what am I saying? Look at Poodle Byng and his dogs!" Filbert stretched out across her letter. "Thank you, you have well and truly blotted it for me." She grinned.

Nonetheless, Belle was more than a little puzzled. How *had* the cat got in here? Could there be another door that she had, somehow, never noticed? She remembered that once or twice, she had turned to find him in her bedroom, when she had been certain she had recently left him elsewhere, but she had not paid much attention at the time. Sitting at the desk, she questioned Filbert again, to no avail. She walked about the large room examining walls that she already knew well. Nothing. Then her eye was caught by some carving in the paneling. She stooped to inspect it more closely. There, in the crease, she saw several long hairs that suspiciously resembled those of Filbert's magnificent plume. She looked at the cat and back at the wall. She tried to remove them, but they were stuck fast. It must be a sliding panel! There was another way into the room and leave it to Filbert to know about it!

Belle looked closely at the panel to find a latch or some sort of trigger to open it, but saw nothing. Well, if the cat can find it, I can, she decided, and began pressing various points in the carving. At length, she heard a soft "whoosh" and the panel swung quickly inward. Belle gasped. She had read about such things as secret rooms and passages, but never seen one. She turned to find Filbert at her side, staring at her. For a moment, she did not speak; then she laughed and said to him, "All right, let's explore!" and, hefting him into her arms, stepped into the passage.

The door slid closed behind them, but Belle did not even notice. The space was dusty, narrow and not very long. Belle sneezed. Some shelves stretched along one side, and she examined them in a cursory fashion in the available dim light. Nothing there but some old newspapers and a lamp. Silly to think that The Bracelet might be here, because the previous occupants, who would have known about the room, surely would have looked here. She was more interested in seeing where the passage led.

Filbert jumped down and sat behind her, blinking in astonishment. Having at last made the decision to let her have The Bracelet, he had hidden it in plain sight just there behind that dusty broken lamp, and she had not even seen it! It did not occur to him that even such a bauble would have little sparkle in this poor light. He had half a mind not to call it to her attention. No, that would be silly, and besides, he was tired of guarding it, of moving it from place to place, of seeing that it sparkled still, just as it had all those years ago, when it had caught Ethelbert's eye. Now, there was a cat, Filbert thought admiringly.

He had listened to all the stories, all the legends about Ethelbert so that, in his turn, he, too, could pass them down. And Ethelbert had, indeed, been an astonishing cat. He had once pilfered a fob from Sebastian's waistcoat without Sebastian's even realizing it! And, more than once, he had sidled between that gentleman's feet causing him to fall quite indecorously. Ethelbert had not liked him. Sebastian had bellowed fit to bring down the house the first time the cat landed him on his bottom. Ethelbert liked him even less then. He hated loud noises, they hurt his ears, and he had an even greater disgust of humans who could not laugh at themselves. After that, he had tripped Sebastian up every quarter or so—just to remind him of his presence and the high esteem in which Virginia held him.

Filbert listened as Belle exclaimed over the existence of the hidden room, the dust, the dim light, everything except The Bracelet. Honestly. He jumped lightly onto the shelf—*Ugh!* No one ever cleaned in here—he would have to wash for hours when he got out. Extracting his treasure with his paw, he picked it up in his mouth. He was turning to show it to Belle, when—

"Belle? Are you in here? Thomasina said you were."

Gore's words drifted faintly from the library, through the panel and into the passage. Belle turned, delighted at the opportunity to show him her discovery. Filbert dropped his treasure and pawed some old newspaper over it. But, when Belle reached the entrance, she could not find the trigger on that side of the panel. She pushed and pressed all round the door to no purpose.

"Gore! I'm in here!" she called.

He had turned to leave the room, deciding that Thomasina was mistaken or Belle had finished whatever she had been doing in there and left, when he heard her voice.

He turned back. "Lillie? Where are you?"

"I told you. I'm in here." Then, realizing how absurd that sounded, and beginning to feel not a little panicked at the possibility of being trapped in the room, she giggled. "Behind the wall."

"What?"

"It's a secret room! But we can't get out! Here, listen!" She beat on the panel to guide him to her location. He beat back from his side.

"In there?"

"Yes!"

"How the devil . . . ?"

"Never mind that now! The trigger is on the right-hand side of the seam, almost midway down the panel. Do you see it?"

"Wait a minute." He, too, pressed and prodded.

"Gore! Can't you find it? Please, get me out of here!"

"Hold on, Lillie." He peered and pushed for what seemed hours, as she grew more frantic. "Just a—there!"

At last, the door swung open to reveal a very flushed Belle.

He stepped inside and took her in his arms. "It's all right, I'm here, my dear. I've gotten you out."

She looked up at him and smiled sheepishly. "Yes, so you have, thank you. It is silly, I know, but I have never cared much for small, closed spaces. I can't think what made me go in there. Curiosity I suppose."

"Yes, no doubt." He smiled down at her.

"Yes, right. Well," she withdrew from him somewhat reluctantly, "I was wondering where the passage led." She explained about Filbert's sudden appearance and her finding of the secret panel. "So, you see, he must have got in from the other side."

"Shall we investigate, then?" He was smiling still, but felt oddly almost bereft, now that she was out of his arms.

"Oh, yes, let's."

They proceeded to the opposite end of the passage, talking softly, as people inexplicably do in such places, about what they might find. Filbert, still lying atop the old newspaper, watched them carefully, for he did not want Gore to have The Bracelet, and he was suspicious of his motives. A close call, he thought, waiting. Once they had gained the rear wall, Belle and Gore repeated the pressing and poking that had proved effective on the other panel, as they muttered to themselves.

"No, that's not it."

"This doesn't work, either."

"Perhaps here. No."

"Oh!" There was a sudden rush of air, and light spilled into the passage, blinding them for a moment, and they found themselves in Belle's bedroom, with the sun coming in through the windows.

"Oh," said Belle again, clearly disappointed.

Gore laughed. "You were expecting a secret, long-forgotten room?" he teased.

Laughing, too, she retorted, "Yes, perhaps I was. I thought I might find Ethelbert's cache, you know."

Unnoticed, Filbert slipped off the shelf with his treasure, raised a large paw to unlatch the door and slipped quietly through the library, worrying over where to hide it this time.

"Still looking for The Bracelet, eh? Do you honestly hope to find it?"

Belle was looking out the window, with her back to him. "Oh, I don't know. Yes, I suppose I *hope* to, but I am not at all certain that I *shall.* Oh, Gore, I do *want* to find it. She would be so pleased if I did."

Belle froze, her eyes wide.

But all thoughts of her duplicity had fled Gore's mind. He viewed her effort now as she did, as a treasure hunt, and so he rescued her.

"Aunt Eulalie, you mean?"

She turned to face him. "Aunt Eulalie! Yes! That is right, Aunt Eulalie. She will be so pleased, I think, for she is the last blood Broadhurst and, so, if I do find it, I shall give it to her." She really had wanted to do this, and knew that Lillie would gladly acquiesce in the plan.

He smiled and smoothed a lock of her hair that had been mussed in her exertions in the passage. "Good, she will like that, I am certain."

"Well I had very little breakfast this morning and vow I am famished. Will you join me for luncheon?"

"Too worked up to eat, were you?"

She sighed. "Yes, I am afraid so."

"Do not worry, B—Lillie, all will go well."

She did not notice his slip. "I pray you are right, Gore."

They were crossing the hall to the front door, when Filbert slipped back into the room, unseen.

"You have quite enough on your plate at the moment, so I shall decline your invitation for lunch. But, I shall see you this evening. Oh!"

A loud thud followed, as Gore landed on the floor, unhurt. They just caught sight of Filbert as he catapulted down the hall. Gore looked up at her and smirked.

"That damned cat, wasn't it?"

"I am afraid so. Are you hurt?"

"Not a bit. I told you he doesn't like me," he muttered, getting to his feet and brushing off his clothes.

"I never disagreed, Gore. Really, you looked so surprised." She laughed.

"I can only be grateful that insidious cartoonist is not looking in your window." He chuckled, and left.

EIGHT

When Gore arrived back at his rooms later that afternoon, he found a message awaiting him. It was a brief note from Maryanne Stockdale telling him that she found herself indisposed and unable to attend the dinner party with him. He snorted. He was, at first, pleased that he would not have to suffer her company. Then, cursing, he realized what the cancellation might mean to Belle and to her other guests. Unfortunately, there was little to be done about it at this stage, as he could hardly invite someone else now. He would just have to hope that the others would attend as promised.

Some of Belle's guests were almost as nervous about the evening as she was. Eulalie, quite uncharacteristically, snapped at her dresser twice while the woman arranged her hair, and, after departing Queen Street for the party, had to send her footman back to the house to fetch the fan she had forgotten.

"Really, Aubrey," she had said to her husband earlier, "I do not know what I shall do if her guests do not attend. Things have already come to a pretty pass, still it is to be hoped that it *may* all be forgotten. But, if people will not honor their invitations, I fear the worst. Lillie will lose all consequence, all of her standing in the *ton*. Oh, it will be just *too bad!*"

Aubrey, who was not up to going to Berkeley Square, shook his head. "I know it, my dear, but there is not a thing we can do about it. To hell with the *ton!*"

"Aubrey! How can you say such a thing? Why, her standing in society is everything! Well, *almost* everything. She must be accepted by people, dear, else where can she go whilst in town? What can she do?"

"Accepted by people! Bah! Damn bunch of snobs! Always was and always will be. Told you a hundred times, that attitude only feeds their egos. Overfed, spoiled and ignorant, most of 'em. Not worth a farthing!"

He was becoming agitated, and his wife crossed the room to soothe him. "There, Aubrey, you have the right of it, I am persuaded."

"Yes, I do." He twinkled up at her. "Besides, our Lillie is a stout thing. She'll come about no matter what those fools do to her. Better than they are."

"Yes, dear," Eulalie sighed. But she was not at all convinced.

"Wake me when you come home, if I am asleep. I want to know what happens."

Meanwhile, at No. 12, Cecily had released her abigail and was putting the final touches to her toilette while William sat nearby keeping her company, his long frame lounging in an armchair. He never tired of watching this ritual, for all that it could take hours before she had accomplished the desired effect, because he still loved her to distraction, and had told her more than once that she could wear a housemaid's dress and still put every other woman to shame.

"What was wrong with the fawn zephyr gown, by the way?" he teased, sipping a glass of wine.

"Not a thing, darling."

He grinned. "Forgive me, I had supposed when you tossed it on the bed along with the heap of other discarded dresses and put on that one," he waved his glass in her direction, "that it was lacking in something. Just a male quirk, you will no doubt tell me."

"And so it is, William," she teased back, conversing with his reflection in her mirror. He laughed. "What I mean is that there is nothing wrong with the gown, only that it is not right for the occasion. One must judge these things carefully, you know."

"I do. Why was it 'not right for the occasion' then?"

"Circumstances call for a gown that is more, oh . . ."

"Yes?"

"Well, vivid, I think."

"Oh, of course. Should I change my black for something in, oh, say, puce, do you think?"

She tossed a slipper at him. "Don't you dare! I meant me, William. You know," she turned on her chair to look at him, her countenance now quite serious, "this evening could turn out to be a disaster."

Assuming her sober mien, he reluctantly concurred.

"And Lillie had been so looking forward to it, that is the worst of it. All those plans, all that work. I do not know what I should do in her shoes. If only she could have postponed it."

"Not possible, Cec. The cats would have been out for certain, then. No, better to brazen it out and hope for the best, I think."

"I stopped in for a moment earlier just to let her know I was thinking of her. She actually seemed rather calm, I thought. Well, no, calm is not precisely the word." She turned back to her mirror to put on her earrings. "No, she was rather, oh, almost glowing. She seemed quite happy." She glanced at William in the glass. "Gore had been there, and I *think* something might have passed between them."

"Indeed?"

"Mmm. A nice gentleman, isn't he? You two get on very well."

William and Gore had become friends since the picnic and had spent much time in one another's company. He had never told her what may have been said between them, and Cecily had not asked, although she had been curious.

William nodded. "A fine fellow, I like him very much."

Finished at last, she rose and pirouetted before him, smiling and awaiting his praise. Her gown was lovely. A stunning marine blue, it was finished with blonde lace upon its numerous flounces and about the neckline.

Never one to disappoint his wife, he eyed her critically, stood up, kissed her and took her in his arms. "Pity Lillie won't at least be the most beautiful woman at her own party," he whispered in her ear.

At No. 7, final preparations for the dinner party were proceeding apace. Belle and Warner had arranged the flowers sent by the florist. Belle had examined the dinner table set with Lillie's finest plate, glassware and silver. It was to be a rather large party. Determined to be optimistic, she was humming a tune as she set the place cards in their stands at the appropriate seats.

Gore would sit at the end of the table opposite her, Cecily and William on her left and right, respectively, then Lord Peter and across from him, Caroline Booth. Then Daphne and Lockwood Farley from No. 1, and Gore's companion—she wondered if it might be Maryanne Stockdale, and shuddered, but she could hardly have told him not to bring her. Then there was Lord Milden, a high stickler, but she had met him so often it seemed right to invite him, across from Aunt Eulalie, and Mr. and Mrs. Ostway—even higher in the instep than Milden, but she had been to dinner at their house,

so it was another social obligation that must be repaid—
and Mr. Harding and his fiancée—she had met them
several times at parties and had thought they would be
a good addition to the group. Then finally the most
proper Earl and Countess of Dawson. Fortunately, the
table would seat all seventeen quite comfortably, once
the leaves were put in, and the room was lovely and
spacious.

The wines had been carefully chosen at Berry Bros.
& Rudd. Belle and Cecily had giggled like schoolgirls
when they had been weighed on the Great Scale there,
in place since the Widow Bourne had opened the shop
as a grocery under The Sign of The Coffee Mill over a
hundred years earlier. The menu, too, had taken considerable planning. She and Cecily, who had hosted so
many such dinners and, thus, had a wealth of valuable
experience, and Mrs. Butter had spent several hours
deliberating over the various courses. They had at last
settled on caviar, turtle soup—Fortnum's boasted that
its turtles were killed in Honduras, although Belle could
not see what that had to do with anything—followed by
salmon, shrimps, round of beef, partridges, biscuits,
salad, and various sweets, ices and fruits. Mrs. Butter,
along with two helpers hired especially for the occasion,
for the household normally was too small to keep a
larger cooking staff, had been working since midmorn-
ing on the repast. The cook had taken Belle's brief visit
to the kitchen in her stride, belying the maid's warning.
The plump, older woman had not prepared such an
elegant and extensive meal for some time, but she was
a good less frazzled than Belle and seemed pleased with
her interest.

In fact, Mrs. Butter was as familiar with the hurtful
cartoons as the next person, and was inclined to indulge
her mistress's fidgets. She had sniffed her disapproval

and leapt to the defense of her lady, when M. Dupré, who was cook next door, had dared to snicker in her presence.

" 'Just you hold your tongue, M. Dupré,' I said to him," she had related to Thomasina after Belle had returned to the upper level. " 'You have no call to say anything so rude about Mrs. Broadhurst, who's a lady born and bred and, indeed, has more refinement and sensibility in her little finger than *some* I could mention. But, of course, I won't, because those of us who are in service to the *quality* know how to behave, unlike *some* I could *mention*, M. Dupré!' Yes, I did, Thomasina," said the cook, who habitually underscored her speech, "you may be sure that I did," she retorted heatedly when the maid had expressed her shock at such an attack. M. Dupré was very high in the instep and never spared a maid so much as a good day, when he passed one in the street, and so Thomasina was more than pleased to hear that the cook had put him in his place.

Up to her elbows in biscuit flour, the cook punched down the soft dough perhaps a little more vigorously than was called for, silently hoping that she had not spoiled its rise. She nodded her head for emphasis, and a lock of cotton white hair escaped her cap and bobbed its agreement. *"That* one is no better than he should be, never mind that he gives himself airs, just like he's someone. *French! I* should say! He's no more French than I am, *which* I thank the good Lord I am *not."* Mrs. Butter had lost a third cousin twice-removed in the late wars and was not about to forget it. "Doesn't even *sound* like a proper Frenchman, if there *is* such a thing, *which* I doubt. And as for his master, *well!"*

"What about him?" Thomasina had begged.

But Mrs. Butter caught herself. It really wouldn't do to be gossiping with the other staff, but she had been so furious with the man next door she had been unable to stop herself. "Never you mind, my girl. It's none of your affair—and not for you to go gossiping about your betters, understand?" she asked sternly.

The poor maid, who had learned nothing concerning the gentleman next door to gossip *about*, had nodded meekly and gone about her business.

Belle was waiting in the drawing room well before the hour at which her guests could be expected to arrive, under strict instructions from Warner to please stop worrying at her fan, else she would have it in tatters before they sat down to table. The yellow silk gown was most becoming and, she realized thankfully, quite comfortable. She looked down at the bodice and adjusted it a bit, wondering if it were cut too low, decided it was too late to do anything about that if it were, then forced herself to sit down and breathe deeply in an effort to calm her nerves. Presently, Thomasina announced Gore, who entered the drawing room smiling.

She rose and went to greet him, hands outstretched. He clasped them in both of his and kissed her cheek, noticing with approval the faint fragrance of lavender. Holding her then at arms' length, he examined her from head to toe with a comically critical eye and grinned broadly.

"You look splendid, Lillie." He kissed her gloved hand for good measure.

Belle let out her breath and smiled back at him. "Thank you, Gore. You are early and—"

"Ha! So you would quiz me for arriving too soon?"

"Oh, wretch, don't tease me, please! I was *going* to say a very pretty 'thank you,' you know for doing just that." She dimpled. "And I *do* thank you. But you have come alone? You had said you were escorting someone, although you never did say who."

"Maryanne Stockdale." Her face fell. "But, I am sorry to say," he hated to break the news, "that she has a megrim or something and sends her regrets."

Belle's face lit up. "Oh, that is too bad."

He looked puzzled. "Well, yes, I suppose it is, but to say the truth, I cannot claim to be very sorry. I had much rather be here to give you all my attention."

"You are most gallant."

"And I have something for you." He withdrew a prettily wrapped package from a pocket and held it out to her.

"Oh!" she exclaimed, tearing off the paper like a child.

"No, no, I beg of you, no need to be shy. Open it right up!"

"You!" She opened the velvet box to find a vinaigrette fashioned of reddish brown carnelian in the shape of a large filbert outlined in gold. "Oh, Gore! A filbert! It is magnificent, thank you!"

He had gone to great trouble and expense to have the trinket made by the jeweler Hamlet, the one the aristocracy laughingly called The Prince of Denmark, and he was most pleased with her reaction. He grinned. "You are so taken with the silly cat that I thought you would find it charming."

"I do! It is the most delightful and thoughtful gift I have ever received. Truly!" She stood on her toes and kissed his cheek. She could feel her heart begin to pound, just as it always did when he was near or touched her. For just a moment, she dared to hope that this was more than just a clever, thoughtful gift to an old and dear friend. He took her shoulders gently and looked into her eyes. As he leaned forward to kiss her, the door began to open, and he released her almost, but not quite, before Cecily and William were shown in. The two arrivals exchanged a meaningful glance, as Gore and Belle looked at one another with slight embarrassment.

"Do look, Cec, at what Gore has given me!" She held out the vinaigrette. William crossed to Gore, and the two men began to converse quietly.

"*Very* pretty." Cecily looked at Gore with an approving smile. "You have excellent taste, Gore, and imagination!"

He nodded his thanks.

She glanced about the room. "Here alone, are you?"

"I am. Maryanne Stockdale was to accompany me, but she is ill."

"Really? Cut herself with her own tongue, did she?"

Before Gore could respond to this baffling comment, the butler hired for the occasion entered to begin serving the champagne. Filbert sashayed into the room behind him, giving the distinct appearance that his arrival was long past due. He looked around appraisingly and sidled up to Belle, who bent down to him.

"Look, Filbert," she cooed, holding her gift out to him, "isn't it lovely?"

Filbert approached it warily. Crossing his eyes, he sniffed, then pulled his head back sharply at the smell and gave a dainty sneeze. Everyone laughed. Offended, he sneered at them and went to rest in the window seat. Some people had very strange ideas of what was amusing. He shut his eyes tight and stretched a large mitten over his face, so that they might not know he was thinking about them. There was to be some sort of do tonight, that much he knew. Not that anyone ever told *him* anything, but he had overheard Belle and Mrs. Butter talking about food and people coming. He always listened when the words had anything to do with food. And he liked Mrs. Butter. She shared what she was cooking and what was left over, and she never told him that he had eaten enough, the way Belle sometimes did. Mrs. Butter understood. Filbert looked at the gathered company through shuttered eyes. Probably more people would be coming, as there was quite a lot of food in the kitchen. Well, he certainly hoped that none of them would expect to sit *here*. The food, he knew, would be delicious, for Mrs. Butter had bestowed on him several samples. He stretched as the voices buzzed and hummed around him, and began to dream about all the scraps that were sure to come his way later that night.

"I commend you, my dear," Cecily teased Belle, "you look lovely and *calm!*"

Belle's fan fluttered like the wings of a nervous humming-bird. "Thank you, I cannot take credit for the dress, for you helped me choose it."

Aunt Eulalie came in quietly, nodded to the gentlemen, and joined Belle and Cecily.

"Mrs. Singleton, I was just saying to Lillie how calm she looks."

"Indeed, Lillith, you do." Eulalie kissed her cheek.

"I am pleased that I at least *appear* calm, for I do not feel so, I assure you."

"Well, none but we shall know it!" Cecily chirped. "This champagne is delightful! Try not to fret too much. Miss Booth and Lord Peter will liven us up, and Mr. Harding and his fiancée—what is that poor child's name again? I declare, she is so timid and boring that I never can recall it."

"Miss Clayton. Anthea Clayton."

"Mmm, yes, but there is no use telling me, I shall only forget it all over again, she is such a milk and water miss. Still, he is a good sort, and I am convinced they will come. And, if they do not, I vow I am so famished that I shall gladly eat their share! What time do we sit down?"

"At eight," Belle replied, glancing at the carriage clock across the room, noting that it lacked but twenty minutes to the appointed hour.

"Well," Cecily hoped she sounded bracing, "the others should arrive any moment."

Gore and William continued to converse in low tones, the former expressing his intention to murder anyone who was not gentleman or lady enough to honor their invitations.

"Just as well that Miss Stockdale decided not to come tonight, my Cecily might have throttled her," William said, only half in jest.

" '*Decided*' not to come?" Gore frowned in puzzlement.

"Yes, that is what I believe. My wife has told me that she and Lillie believe Miss Stockdale to be behind the cartoons. I must say it makes sense. Rings true, I mean to say. I know her and her parents slightly—Father has enough blunt to buy half the town—a thoroughly unpleasant lot. The girl's a spoiled creature, always goes her own way and the devil to pay on those rare occasions when she don't. Just like her parents. Sorry, Lindley, I know you've escorted her once or twice."

Gore had listened in silence, a flush creeping up his neck.

"No, no, it was nothing of significance, I assure you."

William nodded in acknowledgment. "Didn't think it was."

Gore continued. "Well, I cannot say that I am surprised to hear what you say of her disposition. I suppose I should defend the lady, but now you mention it, I must concede that I have noticed hints of that sort of behavior, although I've not seen enough of her parents to have an opinion about them. But, Rafton, while she may be capable of such a nefarious deed, I do not understand *why* she should do it."

William gave a wry grin. "You don't, eh?" Gore shook his head. "It is you, Lindley. She is jealous."

"Jealous? Of what? Of whom? I have given her no cause to expect anything of me."

"I am sure you have not. But that is not to say she don't believe you did, if you know what I mean. If she's decided she wants you, she means to have you. And, no doubt, she sees Lillie standing in her way," he concluded pointedly.

"Lillie? But, why . . . ?"

"I am sure I do not know." There was a decided gleam in Rafton's eye.

The ladies sent a curious look in the direction of their laughter and, presently, resumed their own conversation. Gore returned to the original subject. "Then you believe Miss Stockdale to be behind all this?"

William nodded emphatically. "I do. My wife is quite a good judge of character, and I fancy that Lillie is, as well. Furthermore, who else could, or would, have made such capital of Lillie's, er, mishaps? Still, I wanted to be certain, so I made some discreet inquiries. It was her, all right. Apparently, she knew someone, who knew someone, who knew the cartoonist."

"In the event, I had not intended to see her again, so this actually fits into my plans easily," Gore explained.

That someone she knew, indeed anyone, had treated Lillie in such an underhanded manner infuriated Gore. He wondered if he should confront Maryanne with his knowledge, but after considering the matter, he and

William decided it was best to let it rest, in the hope that the storm soon would be over.

A few moments later, they were joined by Miss Booth and, immediately after her, by Lord Peter. Miss Booth had gardenias in her magnificent red hair and wore an ebony zephyrine gown with the merest wisp of a bodice, which was trimmed in black lace. Lord Peter complemented her in black and white, a ruby pinned in his high, starched neckcloth. As soon as they entered, the level of conversation rose, Lord Peter telling a joke he had heard that afternoon at Tattersall's.

He made his way to where Gore and William stood and said in a low voice, "I say, Lindley, I met Milden when I was at Tatt's, quite accidentally, you understand. Don't know why he was there, the man knows nothing about horseflesh. Anyway, I mentioned that I would see him here this evening, and he looked as if I'd caught him with the under parlormaid. He mumbled something about another engagement he had forgotten, and asked me, *me*, to make his excuses to Lillie. I wanted to tell the old fool to make 'em himself, but I was afraid he wouldn't bother, he apparently had not notified Lillie up to that point, so I said I would. I feel like the devil, but I must tell her." He shook his head in disgust.

"Yes, you must," Gore sighed. "I'll go with you."

Belle was laughing with the three other ladies, but sobered when she caught Lord Peter's eye. She forced the smile back to her lips.

"That is the Mathematical," she gestured to his cravat, "is it not, sir?"

"It is, indeed, Lillie." He smiled back. "I am pleased to have my valet's exertions noticed, and so will he be! Ah, Lillie . . . I happened to meet Lord Milden today, when I was at Tattersall's. He, ah, asked me to convey his very deep regrets," he lied, "said that he remembered he was already promised elsewhere for this evening, and so cannot come." Cecily caught her breath in consternation, and they all watched closely for Belle's reaction.

She cast her eyes down as she felt the blood rush to her cheeks. Was this the beginning of her guests' "regrets" or the end? She recovered quickly, however, and smiled up at him.

"Oh, what a pity. I had so looked forward to seeing him again. Perhaps another time."

Miss Booth broke in. "Thank heavens! He is such a prosy sort, droning on and on about nothing, that I, for one, cannot be disappointed at being deprived of his company. Confess, Mrs. Broadhurst. Tell me you must feel the same. I am certain you asked him only because you had to!"

They all joined in with their own stories of the tedious Lord Milden, and the moment was saved. Not much more time elapsed, however, before it became clear that none of Belle's other guests would come. She was the most surprised at the Farleys' snubbing. For pity's sake, did they not realize how likely it was they would meet in the square? What would they say to her if they did? Mr. Harding, too, she had thought would come, he seemed such an easy, genial person.

Presently, Belle excused herself to speak with the servants about removing some of the leaves from the dining table and to instruct Mrs. Butter that only seven would sit down to dinner so she could adjust the servings accordingly. Eulalie shook her head in distress. While she was out of the room, Cecily swore vengeance on all those who had insulted her friend. Miss Booth seconded this intention, and the gentlemen were at pains to calm them.

Belle ushered them into the dining room, grateful

for the company and loyalty of her real friends. She could not say she was undisturbed by the failure of so many of her invited guests to come to dinner, but the party turned out well, for all of that. Her friends, true friends, she knew, all had rallied to support her. Initially, it had been awkward, all of them trying too hard and talking at once, as if all that sound could cover the absence of half her company.

William told two or three silly jokes that had them groaning, all except Miss Booth, who suffered a fit of the giggles. Lord Peter did a hilarious imitation of an aging dandy who, unable to see beyond his extravagantly high shirt points, failed to see that he had left half his supper on his vermillion waistcoat. Once the gentlemen had rejoined the ladies in the parlor after dinner, Aunt Eulalie, inspired by Lord Peter, amazed them all with a riotous account of a disastrous ball given by the absent Earl and Countess of Dawson many years before. The assembled company laughed in appreciation of her story and her previously hidden sense of humor.

Belle was pleased to notice Lord Peter look more than once in the direction of Caroline Booth. While she had grown very fond of that gentleman, she could not think of him as a possible suitor, and so was happy to see that his attention might be caught by the admirable Miss Booth. Over the course of the evening, she had gotten to know that lady much better and, on reflection, thought that she might be just right for him. Cecily liked her quite as much as Belle did, and not much time had passed before the three had made plans to go shopping and visit the Horticultural Society together during the coming week.

NINE

The day after Belle's dinner party, Gore was crossing St. James's Street, having just left his tailor. Midway through this somewhat perilous navigation, he spied, between a precariously laden farmer's cart and a drag, the figure of Miss Stockdale accompanied by her maid and two ladies with whom he was slightly acquainted. Following his sotto voce conversation the previous evening with William, and his own lately acknowledged intent to separate himself from Miss Stockdale's company, he felt a natural desire, in fact, an instinct, to avoid a meeting with her, but Miss Stockdale had caught his eye and, smiling, nodded to him, not too vigorously of course, for that would have been ill bred. Thus, he was forced to continue in his present direction and to suffer the encounter, or to make the rude and, considering the relentless onrush of traffic behind him, foolhardy, attempt to return to the other side whence he had come. He did wonder, as the cart finally lumbered past, if good manners would prevent his telling the lady his new opinion of her.

She smiled coquettishly as Gore reached the curb. "Why, Major Lindley, how nice to see you."

He inclined his head, tipping his hat. "Miss Stockdale," he said, his own smile no more than courtesy required. "Miss Brent. Miss Davies," he added, nodding to each of the young ladies and the maid in turn, and observing the parcels each carried. "Shopping, I see. I take it you are quite recovered from your indisposition, Miss Stockdale?" he asked innocently, brows raised slightly.

She had not even the grace to look abashed. "Oh, yes, I am much better this morning, thank you. How was Mrs. Broadhurst's dinner party? Was there a crowd?" She smiled sweetly, and her friends giggled.

Gore smiled. "A delightful evening," he assured her.

"Indeed? I can understand why you would attend, she is, after all, your cousin, so to speak, but I cannot imagine that anyone else of consequence would have done so, for I must say, sir, that her behavior is quite *farouche.* I hope I do not offend." She fluttered her lashes and managed to look concerned. She naturally did not want to provoke him, for that would ruin her chances at bringing him up to scratch, but she did wish to lower Lillie in his esteem.

"It is no wonder that they are calling her The Provincial Lily," put in Miss Brent with a smirk.

" 'They,' Miss Brent?" He looked at her coldly, then turned to Maryanne, to respond to her remarks. "Do you think her behavior lacking, Miss Stockdale? I do not. I believe that a great deal of noise has been made about nothing." He heard her friends gasp at this heresy.

"And it is commendable of you to defend her so, Major."

"Someone must. Whoever instigated these ridiculous cartoons has too high an opinion of himself, or *herself,* " he added pointedly, "and a great deal too much time to spend in spiteful, childish pranks that harm innocent people." He itched to confront her, but knew she would deny culpability, and in any case, he would not do so here in the street. Not that she deserved to suffer her comeuppance in private.

"And so," he continued smoothly, "I think you must have been relieved when your indisposition prevented your accompanying me last evening."

Maryanne feigned wounded surprise beautifully. "Why, sir, how can you say so? I would have gone for your sake, you know, had I felt up to it."

Gore decided to ignore this. He inclined his head. "As you say, Miss Stockdale."

"There, I am glad to know that I am not in your black books, sir. We hear that Gunter's has just got in a shipment of ice and were talking of going there for cream ices."

"Yes, I saw their advertisement in *The Times.*"

"Shall you join us?" Her friends, who were as envious of his attentions as she had wanted them to be, begged him to agree.

"Oh, yes, please, Major!"

"Do come!"

"I am promised elsewhere. You must forgive me." He tipped his hat again, nodded to all of them, and departed.

Maryanne watched him go, eyes narrowed, as her friends looked at her with speculation. Perhaps the Major was not the prize she had believed him to be. She would give the matter more consideration later, as she had planned a rare quiet evening at home.

"La," said Miss Brent, whose haughtiness was exceeded only by Miss Stockdale's, "I think he may be rather miffed with you, Maryanne." The remark contained a spiteful satisfaction.

Maryanne turned to deliver the setdown appropriate for keeping Miss Brent in her place. "Esmé, you—"

She was interrupted, however.

"Oh, my." Miss Davies sighed dramatically and cast an arch look at her companions. "Major Lindley is all a lady could want—handsome, rich. . . ."

"Rich?" echoed the two young ladies in unison. Even the maid raised her eyebrows.

Miss Davies, always behind times with the latest news, was not a little pleased that she was, for once, a step ahead of them. "Rich," she repeated smugly. "Very. My papa says he's rich as Croesus."

So the truth was out. The size of the property that Gore sought, was far grander, indeed, than he had led Cecily to believe, and would be much more costly than he was commonly thought capable of paying. When he had drawn a large sum from his account as a deposit on a potential purchase, whose rotted timbers, when they came to light, removed it from his consideration, he had disclosed his plan and the astonishing cost to his banker, a gentleman whose services he did not know he shared with Edward Davies. Unfortunately, Gore had made the mistake of not changing bankers, as he had promised himself he would do, and it was not long before the information had been inadvertently slipped to Davies and, subsequently, to half the town.

Maryanne's brain was working at a fever pitch. If this were true, it put an entirely different face on the matter. She had previously never entertained the possibility of marrying Major Lindley, as she had explained to her mother, but if he were, indeed, *rich* as well as handsome and charming, why should she not? Certainly, there were no better prospects in town this Season, none that had come her way, in any event. She had some work to do.

"I must return home," she told Miss Brent and Miss Davies.

"But we are going to *Gunter's!*" they exclaimed.

"I have just remembered something I need to do," she said loftily, "something more important than cream ices. You two go. I am certain there is nothing of significance to otherwise claim *your* time." And she and her maid walked off, blithely leaving her two friends without a chaperone.

The news of Gore's wealth had spread quickly through the *ton*. Suddenly, mamas were reassessing his merits as a husband, sharps tried to engage him in games of chance and tricksters wanted to enlist his involvement in a host of specious "investments." Invitations, never sparse, began to pile up faster than Alvanley's bills from his tradesmen, and any taint that might have attached itself to him from his relationship with The Provincial Lily was, of course, not to be considered.

He tossed his gloves into the tall beaver hat that Riddell held upside down for this purpose and chuckled tiredly.

"Riddell, you have no idea how trying it is to be so sought after." He had just come in from White's, and in his perambulations both to and from that august club, had been accosted by no fewer than four young ladies and their zealous mamas, only barely, he was convinced, escaping with his skin.

"No, sir, I have not," his man replied dryly. "Shall I bring you anything, Major?"

"Laudanum, Riddell, laudanum. Perhaps I can sleep until all this nonsense has passed." He shut himself in the library, his mind in a fuss. All this attention was galling him. He had been accepted well enough before, but now people were falling all over themselves for his

attention. It was so transparent that it almost sickened
him. He did not care a fig for their opinions or their
so-called good wishes. The only opinion that mattered
to him, the only *person* who mattered was Belle. He had
come to use her own name in his thoughts of late. Gore
gave a wry smile. After he had begun to do so, quite
inadvertently, he had been concerned that he might
slip in her presence. And he had come close once, although she apparently had not noticed it.

He had known for some time that Belle was the
woman he had been seeking to share his life. His fortune, as sizeable as the gossips believed it to be, ensured
that he could give them both a life of luxury, but how
could he win her? Obviously, they could not be wed—
no, he could not even declare his love for her—whilst
continuing this charade, though he feared what telling
her of his knowledge might mean. Would she be frightened off? Or, perhaps, think he had been laughing at
her all along and hate him for it? He must do something. Of late, his sleep had been disturbed by too many
visions of her smiling face, her soft voice . . . And he
believed, though aware that it might be only because
he wanted to, that she must care for him. He had seen
a look in her eyes more than once, heard an inflection
in her voice that, surely, must be meant only for the
man she would love. Yes, he instructed himself, it is
time to tell her, time to take her in your arms once and
for all.

But even now, even after acknowledging his feelings
and dismissing the suspicions he had harbored about
her, even now a question tickled at a corner of his brain.
What if he had been wrong in revising his opinions of
her? What if she were the fortune hunter he had believed her to be? If so, would she be reaching for him

or his fortune? No, he would wait. The time was not yet right.

At No. 12, William and Cecily were having a quiet dinner and chatting over the last remnants of Belle's party, the previous evening.

"And, oh darling, the most interesting *on-dit* of all!" Cecily was fairly bursting with her news. "Gore is rich!" She laughed, but stopped when she noticed the lack of surprise on her husband's face. "Did you hear what I said? I heard it over tea at Lady Clutterbuck's. She heard it from her husband, who heard it from someone at his club. It must be all over town."

William remained maddeningly calm as he idly turned the pages of a book on ornithology, his wife not being the stiff-necked sort who always demanded her husband's total attention when enjoying a quiet dinner *à deux*. "Yes, dear. Would you pass me one of those biscuits, please?"

She tossed one at his head. He caught it and laughed at her.

"William!"

"Yes, dear?"

"William! Did you know?"

He slowly spread butter on the bread, making a great show of examining a drawing of a finch. "Happens I did, Cecily."

"You . . ." She choked, as he bit back a chuckle. Her toleration of his books apparently having reached its limit, she raised her voice one or two octaves. "William, do shut that stupid book!"

He complied and sat back in his chair, grinning.

"You *knew*?" He nodded. "Well, you mean that you heard it at your club today?"

He shook his head, lips tight, then took pity on her. "I have known it for some time, darling."

"And never told me?"

"Oh, don't look at me that way, Cec. Lindley wanted it kept secret. Didn't want to be courted for his blunt."

"Oh, I see." Her tone was injured. "Obviously, you did not trust me to keep silent."

"Now, darling, that had nothing to do with it. It was not my secret to tell, and after all, there was no need for you to know."

"Indeed?" she replied coolly.

"Come, don't cut up stiff. Think of poor Lindley. Certainly, he's enjoyed his last day of peace, now that the news is out." He chuckled and sipped his wine. "I don't envy him. What is it? You're looking very pleased with yourself all of a sudden."

"Humph. You are not the only one who can keep a secret, William."

He poured more wine into her glass and asked with a casualness that was hopelessly transparent, "And what is your secret, pray?"

"I am not sure I shall tell you."

Laughing, he pointed out that it was unlikely she could keep her silence, and he confessed his curiosity, hoping that would help to loosen her tongue. For a moment, she experienced a twinge of guilt at disclosing Belle's tale. She told herself, however, that she had her friend's permission and that, while her disclosure certainly would allow her to get her own back with her husband, she rather hoped instead to somehow further what she saw as the burgeoning romance between Belle and Gore.

It was her turn to chuckle. "Oh, very well." And she told him all she knew of Belle.

Her husband's astonishment was most gratifying. Cecily grinned at him impishly, and they both laughed.

"And you say Lindley knows nothing of this?" By now,

they had settled into comfortable chairs in the drawing room, where a breeze cooled the heavy air.

"Not so far as we can tell, but perhaps you have better knowledge of that, too?" She was only half teasing for, if Gore had told William of his fortune, he might also have told him that he had discovered "Lillie's" true identity.

"No, no," William assured her. "He has not uttered a word to me. I am convinced he does not know."

"Mmm."

"Cec," he said pointedly, but with a hint of a smile, "we cannot interfere in this."

"William," she admonished him, "as if I ever would."

Gore and Belle brought the horses to a halt in a grove of oaks and dismounted. Thistle and Orion moved off a few paces and began to champ the grass. He turned to Belle and smiled.

"Spending time with you like this means a very great deal to me." His voice was low and soft.

The grove was off the bridle path and, in any case, one o'clock in the afternoon was not an hour that the *beau monde* considered fashionable for riding in Hyde Park, so they were unencumbered by human company. Some bees hummed in the sweet clover, and a harlequin-patterned butterfly floated past.

She looked into his green eyes, at last finding what she had hoped for all these weeks, and forgot all the lectures she had given herself. None of that mattered now. She looked up at him and whispered, "And to me, Gore."

He drew her gently into his arms, softly kissing her eyes, her nose and, at last, her lips. "My lovely Lillie."

She sighed.

"Lillie. Lillie!"

Belle woke with a startled "Oh!" and looked into Cecily's laughing eyes, then around herself at the drawing room. She put a hand to her forehead and brushed back tendrils of damp hair. "Oh," she said again, "I must have nodded off. This heat," she said by way of explanation.

"Yes, awful, isn't it? You were dreaming, I think. And quite a pleasant dream, judging from the smile on your face," her friend teased.

"I was."

"Let me guess. It was about Gore, was it not?"

"Yes," Belle confessed with another smile.

Cecily made herself comfortable on a fragile-looking chair, put down her reticule and asked eagerly, "Tell me, my dear, what do you think of the news? About his money, I mean. You have heard?"

Belle had, having received the information from Lord Peter. "It would seem I am not the only one who is keeping secrets."

"Indeed you are not. I said much the same thing to William just last evening. My husband, you see, tells me he has known for some time. Imagine!"

"He did? Well, but, you have kept our secret from him, too," Belle reminded her with a grin.

"Not anymore. I told him last night, when we were discussing Gore. I just could not bear that smug look on his face, so I told him about you. Hardly noble of me, was it?" She chuckled.

"Don't be a goose, Cecily. We both agreed you would tell him eventually." Her eyes twinkled at her friend. "I am pleased that you were able to use my story to your advantage. And I am also happy that William knows. He will not tell Gore, will he?" she asked as an afterthought.

"He promised not to. Although, he did tell him of that creature's role in your disgrace."

Belle's eyes opened wide. "He has not mentioned it to me."

"No, very likely he does not want to disturb you with resurrecting the matter. But here, I also came to tell you that I am on my way to Mrs. Niven's. I am putting my plan into motion, Lillie," she said gaily, "and I wanted you to know it."

Belle looked rather doubtful. "I know we discussed it, Cecily, but, now I have had time to think on it . . . well, are you certain it can work? That is, oh dear, Cec, it just seems, after some thought, that it might be rather, um, unusual." This circumlocution reflected her uncertain feelings about her friend's intended machinations. She had not wanted to hurt Cecily's feelings. Her friend was, after all, doing her best to help, but in the cold light of day, the scheme seemed rather cork-brained. Not that she would have put it into just those words, of course.

"It will work, I promise," Cecily trilled. "Now, I am off, and you do not even have to wish me luck!"

TEN

All *ton* parties were, by definition, exclusive, but the Remington ball promised to be one of the grandest events of the Season. Everyone who mattered was in attendance, and carriages still were lined up in the street waiting to dislodge their passengers well past the hour when the festivities had commenced.

Cecily's appearance at any *fête* was always noticed. Her height not only made her difficult to overlook, but blessed her with the good fortune to shine in any garment she chose to wear, and her choices always were of the first stare. On this night, however, she outdid not only every other lady present, but her own reputation, as well. She and Mrs. Niven had labored happily for hours over patterns and fabrics.

"Mrs. Niven, you must make for me the most beautiful ball dress you have ever created. So beautiful that the ladies of the *ton* will line up at your door!"

"But, Mrs. Rafton, I have already enjoyed much custom, thanks to your good words."

"Thanks to your wonderful work!" Cecily corrected her. "But, this time, I am interested in your receiving the custom of one *particular* lady. It is very important. You do not dress Miss Maryanne Stockdale, I think?"

Mrs. Niven, who had heard of that young lady, wrinkled her nose. "No, I do not."

Cecily noticed her grimace of distaste and was pleased. "Splendid."

Miss Stockdale's difficult reputation had preceded her in dressmaking circles, and Mrs. Niven was somewhat surprised that the considerate Mrs. Rafton would associate with such a person, much less give her the name of her milliner. "You wish me to dress her as I do your friend, Mrs. Broadhurst?" she asked dubiously.

"Hardly," she replied dryly. "Mrs. Niven, I have a favor to ask of you." She gave her most quelling look to a matron who was signaling for Mrs. Niven's attention. "Allow me to explain," she said, taking the dressmaker's elbow and leading her to a quiet corner of the salon.

A short time later, Mrs. Niven had agreed to grant Cecily's wish. Not only would she never have dreamt of alienating her best client by denying such a request, but after many years of quietly deferring to the demands of too many snobbish customers, she was happy at the prospect of getting back a little of her own. In addition, when she heard what Miss Stockdale had done to one of her creations, she was not a little offended.

Mrs. Niven had succeeded so well in the first part of Cecily's request, that she had surprised even herself. The sarcenet slip of hyacinth blue was spotted with oyster-colored satin and decorated at the bottom with small hyacinth flowers of the same off-white color. A robe of the finest white lace, open on one side, was finished all around with a scalloped hem. The tiny sleeves were narrow bands of the same lace and the corsage covered barely enough to justify its name. A band of sapphires and diamonds adorned Cecily's hair, neck, ears and wrists. (William would have been offended by feathers of any kind and, after years of living with him, so would she.) The whole effect on another lady, especially a short one, would have been overpowering, but on Cecily Rafton, it was exquisite. Even William, who was used to seeing his lady decked out in the highest kick of fashion, was impressed, but he was most struck by the tiny wisp of a bodice.

As they made ready to depart Berkeley Square, he blinked. "God, Cec, you look—that is . . ."

Kissing his cheek, she took his arm and, smiling, led him to their carriage. "Thank you, darling, I am so pleased that you like it." William shook his head and went along quietly. He was a lucky man, and he knew it.

Even in the crush that was the Remington ball, Cecily turned heads. It was not long before, much to her delight, she had attracted any number of ladies who exclaimed over her gown, examined its details up close and begged for the name of her dressmaker. She gladly complied. Eventually, Cecily's real quarry slid over to her.

"Oh, Mrs. Rafton, is it not? You will remember me, I am convinced. I am Maryanne Stockdale. We met at that frightful do at Mrs. Carling's the other week."

Cecily looked down her rather long nose—she had bewailed that appendage more than once, but it had its purposes—and raised her brows. "Stockton?"

"Stock*dale*, ma'am."

"Stockdale, you say? I am not—oh, wait, perhaps I remember." She also recalled how once, in her first Season, when she had been all giddiness, arms and legs, she had been subjected to the rudest examination through the quizzing glass of a veritable empress of the *beau monde*, the Countess of Hopwood. Cecily had nearly shriveled up in embarrassment at the dowager's temerity. Now, giving her best imitation of the Countess, she scrutinized Maryanne Stockdale with as much effrontery as she could muster. At length, as her victim squirmed, she gave a little *moue* of distaste and replied, "Ah, yes, I think I remember you."

Maryanne wanted to slap her face. How dare the woman treat her this way? How dare she claim not to recall her? But, she said nothing for fear it might deprive her of the information she sought. She merely raised her own brows and said silkily, "Thank you, Mrs. Rafton, I am so pleased that you do."

Cecily nodded regally.

"Mrs. Rafton, I must tell you that I think your gown the most magnificent creation I have ever seen."

Cecily's look seemed to ask if she were expected to find any satisfaction in that. She gave the ghost of a smile. "How . . . nice, Miss Stockwood."

"Stock*dale.*"

"Of course."

Maryanne swallowed a biting retort. "Mrs. Rafton," she began, "I wonder if you might be willing to share the name of your dressmaker . . ."

Cecily eyed the length of Maryanne's figure again and smiled sympathetically. "You are in need of a new one?"

Maryanne gasped not just because of the other woman's audacity, but because her own ivory silk dress was quite lovely and she knew it. "Mrs. Rafton, I would have you know . . ." She stopped herself just in time, as Cecily waited with innocent patience. "That is, well, we all must strive to look our best, after all, and your gown puts the rest of us," here she swept an all-encompassing wave in the general direction of the ballroom on whose perimeter they stood, "in the shade. So, I hoped you would share with me the name of the person who dresses you."

Cecily pretended to be taken aback by this request and put a white-gloved hand to her breast to lend the proper effect. "Why, Miss Stock—*dale* is it? I am not sure." She looked down her nose again, this was *such* fun. "Her services come *very* dear, you know. And then, you know, she does not dress just *anybody.*"

Maryanne managed a laugh. "Oh, Mrs. Rafton, I promise you that cost is not a consideration to me. And I am, after all, *someone.*"

"Of *course* you are, my dear. Although, you know, the more I look at you, I am less certain that I do know who you are." Maryanne seethed. "Well, no matter. My woman's name is Mrs. Niven, in Oxford Street. Doubtless," she cast one last speculative look at Maryanne's person and shrugged, "she will be able to help you. The woman is a wonder."

When Cecily later shared this story, in every delicious detail, with Belle and Warner, they all went into gales of laughter. "I cannot believe that I had the cheek to do it, Lillie, but I kept reminding myself how terribly she had treated you. You should have seen her face! I thought she would strangle me at any moment!"

Maryanne Stockdale and her mother appeared at Mrs. Niven's shop the next day, but so did most every other lady who had cadged her name from Cecily, and the premises were full to bursting. After cooling their heels for well over an hour—many ladies, including some that entered after they had, waited much longer, but Cecily had asked Mrs. Niven to keep this one waiting only long enough to infuriate her—they were ushered into the dressmaker's presence. Once again, Maryanne suffered a lengthy and disdainful scrutiny.

"Well," Mrs. Niven sighed, "I think I can dress you nicely, Miss Stockdale."

"Marvelous. Now, Mrs. Niven, I shall be needing, among other things, the most perfect gown that you can create. It is for my birthday ball."

"Ah. My felicitations, Miss Stockdale. Well, yes, I am certain that I shall be able to accommodate you. Why do you not look at these patterns on my table? Do you have any particular fabrics in mind yet?" Maryanne replied that she had an idea or two. "Good. Look through these, then, and I shall have one of my assistants measure you. You may have the fabric sent over from the warehouse and come in for your first fitting, shall we say . . . Thursday week?"

"Impossible, Mrs. Niven. My birthday ball is this Friday night!" Her mother nodded.

"Friday? Why, this is Monday, Miss Stockdale, I cannot possibly have anything completely ready by then. It is not nearly enough time."

"But you must!"

Mrs. Niven shook her head firmly and shut her eyes. "It cannot be done."

"Mama!"

"Mrs. Niven, I do not think you realize how important this occasion is," Mrs. Stockdale sputtered.

"I am sorry, ma'am. But, I could not properly finish such a gown, any gown, in that short a time. And, as you can see," she waved her arm toward the public environs of the shop, "today I have been besieged by ladies wishing me to dress them. It is quite extraordinary." Indeed, it was. Cecily had sent around a note first thing that morning that Mrs. Niven could expect her services to be in high demand, but she had never expected anything like this. "Some of these ladies arrived here before you did and have already put in their orders—not to mention those commissions I already had before today. Friday I cannot do."

"Mrs. Niven, I simply must have you make my dress for my party. I *must.*" Maryanne's voice was rising.

Her mother interjected. "Mrs. Niven, perhaps we did

not explain clearly enough. We were sent here by Mrs. William Rafton." So were the other ladies, but the dressmaker was not about to tell them that. "I understand she is a particularly good client of yours," Mrs. Stockdale continued pointedly. "And she is a very close friend of Miss Stockdale's."

Mrs. Niven had been instructed to make them beg for her help, that would serve both her purposes and Cecily's, but to relent when the time appeared right. "Mrs. Rafton, you say. Very well, I may be able to contrive something, but not too extravagant, mind you, for *that* even for Mrs. Rafton's sake, I cannot do."

The two ladies gladly agreed, and the arrangements were duly made according to Mrs. Niven's direction—nothing too fancy or detailed. When left alone to pore over patterns, however, they devised their own plan.

Maryanne and her mother appeared in the shop late on Friday morning for her final fitting. The gown was just what Cecily had suggested to the dressmaker. It was made of aquamarine silk, beautifully, but very simply fashioned. Maryanne had realized its simplicity all along, through two previous fittings, and had, in fact, chosen the pattern for that very reason. Now, standing before the full-length glass in the dressing room, she exchanged a conspiratorial look with her mother.

"That looks very well on you, Miss Stockdale. Just a few touches left and it shall be ready for tonight. I shall have it sent round to you."

"I think not, Mrs. Niven. Not like this, at any rate. It is just too plain."

"It is, but it becomes you, Miss Stockdale. And it is just what we agreed—"

The Stockdales did not let her finish. "Mrs. Niven, my daughter feels it is too plain, and she must have what she wants. This is a very important evening for her, after all. You must do something."

"Do something? What would you have me do at this hour, ma'am? The gown is finished."

"You said yourself that you had work left to do."

"Oh, but that is nothing, a stitch here and there, nothing more."

"Be that as it may, you must add something to the dress."

"Yes, you must," Maryanne added. "You would not want me to decide not to take it, would you? I do have others, much lovelier than this is now," she held out the skirt with a sneer, "that will do much better. I shan't take this dress if you cannot accommodate me."

Mrs. Niven was aghast, then suddenly realized that this could work out better than she or Cecily had ever dreamed. "Very well, I can, perhaps, add a *rouleau* just below the bodice, here," she demonstrated, "and at the sleeves and above the hem."

"Above the *flounce* on the hem, Mrs. Niven, I think," Maryanne said slyly.

"Of course, Miss Stockdale, you shall have a flounce. However, I must say again that you have left me but a short time. Adding touches such as these takes time and, while the dress will look well enough, I cannot promise you that the work will be of the high quality for which I am known," she added proudly.

Maryanne and her mother were too pleased with the success of their plan to pay sufficient attention, and Mrs. Niven did not bother to repeat her warning. *Her* reputation would survive, of that much she was certain, and she set her seamstresses to work with very unusual instructions. Cecily, who had wanted only that the Stockdale creature be made to grovel at Mrs. Niven's feet and, perhaps, if Mrs. Niven were not too averse to the notion, to end up with a dress that was nothing more than acceptable for all her trouble and blunt, could not have thought of a better scheme.

ELEVEN

Cecily regaled Belle and Warner with the note she subsequently received from Mrs. Niven which explained all that had taken place that morning, but she did not give them all the details of the plan; those she would save for after the ball. "This is too delicious." She laughed. "You know, that awful creature actually invited us to her party as thanks for my giving her Mrs. Niven's name. We had not intended to go, but I would not miss this for a hundred new gowns!"

"Oh, my, this is serious!" teased Belle.

Cecily hugged her. "I promised you we would fix that minx, Lillie, and tonight is the night!"

She laughed. "I almost wish I could be there."

"I, too," Warner added.

"Do not worry. I shall remember every last detail and come back tomorrow to tell all!"

Filbert was determined. He had worried about, and cared for, The Bracelet long enough. He was sick of the very thought of it, tired of the weight of responsibility. And so, he rose long before Belle the next morning to retrieve it from its latest hiding place—a now-to-let mouse hole in one of the unused bedrooms—and place it carefully in a half-open drawer of her dressing table, where it nestled among her handkerchiefs. That done, he went to rest on the foot of her bed until she finally decided to get up.

The previous evening, Belle had attended a *soirée* that lasted into the wee hours of the morning. Just as all her friends had predicted, her trial had passed. The *ton* were now feeding on a nabob, Mr. Penworth, recently returned from India with newfound wealth beyond his wildest dreams. Poor Mr. and Mrs. Penworth had actually believed that said riches would allow them to establish their family in London society, and the *ton* were too busy humiliating them to pay any attention to The Provincial Lily. Their thick Yorkshire accents and rustic ways were burlesqued in drawing rooms all over town, while the dandies mocked his style and the ladies laughed at her unbecoming gowns. In short, the pair were the latest *divertissement* of the *beau monde,* who sank their fangs and dug their claws into the flesh of the naive Penworths as if they had not feasted for weeks.

Belle had encountered the Penworths at Hatchards just the day before, and had recognized them easily, their accents and manners, which in no way offended, giving them away immediately. She made so bold as to introduce herself, believing both that their country ways would not consider such contact *outré* and that, surely, they stood in need of kindness. Cecily, who had accompanied her to the bookshop, put them at their ease at once with her outgoing manner, and their relief at an honest gesture of friendship was plain on their faces. Mrs. Penworth complimented Cecily on her pale blue walking dress.

"Mrs. Rafton, I have never seen anything so lovely." She held out the fabric of the gown that covered her ample frame and, with a self-deprecating laugh, added, "I never seem to turn myself out so well, try as I might."

"Now, Helen, never you mind what those cats have been saying. Aye, you look well enough," her husband reassured her fondly. "That silly dressmaker of yours just doesn't know what to do with a figure as wholesome as yours."

Cecily smiled. "Mrs. Penworth, I should be most happy to give you the name of my dressmaker, if you do not think me too bold."

"I should be in your debt, Mrs. Rafton," said Mrs. Penworth, trying not to display too much eagerness. She had received in return not only Mrs. Niven's name, but a personal recommendation, as well. Cecily even managed, without offense to anyone's feelings, to give Mr. Penworth the name of William's tailor. Well, Belle thought, the *ton* probably never will accept them, but at least there will be less about them to mock.

Now, sitting at her dressing table, Belle yawned and examined her face in the glass. She had stayed much too late at the party. Glaring at the dark circles that underlined her eyes, she decided she would have to apply some powder to mask them.

Warner poured water into the bowl on the wash stand, and Belle splashed her face hoping to clear away the cobwebs in her head.

"I cannot believe how exhausted I am. I feel as if I had spent the entire night dancing one Scotch reel after another."

"While you finish washing, I shall get your coffee, so you can sip it while you dress. You'll feel better soon," Warner assured her with a smile.

A short while later, feeling much more the thing,

Belle sat at her dressing table as Warner finished her hair. Filbert sat on the table, watching her intently. She and Warner were chatting quietly, and he was not a little miffed.

"Major Lindley is taking me riding later this morning. Much as I have come to enjoy it, I cannot say that I am anticipating riding again—not after the last time."

Warner was sympathetic, but preoccupied with her mistress's hair. "Now, I am certain you will have a nice, *uneventful* ride, ma'am. Shall we try the curls drawn back like this, do you think?" She demonstrated her idea. "That way, with the bonnet tilted forward, as it is intended to be, like this," she placed the hat momentarily on Belle's head, "the curls will show up quite nicely from behind."

"Oh, yes. And, perhaps we could pull it up just a bit higher . . ."

Filbert glared in exasperation. What were they doing?

"That's lovely, Warner. Thank you."

"Here is your reticule, ma'am."

"Thank you again. I just need a fresh handkerchief," she said, reaching into the drawer. "What time is . . . ? Oh, what is this?" She peered into the drawer and withdrew the foreign object her fingers had encountered.

"Good God! Warner, look!"

Warner, who had just retrieved Belle's riding boots from the armoire, came to her side and gasped.

"It's The Bracelet!" they exclaimed in unison.

Filbert had kept the faith of all the Broadhurst cats. Although he had wavered for so long about giving back his treasure, at length, he'd known it was time to relinquish it. He had worried, for a time, whether Ethelbert would approve, but had ultimately decided that if he did not, his ancestor was in no position to do much about it.

Belle held The Bracelet up with both hands, and it sparkled in the sunlight.

"Oh, Mrs. Broadhurst, it's—"

"Beautiful," Belle finished.

It was. Three rows of stones were fashioned into a graceful, elegant pattern of scallop shells. There were dozens of small, perfect diamonds, but the craftsmanship was such that the piece was not garish or heavy; in fact, it appeared quite delicate.

Filbert watched from the window. Good. It still glittered just as it ought. Well, it should, after all, for he had followed to the letter the old instructions for polishing it. Filbert had heard Belle speak of a gentleman called Beau something, who bragged about using champagne to keep the high luster of his boots. Champagne, indeed! He sniffed in disdain. If the man only knew.

"Oh, you must put it on, you know." Warner breathed the words eagerly.

"Yes! Help me, Warner." In a moment, the platinum catch was closed and The Bracelet dangled loosely from Belle's wrist. The bedroom was filled with "Ohs" and "Ahs," as the two women admired the cat's treasure. Filbert blinked from his vantage point. He never had understood what all the fuss and subterfuge was about. It was just a bunch of bright stones of some kind, wasn't it? Why did people want it so badly? And why did Belle want to hang it on her person? He blinked again. Someone had tried to put a collar on him once, but Filbert had sent him to the roundabout soon enough. And with a nice scratch on his hand for his pains.

"Now you, Warner. You must try it on."

"Oh, ma'am, I should love to."

Belle put it on her maid's wrist, and the "Ohs" and "Ahs" were repeated.

"I cannot believe I have finally found it." Belle giggled. Warner removed The Bracelet and returned it to her mistress.

Filbert sat up and glowered at her. *I?* The silly creature thought that *she* had found it? How dare she? If it were not for him, she would still be on her hands and knees searching under tables and in old closets! He had hidden the thing in plain sight in the secret passage and she still had missed it. He would have posted a sign if he knew how to write, but after that episode, he was not entirely convinced that Belle was bright enough to read, as most humans seemed able to do. Why, if it hadn't been for him . . . Thoroughly disgusted, and impatient for his share of the glory, Filbert slipped from the window seat with a squeak and back onto the dressing table, where he sat between them and stared at Belle. He wanted very much to scowl, but had gotten to know human temperaments quite well by this time, so he rubbed up against her and uttered his most charming soft purr.

"Filbert, look! It's beautiful, isn't it? Oh, Warner, how silly of me! He knows quite well how lovely it . . ." She looked from the cat to Warner, and they both laughed. "What am I saying, Warner? I did not *find* The Bracelet. Well, not precisely. He put it where I could not miss it! Didn't you, my darling?" she cooed at him. "It was so cleverly hidden that you knew I should never find it otherwise!" She gathered him into her arms and kissed his head with great affection. "Wonderful, clever Filbert."

"Indeed, clever he is, ma'am." Warner chuckled.

Filbert rolled over and exposed his tummy which Belle dutifully rubbed until his purr nearly brought down the house.

A rap at the door signaled Thomasina's entrance. "Major Lindley has arrived, Mrs. Broadhurst."

"Gore! Oh, I cannot wait to show him!" She kissed Filbert soundly once more and placed him back on his cushion in the window, picked up The Bracelet, then flew past the maid and down the stairs. Warner and

Thomasina followed her, the former explaining what had occurred.

Filbert yawned and stretched in the sun. His duty finally accomplished, he needed to rest.

She burst into the drawing room, laughing. "Gore! You will never guess! Look, The Bracelet! I have found it! Well, that is, Filbert allowed me to find it. Isn't it beautiful?"

Gore took it from her outstretched hand and brought it to the window to examine in the sunlight. He grinned at her. "Congratulations, my dear, the treasure is found. You are looking very pleased with yourself," he teased.

She joined him at the window. "Well, I am, actually. Even if I did not manage to do it alone. I should have known that Filbert would help me. Eulalie said he would."

"Ah, yes, Filbert. Come closer, Lillie." She did so and gazed up at him, wanting to touch his cheek, his soft brown coat, anything that would draw him closer still. "Hold out your hand. There," he placed The Bracelet on her wrist, "that is where it belongs."

"Oh, no."

"No?"

"I am not going to keep it, Gore. It should go to Aunt Eulalie, for it really belongs to her, after all."

He put his arms around her then and sighed. She had confirmed his trust in her. She would not keep the piece; he had finally known she would not. Gore wanted desperately to kiss her, to tell her that he knew her secret, but now was not the time.

Belle looked up into his eyes and, for a moment, hoped foolishly that now he might kiss her.

Instead, he only said, "Yes, you have the right of it, Lillie. A less generous woman would have kept it for herself and been perfectly justified in doing so. I admire you, and so will Eulalie. Shall we go there now and give it to her?"

"Oh, yes, let's. I cannot wait to see her face!"

She was not disappointed, Eulalie was ecstatic and eager to know how she had finally found it.

Belle hugged her and said lightly, "Just as you promised, Aunt, Filbert helped. Evidently, he put it in one of my drawers, and then, thanks to my boundless powers of intelligence, I managed to find it. It makes me wonder if the poor creature might not have been trying to give it to me for weeks!" They all laughed.

"Well, Lillie, good for you," Uncle Aubrey put in. "To say the truth, I always wondered how much of that bracelet was legend and how much was real. After all, it had been lost for generations. But, my dear wife," he said as he patted Eulalie's hand, "never doubted it. Always knew it would be found, she said. Didn't you, Eulalie?"

"Be sure that I did, Aubrey."

Belle glanced at Gore, and they exchanged a private smile. "And now, Aunt Eulalie, I restore it to its rightful owner." She sat down beside the older woman, took her hand, and put The Bracelet in it. "There."

Eulalie looked at her, wide-eyed. "You want to give it to me?"

"Indeed I do. You are the last blood Broadhurst, and as such, it is rightfully yours, Aunt."

Eulalie tried to give it back. "No. No, that is not right. For one thing, Lillith, you found it . . ."

"Pooh," interjected Belle.

The older woman held up her hand. "And for another—well, to be honest, I am not certain of the other. But, I do know that you should have it. How should an old woman like me look wearing such an extravagant piece of jewelry?" This made no sense at all. Eulalie's magnificent jewels were the envy of many of her set;

the Singleton pearls alone could have bought a man an abbey.

"Oh, Aunt, you are being silly."

"Gore?" Eulalie looked to him for support.

He shook his head and smiled. "I am afraid she is determined, ma'am. You really must accept it, you know."

She was clearly weakening, then thought of something else. "But what use shall I have of them in Minster Lovell?"

"Aunt? Have you and Uncle Aubrey finally found a house, then? You are leaving London?"

The older couple exchanged looks. "Yes, my dear," Aubrey replied. "We were planning to have you and Gore to supper this week to tell you all about it."

"Oh, but I shall miss you both so," Belle said, then remembered she would be gone in any event and, likely, would never see either of them again. Or anyone else in London who mattered to her. Suddenly, her eyes filled with tears and she fussed for a handkerchief. She had developed a great fondness for both Eulalie and Aubrey, Eulalie especially, and the prospect of never seeing them again pained her more than she would have thought.

"Now, now, Lillith. We are not going to the ends of the earth, you know. Why, Minster Lovell is not far from Burford at all, and you will be repairing there anyway, as soon as the Season ends." Eulalie looked at Aubrey helplessly. "We, ah, leave Tuesday week," she finished softly.

"Oh! As soon as that?" Belle's voice caught in her throat.

"Come, my dear, no tears now," Aubrey said gruffly.

"I am sorry, Uncle." She brightened and lied, "Of course we shall see one another often, and, Aunt, you know perfectly well that you can wear The Bracelet when you socialize there. After all, you will make new friends. You can dazzle them with it and with its story." As a last resort, she added with a twinkle in her eyes, "And I know that you will let me borrow it from time to time, will you not?"

"Naturally, Lillie."

"It is settled, then."

Eulalie hugged her then and, sniffing, said with a little laugh, "I confess, I would very much like to have it. Thank you, Lillith."

"You are most welcome, Aunt Eulalie."

TWELVE

Had he been less humble and given the matter much thought at all, Gore might have thought of crying off from Miss Stockdale's birthday ball, an invitation he had accepted weeks earlier. Still, he considered, his manners would not allow him that luxury. She had invited many gentlemen, and he was not best pleased by the way in which she hung on his sleeve for most of the evening. Indeed, he was puzzled that her mama had not stepped in when the girl tried to cozen him into yet another dance with her. He had politely, but firmly, declined that request, reminding her that for them to stand up for so many dances together was not altogether proper, and that, perhaps, she might distribute her charms more equally among her other male guests. She did not take either his repulse, couched as it was in the most civil terms, or his suggestion, well.

"But, Major," she had pouted, "I wish to dance with *you,* not the others."

"Miss Stockdale, I must decline. You do not want people to talk, do you?"

"Major Lindley—Gore—you are, after all, my *particular* guest, as I am certain you know." She smiled sweetly and put a hand on his ebony sleeve. "I hope that I may not have to care a fig for what the *ton* may say, Or, perhaps," she said as she bit her lip and looked up at him through her lashes, "I am speaking too plainly, sir."

Good God, what was the silly creature saying? He knew he had given her no cause to expect a proposal from him, and was astonished at her boldness. Did she really think she could bamboozle him into parson's mousetrap? He decided that his safest tactic was to feign obtuseness.

"Miss Stockdale, I have no idea to what you can be referring. I must tell you that I am aware of your, shall I say, *involvement*, in those scurrilous attacks on Mrs. Broadhurst. And, if you do not release your hold on my arm this instant, I shall see to it that the rest of the town knows, as well."

"I . . . but I assure you, Major, I would never do such a thing! How can you think it? Doubtless, it was that very *lady* who has libeled me in this way, she—"

"The term you are looking for is *slander. Libel*, on the other hand, is what you have done to Mrs. Broadhurst, or at least, instigated." She stamped her foot with rage. "Careful, or you will not be able to dance for the rest of your party. Goodbye, Miss Stockdale."

On his way out, he encountered William and Cecily. "Good God, the chit's worse than a quack's leech."

William raised his brows in sympathy. "Can't say I envy you, Lindley."

Gore was baffled by Cecily's smug smile.

"What are you two doing here, by the way? From what you said to me, William, I would have thought that nothing could drag you here tonight."

"Ask my wife," his friend drawled. "She's done something to put the cat among the pigeons, I know she has, but she won't tell me what."

They both gave Cecily a questioning look, but she

merely continued to smile and shook her head. "Just you wait."

"See what I mean? There's no prying it out of her. We just have to wait. God knows for what."

Until now, the ball had been uneventful, much to Cecily's consternation. Maryanne had accepted the felicitations of her friends and relations as only her due, and had enjoyed herself tremendously in dance after dance with Gore. Her guests ate and drank, danced and laughed, gossiped and flirted. So pleased was she, that Maryanne even danced a Scotch reel with her father and a country dance with her cousin, Neville. And that was, indeed, unfortunate. For Mrs. Niven had been able to do little more than baste the flounce and *rouleaux*, and those stitches were tugged at terribly during the vigorous dances which Maryanne, under other circumstances, never would have performed. So, when she and her father took the floor alone for her birthday waltz, following her conversation with Gore, she was quite unprepared for what happened.

The *rouleaux* that formed the band at the bottom of her bodice came loose first, when she reached up to put her hand on her father's shoulder. It took a few moments for anyone to notice, but, by the time they did, most of it had come away and hung down her back like a tail. At first, she assumed the sounds were murmurs of admiration, but then she began to discern titters and gasps. She looked into her father's eyes to see if he knew what was happening, but he shrugged and continued to smile down at her. Until she tripped. The flounce was a deep one, just as Maryanne had ordered, and despite her father's efforts to grab her, it too came loose and entwined itself around her ankles as she twirled into the next pattern of the dance.

Cecily's laughter was, perhaps, the first to be heard—

she had, after all, been watching and waiting for this moment—it certainly was the loudest, as the young woman, her face purple with rage, sat in a ridiculous heap and cursed Mrs. Niven. Someone was heard to remark, loudly enough for most to hear, "Oho! A new Provincial Lily, as I live and breathe!"

Miss Brent and Miss Davies rushed to the side of their friend, who was being helped to her feet by Mr. Stockdale. "Why, Maryanne, you've come all undone!" they cried with barely concealed glee.

Maryanne Stockdale's social disgrace was complete, and Cecily and William departed the house in Grosvenor Square and repaired to No. 12 to replay the events of the evening.

Late in the afternoon after the soon-to-be-famous birthday ball, Cecily could be found at No. 7, her audience in rapt attention as she told her story.

"That is perfect!" Warner exclaimed. "No one could be more deserving of such a come-down."

"Yes, there is justice in the world, after all." Belle wiped a mirthful tear from one eye. "You know, I almost feel sorry for her."

"Don't!" Cecily and Warner cried in unison.

Belle laughingly agreed that only a block would be so magnanimous.

Cecily chuckled. "And, when Gore—"

"Gore was there?" Belle's heart stopped momentarily. Why, he had been with her earlier today, as they exclaimed over The Bracelet and visited Aunt Eulalie, and he had never mentioned it. She supposed that he could not be expected to hold Miss Stockdale in the same disdain that she did, but she still felt betrayed by his attendance at the ball. He had looked at her in such a way, spoken so sweetly to her just that morning, and had been *there* last night.

"Well, yes, Lillie, but it was of no significance, honestly. I promise you, he was less than charmed by the affair." She knew her words would do little to ease Belle's discomfort, but had nothing to add to them, since manners had prevented Gore's telling either her or William of the setdown he'd delivered to Miss Stockdale. Belle did not believe that Gore actually harbored a *tendre* for Miss Stockdale, simply because she believed he had more common sense than to leg-shackle himself to an empty-headed woman, but that he still would seek out her company after hearing what she had done, cut her. Surely, this told her clearly enough, if nothing else had, that Gore had no particular feelings for her.

"Do not refine on it, Lillie," Cecily said firmly and changed the subject.

"I called to see Mrs. Niven before I came here," she told them. "I wanted to thank her for all her hard work! Evidently, only two or three clients had seen or heard what happened to Miss Stockdale's gown, and Mrs. Niven told them the truth—that the girl had demanded it be given her, even when she knew it was not her best work. I am happy to say that all their sympathy lay with Mrs. Niven. In fact, she said, all those ladies had given her additional orders, so that others would see that their confidence in her had not diminished!"

"I am happy to know it," Belle remarked, genuinely pleased that the milliner would not suffer any repercussions from Miss Stockdale's disgrace.

Thomasina came in and handed her the morning post, which consisted entirely of a single letter. "Here! A letter from Lillie. I shall read it to you, so that you can hear all her news. What few letters I have received have been fascinating, and I know she would not object to your hearing this." Belle had, eventually, finished her own letter to Lillie, but she never had the chance to post it. She scanned the first few lines before beginning to read aloud, and her face fell.

"What is it, ma'am? Has some harm come to Mrs. Broadhurst?"

"No, not at all." She looked up at them. "Lillie is coming home."

"Oh!" said Warner.

"Coming home?" echoed Cecily.

"Yes, she sounds rather embarrassed, really. Says she cannot believe it herself." Belle searched for the appropriate lines. " 'You will, doubtless decide that I have gone completely round the twist, Belle, but I find that I have had enough of travel—at least for now. Italy has been beautiful, but, somehow, I have tired of ruins and strange foods and olive trees—my dear, they are simply *everywhere* in the countryside. I am homesick, Belle. *There*, I have said it and, believe me, you can be no more shocked to read it than I am to write it!' Well, she goes on, of course, but that is the gist of it, except that 'By the time you read this, dear Belle, I shall be well on my way back to England. I expect to arrive around the fifteenth.' That is less than two weeks away," she said quietly.

The room was silent for several moments. "Oh," Cecily said at last. "Well, that is nice, isn't it? I have wanted so much to meet . . ." Her voice dropped off. Warner watched her mistress carefully.

Belle forced a smile to her lips. "Well, naturally you have. And you will adore her, I promise you. I am looking forward to seeing her very much myself. Are you not, Warner?"

"Of course, ma'am."

Cecily did not know what to say. What would her friend do now? Go into service as a companion, as she had originally intended? But that was not to be thought of! If that fool, Gore Lindley, would simply marry her, a solution that Cecily was convinced both of them wished, the problem would be eliminated. But, he had not, and adding Lillie, the *real* Lillie to the equation could only muddle things further. She and William would, of course, ask Belle to live with them, but she knew full well that their offer would be graciously declined.

"Well," Belle said at length. "I have much to do."

"What do you mean?" asked Cecily, eyes wide.

"I have arrangements to make, Cec. The house must be got in readiness for Lillie, and—"

"The house is quite fine the way it is. It is fine. Just fine. Is it not, Warner?"

"Yes, 'tis, ma'am."

"There, you see?"

"And, I must find a place to go." When her friend began to interrupt this ridiculous plan, she held up a hand and smiled. "Come, Cec. We all knew it would come to this eventually. I have foolishly put it off, partly because I honestly did not expect her return so soon. And partly, I confess, because I did not want to think of it. I suppose that I had hoped . . . Well, no matter." She leaned over and kissed Cecily's cheek, which she found wet with a few tears. "Stop that, you goose. It is not as if I were leaving tomorrow, you know. We shall have lots of time together yet. You will excuse me, now, will you not?"

Warner found her curled up like a child in the window seat in her bedroom. The room was in darkness owing to the thunderstorm that had been tearing through the city for the past two hours.

"Mrs. Broadhurst?" Her voice was almost a whisper, but she knew that was not the reason Belle did not respond. She sat down beside her in the embrasure.

Belle looked at her. "Warner, it has just occurred to me that I do not even know your given name. How arrogant I must be."

"It is Leonie, ma'am, and I do not think you arrogant at all. Nor should you."

A brilliant flash of lightning illuminated Belle's garden, and, for a moment, she could see the branches of the medlar tree cringing in the high wind. No one would make the preserves now, she thought. Thunder crashed once, twice, three times, and the percussion reverberated throughout the bedroom.

"I love thunderstorms," she said absently, then glanced at the room and shook her head. "How easily I fell into all this."

"I should have done the same, Mrs. Broadhurst, had I been given the opportunity," the abigail smiled.

"Please do not call me that. Not anymore."

"What shall I call you, then?" Warner kept her voice light, hoping to tease her mistress into a smile.

"Very soon, I shall be just Annabelle Makepeace again. And I shall have to make my way in the world, just as you have had to do. You must call me Belle."

"If that is what you wish. Belle."

She nodded. Thunder bellowed into the room once again, and she put her head down on knees already drawn up to her chest. "I had so hoped—I—I love him so very much. Oh!" Her shoulders heaved, and she wept great, wrenching sobs, as if her heart were broken.

The maid put her arms around her, her own cheeks quite wet. "Shhh. I know, I know."

The storm did not end for some time.

THIRTEEN

Over the ensuing days, the staff at No. 7 were engaged in putting the house in readiness for Lillie's arrival. Belle recognized that there was, truly, little point in such a flurry of activity, since the place was quite presentable as it was and since Lillie would, doubtless, be too exhausted from her journey to pay much attention to the niceties in any event. And then, the surroundings had been considerably improved since last she had viewed them, all those weeks ago. Still, it seemed the proper thing to do. So, unmusty rooms were aired, tables were polished to a higher luster, still-clean draperies were taken down and refreshed, and flowers from the garden were replaced daily.

Belle wanted to be quit of the house, of London, before her friend returned, for she knew that Lillie would try to talk her out of leaving, that she would try to contrive some reason either to keep Belle with her or to assist in her support, and she was afraid that she might just weaken and accept. And so, she visited the Employment Registry the Monday after the arrival of Lillie's letter, knowing that it might prove difficult to secure a position in the short time left to her.

She had put on one of her own plain frocks, dressed her own hair—I must get used to this again, she told herself—in a simpler style and gone to Mrs. Cosway's Employment Office for Women. Her job as companion, the one she had been going to when she and Lillie met, had been found via a discreet ad in the newspaper. When a look at the London papers had been fruitless, Belle had discussed the matter with Warner. The maid had recommended the Employment Registry, for that was how she had found her position with Lillie, but experience had taught her that some such offices were unscrupulous. Belle sat for some time on a hard-backed chair in Mrs. Cosway's establishment, waiting her turn, and unobtrusively examining the large number of women who occupied the waiting room with her. She was relieved to see that they all appeared to be neat and presentable.

At length, she was shown into a small office where sat a pleasant-faced, grey-haired woman of some sixty years. Belle clutched her reticule, the plain brown corduroy one she had brought from Whichford, and tried to look capable, presentable and worthy of employment, as the older woman examined her with a critical but not unfriendly eye. Mrs. Cosway asked her numerous questions about her background, education and experience, then consulted some papers stacked on the table in front of her.

"Well, let me see what we may have for you, although I must tell you that good positions are hard to come by and, as you no doubt saw, there are more applicants than jobs. She smiled encouragingly. "So, you have not worked before, Mrs. Makepeace?" Belle shook her head. "Well, that is not necessarily a drawback, except in some circumstances . . ." Her voice trailed off as she thumbed through the pages. "And you do not wish to work in London, you have said?"

Belle found it odd to be addressed by her own name

again. She shook her head once more. Staying in London would mean the possibility of meeting people she knew from her other life, the life she would have to abandon in just a few days. No, she could not subject herself or them to that. And she certainly could not cause any more problems for Lillie by assuming her own identity while still in town.

"No, Mrs. Cosway, as I have said, I have been staying with a friend while I have been in London, but, now that my visit is ending, I think I would prefer the country."

"Just so. Ah, here. A position as companion in East Grinstead for the wife of . . ." She turned the page and shook her head. "No, that will not do."

"What, Mrs. Cosway? I think I should make a competent companion and—"

"Not for this household, Mrs. Makepeace. We have filled more than one position for Mr. and Mrs. . . . ahem, well, their name is no matter. I assure you, Mrs. Makepeace, it is not the job for you. He is a, well, let me say that the last woman whom we put there told me a tale that . . . Well, you are just too pretty, Mrs. Makepeace. It just wouldn't do. No, not at all. I need say no more on that head, need I?"

Good heavens, did the woman never finish a sentence? But Belle caught her meaning well enough. She could be referring to any manner of problem, but very likely Mr. Whatever was a rake who wanted his way with the female servants, and Mrs. Whatever evidently blamed his victims for his lust. Mrs. Cosway was right, she did not want to go there. The older woman continued to sort through her papers, muttering all the while.

"Ah, do you speak German? Because if you do—"

"I am afraid I do not."

"Oh. Pity. Hmm." Two more papers were rejected

and turned over. "Parlormaid?" she offered, eying Belle from above her spectacles.

"I had hoped, as I said, for work as a companion or governess."

"I know you did, however, there is so little, and you do not have the education yourself to be a governess. This position is in a very large household, so your duties as parlormaid likely would not be onerous—oh, never mind, I see the address now. It is in Grosvenor Square. Too bad." She disposed of the rest of the sheets and looked up at Belle. "I am sorry, Mrs. Makepeace, I do not have anything for you at present."

Belle's face fell. She had not expected it would be easy, but neither had she foreseen that her search would be fruitless. "There is, truly, nothing?"

"I am afraid not. But do check back with us again. Say in a few days. We might have something then."

"Did you have any luck, Mrs. Broadhurst?" Warner asked her later. The abigail was helping her to change back into a fashionable afternoon dress, for the masquerade had to continue for the present.

"None, I am afraid, Warner. I must confess that I am discouraged, but I shall go back in two days' time to see if the situation has changed."

On her second visit, Belle had better luck.

"Ah, Mrs. Makepeace, I was just saying to Miss Grantham, that is my assistant, you know, that I hoped you would come again, for I think I have the sort of position you would like. It is as companion to a young female invalid. Let me see . . ." She scanned the paper in her hand. "Ah, Miss Diane Fallows. You are to see her mother, Mrs. Fallows. Here," smiling, she handed Belle a slip of paper with a name and address written on it.

'Go round to this house and tell Mrs. Fallows that the agency has sent you. They are in London now, but will shortly be removing to Peterborough. I do, yes, I do, think that you will find this is exactly what you have been looking for.'

Before long, Belle found herself in an elegantly appointed drawing room in Mayfair. After what seemed an interminable wait, for all the windows were closed tight and the draperies drawn shut against any fresh air that might, somehow, wheedle its way in, making the room stifling hot. She withdrew a handkerchief from her reticule and quickly pressed it against her temples and neck, hoping that she did not appear as distressed by the heat as she felt.

Eventually, a very tall, regal-looking woman appeared and, unsmiling, looked down her nose at her. Belle smiled as she rose and curtsied. "Good day, Mrs. Fallows, I am Annabelle Makepeace. Mrs. Cosway sent me to see you about the job as companion to your daughter."

The woman arched a thin brow and sneered. "I am not Mrs. Fallows. I am her aunt, Mrs. Laughton. You will come with me, and I shall bring you to her and to her daughter. They are in dear Diane's bedroom."

As they turned into the corridor which, evidently, housed the bedchambers, Belle heard a loud crash followed by a voice that fairly screamed, "I shall not!" She gave a small start. "Oh, my, what was that?"

Mrs. Laughton did not answer, but knocked gently on the door. "Diane, my darling, I have someone here for you to meet."

This room was even hotter than the drawing room had been, but thankfully, the draperies were open. A matron of middle years, looking much put upon, flitted about a younger woman seated in a chair and sur-

rounded by pillows. Diane, for surely this was the invalid
mentioned by Mrs. Cosway, was of some twenty summers
and did not give the appearance, at least, of being ill;
her color was not bad and her arms did not have the
emaciated look of the chronic invalid. She examined
Belle from head to foot with a haughty, rude eye and
looked at her aunt.

"Well, does she have a name, Aunt, this potential
playmate you have brought me?" she asked snidely.

"Of course she has a name, darling. It is Annabelle
Makepeace. Mrs. Makepeace," she turned to Belle,
"make your curtsy to Miss Diane Fallows."

Belle had not had to be so instructed for many years,
and she wanted very much to tell Mrs. Laughton so.
Instead, she made her bow and smiled. "How do you
do, Miss Fallows?" Evidently, Mrs. Fallows did not have
sufficient significance in her own household to deserve
an introduction, but Belle decided to extend the courtesy anyway. She turned to the woman still fidgeting
behind her daughter's chair. "Mrs. Fallows? It is a plea-
sure to meet you, ma'am." The woman looked rather
surprised and nodded.

"You will address your remarks to me, Mrs. Makepeace, for it is I you shall serve, and it is I who will
decide whether or not to employ you," Miss Fallows
said in strident tones.

At least there is nothing wrong with her lungs, Belle
decided, biting back a retort. She inclined her head.
"Very good, Miss Fallows."

"Aunt, get someone to clean that up," she pointed
to the remains of a china shepardess on the floor by
the wall.

"Yes, dear." Her aunt extended a hand toward the
nearby bellpull, then pulled it back sharply, as her niece
screeched. "I said 'get' someone, did I not?" Diane Fal-

lows leaned forward in her chair. "That means, Aunt, go and *get* someone. I am perfectly capable of walking to the bellpull myself, as well you know."

Mrs. Laughton drew herself up and, with an injured look, left the room.

"Silly old fool," Diane spat out. "Mother," she ordered over her shoulder, "for God's sake, stop hovering and sit down!"

Mrs. Fallows, too, followed instructions.

"Now, Mrs. Makepeace. You wish to be my companion, is that correct?"

Belle wanted more than anything to say that she would rather have all her teeth drawn out, but she realized that this could be the only position that might present itself. She nodded.

"Well, tell me your skills."

Belle complied, and the young woman sniffed. "Have you any experience in looking after an invalid?"

"I cared for my husband for several weeks before he died, Miss Fallows." She was at a loss to see what Miss Fallows' malady might be, for the young woman seemed in the pink of health. "If I am not too bold, Miss Fallows, may I inquire as to the nature of your, um, ailment?"

There was a long pause as the young lady looked at her through narrowed eyes. A few moments passed and then her mother spoke. "My poor Diane has spells, Mrs. Makepeace," was all she said, as if those few words conveyed any meaning at all.

"Spells. I see. What—"

"You are here to *answer* questions, Makepeace, not to *ask* them." The use of her last name in these circumstances, given that she did not yet have the position, was, Belle knew, intended to offend. It seemed clear that any physical complaint that Miss Fallows had was used as a weapon to act the tyrant with the rest of the household, although why a young lady with all the advantages this one appeared to have should prefer to spend her life as an "invalid," rather than enjoying a Season in town, she had no idea.

"Of course, Miss Fallows."

"Now, as you no doubt know, we shall be removing to Peterborough within a se'enight. More time in London is too much for me to bear. And," she gave her mother a nasty look, "we are *not* ever coming back to this vile city." That lady emitted a soft mew of disappointment. "That is correct, Mother. I have told you before. *Never.*"

"But, dearest—"

Another porcelain figure joined the remains of its sister on the floor. "I said *never!*"

Her mother cringed back into her chair.

"If I should decide to hire you, Makepeace, you will see to all my needs, for I do not intend to employ a dresser as well as a companion. That means you will be responsible for my clothes, as well as my amusement."

How could she bear it? Belle swallowed. Did she have a choice?

"Your salary is, I am sure you will agree, generous." She named an insultingly paltry sum. "And you will have a half-day every month for yourself."

"A half-day?"

"That is what I said, is it not? Are you deaf, Makepeace?"

"No, Miss Fallows, but—"

"Do . . . not . . . ever . . . question me, Makepeace."

Belle waited for her to finish this last order before politely explaining to Miss Fallows that she would sooner starve than be accepted into her employ.

The satisfaction she derived from this action did not

last long, and her mood was not lightened by the departure the same day of Aunt Eulalie and Uncle Aubrey. Belle had seen them off with a tearful goodbye and deceitful promises of making a long visit soon. The next day, she called on Cecily and related her tale of the terrible Miss Fallows, and her friend laughed at Belle's impersonation.

"Humph, I can assure you it was no laughing matter, madam," she reproached Cecily with mock severity, then joined in her friend's giggles.

Suddenly, Cecily became serious. "Oh, Lillie, what are you going to do? Please," she held up a hand, "please do not tell me that you really do mean to go into service. It is too awful. I cannot bear to think of you at someone's beck and call, curtsying to everyone and his dog, and wearing deadly dull gowns, and I shall probably never see you again, and . . . Oh!" She had broken off in tears.

"Oh, Cec, please do not. For, if you cry, I shall too. And I do not wish to cry anymore, Cec. I am trying very hard to accept all this, for—"

"For pity's sake, Lillie, you cannot do this! You can, you *must,* come to William and me. You would live as one of the family, for I have come to think of you as a sister, you know. And William wants you to come, also." She sniffed and dabbed her handkerchief in the direction of tear-stained cheeks. "I cannot bear it."

Belle took her hands and kissed her wet cheek. "I feel the same way, Cec. And I thank both you and William for your generosity—your kindness. To say the truth, I would like very much to come to you," Cecily brightened. "But you must know I cannot."

A thought had occurred to Cecily. "I have it! You could be governess to Phillip. You know that we should never treat you as *some* people would. You would truly be like one of the family!"

But Belle was already shaking her head. "I thank you again. However, Mrs. Cosway has explained to me what I really already knew, which is that I was never educated enough myself to teach someone else."

"Of course you are! Why, you are one of the most intelligent people I know."

"Well, thank you, Cec. But that is not the same as knowing foreign languages and mathematics and history, and all those things you would want Phillip to know. No. A companion is what I am fit for. I shall find such a position, I am convinced of it."

But the days passed, and despite repeated visits to Mrs. Cosway, Belle could not find a suitable position. By the twelfth of the month, three days before Lillie's anticipated arrival, Belle had made her decision. She and Cecily were strolling in the square, and she knew that the time was right to tell her friend of her plan.

"Cecily, I am going away," she said carefully.

Cecily blanched. "Oh, you have found a position, then? Is it at least near Gloucestershire? Because then, at least, we could visit more easily."

Belle tilted the brim of her straw hat to better shade her eyes from the bright sun. She shook her head.

"I have not found a position, I am afraid."

"Well, then, what—"

"I must leave, Cec. Everything will be in such chaos when Lillie returns. Heaven knows how she is going to handle it all, and I cannot add to that."

Cecily nodded her understanding. "But where will you go?"

"To Aunt Eulalie and Uncle Aubrey."

"What?"

"Yes. It suddenly occurred to me yesterday. Oh, I

know it will be terribly awkward when I tell them who I am and how I have deceived them. They may even consign me to the devil, and I should not blame them if they did, but they are so kind that I dare to hope they will forgive me and hire me as companion to Uncle Aubrey."

Cecily grudgingly admired the plan. "I must admit it makes sense. And I cannot believe that they will not forgive you. Although I should not want to be in the room when Eulalie gives you the trimming she is bound to!" She chuckled. "At least it is not *all* that far from Gloucestershire. And you know that Eulalie and Aubrey would treat you as a daughter!" She was definitely warming to the idea.

"I think that is a bit too much to hope for, Cec. But if they do accept me as Annabelle Makepeace, I could not ask for kinder employers, I am certain."

"When do you leave?"

"Tomorrow."

"That soon?"

"I dare not delay any longer. I must be sure to be gone before Lillie comes home."

"Oh, yes," Cecily said softly. "Will you tell Gore?"

"No. How could I explain it? Lillie never would leave London before the end of the Season, especially not now that her trial has come to an end." She smiled. "Besides, what would be the point of it? You know, Cecily, a few times, I actually thought that he might care for me. Oh, I cannot put it into words exactly, but it was there, I thought, sometimes, in his words or his look." She sighed and swallowed. "I was wrong. Oh, how could I not be? I am just the Lillie he grew up with, and I shall never be anything more. I know that he will learn, eventually, where I am, for Eulalie and Lillie must meet at some point. Once Lillie knows what I have done, she is bound to mention it to him, but I shall deal with that situation when it arises."

"Are you so sure that he does not care?"

"How can I be otherwise? I had hoped, foolishly I know, that, given time, he might come to love me. As I do him," she ended softly. "But he has not, and, Cecily, even if I believed that time would answer my prayer, I have none left to give. I must leave here."

Cecily touched her hand. "I am sorry, Lillie." She gave a determined smile. "We shall write often."

"Of course we shall! Every week!"

That evening, Belle and Gore dined with Cecily and William. Cecily knew of her plan to leave London, but she had not yet disclosed it to William, and of course, neither of them had informed Gore. He had looked forward to tonight, when, in the company of their dearest friends, he would begin his subtle but determined efforts to, finally, woo Belle.

Despite Belle's resolution to maintain a cheerful facade, Gore sensed a disturbing remoteness in her behavior. After supper, Cecily suggested a few hands of whist, and Belle quickly asked William to partner her. Gore was rather piqued. He had been solicitous all evening—refilling Belle's wine glass, taking particular notice of her oyster white evening dress—but she had seemed to notice none of it. When he took her arm to go in to dinner, she had almost recoiled from his touch. Had he been wrong in his surmise that she might care for him? Tonight, she hardly seemed to care that he was there.

He could not know that every bite of Cecily's fine meal stuck in Belle's throat. That it cost her every ounce of strength she had to keep from crying and throwing her arms about him, to beg him to have her. That she could not, dare not, think about him or let him nearer than convention required. Whenever he looked at her—just so—when his eyes seemed to see only her in the room, she believed her mind must be playing tricks. I must get through this last evening, she thought. I cannot think of him or, dear God, of losing him. And so, when the last hand of whist was finished at eleven o'clock, she knew she must make her escape.

"Cecily, William, it has been a wonderful evening, and a delicious supper, as always." She stood up to leave.

Although her friend desperately wanted her to stay, she knew what a trial the evening had been, and what she had to do the next day.

"Of course, Lillie. Thank you so much for coming." Cecily kept from hugging her too hard and whispered in her ear, "I shall see you in the morning," then sniffed.

"Something wrong, darling?" William asked.

"No, no. I may be getting a cold, that is all."

"I shall see you home," Gore said.

She had known he would do so, and there was no way she could refuse. As they walked the few steps to No. 7, he made several attempts at conversation, but she was still distracted. Well, he decided, probably she has a megrim, I shall be back tomorrow and, damn the consequences, just ask her to marry me straight out. Arriving at her door, she turned to thank him for his escort. He held her hand a moment, then raised it to his lips.

"Good night, Lillie." Tomorrow, he could finally call her Belle.

"Goodbye, Gore."

FOURTEEN

There was no more reason to delay, everything had been done and the carriage would arrive soon. Belle knew that, at all costs, she must not cry again, for she feared that, if she did, she might never stop. She sat in the sunny morning room with Cecily, Warner and Filbert, her cases at the front door and her gloves and reticule in her lap. She had expected to toss and turn all night, but she had fallen into a deep sleep and had woken emotionally exhausted.

Earlier that morning, she had given Warner the earrings she had seen her admiring on one of their expeditions to the Burlington Arcade, and had fastened around Filbert's neck a collar set with shining pieces of smooth glass, as a remembrance of The Bracelet. Warner was deeply touched by her gift. The two women hugged and Warner wept for some minutes.

"I shall miss you, Belle."

"And I you, Leonie. Thank you for all you have done for me. I cannot say how grateful I am."

She picked up Filbert and held him hard, heedless of the grey and white fur he deposited all over her dress. "And I shall miss you, Filbert," she rubbed his tummy, "so very much."

Filbert agreed to wear the collar, and allowed himself

to be cuddled, even though he did not wish to be held at that particular moment, because he knew that something was amiss. He had seen some large objects set by the front door and sniffed them for several minutes before deciding that they were very like the things that Lillie took with her when she went away. And everyone seemed to be having a fit of the dismals this morning. He looked at her and blinked. Could Belle be going away? That must be it! But no one had said a word to him about it. I have not been *informed,* he wanted to point out to her. You cannot just leave. He decided to keep the collar on for just a little while, and purred loudly and touched a large, soft paw to her chin. Belle had buried her face in his scruffy fur and sobbed.

"And you will write to me, to us," Cecily included Warner in her instruction, "just as soon as you arrive to tell us how things turn out with Eulalie and Aubrey?"

Belle smiled and nodded. "Yes, Cecily, for the tenth time this morning, I promise that I shall write to both of you and tell you what has happened."

"Mrs. Broadhurst, the carriage is here."

"Thank you, Thomasina." Belle stood. Cecily, Warner and Filbert followed her to the door. "Thomasina, as I explained, Mrs. Makepeace will be arriving quite soon. Warner will explain to her that I have gone to visit friends."

"Yes, Mrs. Broadhurst. Have a safe journey." The maid dipped a curtsy and returned to her duties upstairs.

Belle turned to her friends and smiled. "You both are very dear to me. I shall never forget you." Quickly hugging each of the women in turn and bestowing a last pat on Filbert, she left the house.

* * *

Not three hours had passed before another carriage drew up before the door of No. 7 Berkeley Square.

"Oh, Mrs. Makepeace, Mrs. Broadhurst said you would be here soon. Did you have a pleasant journey?"

"I did, Thomasina, thank you. Where—oh, Warner!"

"Welcome home—Mrs. Makepeace." She had almost stumbled over the name, not that it mattered much at this point. "Thank you, Thomasina," she dismissed the maid.

"Warner . . ."

"If you would come upstairs, ma'am. I have something to give you."

Puzzled, Lillie followed. When they had reached the privacy of the bedroom, she tried again to ask her question. "Warner, where . . . ?"

"Here, ma'am. I think this will answer your question." She handed Lillie the letter that Belle had left in her care.

"Warner, for heaven's sake, you look absolutely ghastly. What is wrong? What has happened? Is Belle all right?"

"She has left, Mrs. Broadhurst."

"What?"

Warner nodded.

"But when? Why?"

"Just a few hours ago, as it happens. She told me that her letter," she said as she inclined her head in the direction of Lillie's hand, "would explain it all to you."

"Wh—Oh, very well. Please stay, Warner." Lillie sat in the window seat and read. Belle had taken great pains to compose a letter that would tell Lillie what she was entitled to know, while not giving away her feelings about Gore or causing any distress. Her departure she explained only as

. . . the best and only sensible thing to do, Lillie, for we could never both of us continue to deceive people. I am deeply sorry for leaving you to bear this alone, and I hope that you will not think me too craven. In any event, you have no further need of a double, for you have had your adventure—and a wonderful one I hope it was!—and I believe you may be able to better deal with all this with one less of "you" around to further complicate matters, if such is even possible! Then, too, once Gore does learn my real identity, I am convinced he will truly hate me. If I am removed, you will at least be spared having to take sides between us, as I fear you might feel compelled to do.

Lillie's eyes grew wider and wider, as she read. Warner watched from her perch on the edge of the bed as her mistress shook her head, "Tsk'd" repeatedly, muttering and sputtering, "Foolish creature, thinks I shall believe her flummery" and "What a humbug." Finished at last, she held the pages out to Warner, one brow raised archly, and demanded, "Well? I assume you do not even have to read this."

The maid shook her head. "I should not think so, ma'am," she said softly.

"Don't come all milk and water with me, my girl! I want to know what has been happening. Perhaps Belle thinks she can fob me off with this Banbury tale, but I cut my teeth a long time ago, thank you very much."

Warner gave a small smile that Lillie returned quickly.

"I knew it! What happened? What could have compelled her to go haring off to Eulalie? Belle knows that she must confess all to them—she says so right here." She brandished the letter again. "And we always realized that, when I returned, everyone should know the truth. Since I know she has more bottom than to turn coward when faced with our consequences, she must have had another reason." She paused. "Out with it, Warner. It was Gore, was it not?"

Her answer was a reluctant nod.

"But what occurred? Did he find us out?"

"I do not believe that he did, ma'am."

Lillie flopped back against the cushions and stared at Warner. "Fell in love with him, didn't she?"

Another nod.

"Oh, my, that would put the serpent in the Garden, would it not? Did he know?"

Again, Warner replied that she did not think he did.

"Hmm. Couldn't face him, then." She sighed. "I don't know that I would not have done the same thing. Well, Warner, you must give me all the details, so that we can decide what we must do."

Gore had considered the possibility that Belle might turn his proposal down flat. He had not considered the possibility that she might have fled. Business had kept him from calling at No. 7 as he had intended to do the day after Cecily's dinner. When he did present himself at No. 7 the morning after Belle's departure and Lillie's return and ask for Mrs. Broadhurst, Thomasina, who by this time had been apprised of her real mistress's real identity, hesitated, a baffled expression on her face.

"Mrs. Broadhurst? Um, well, that is, ah, would that be Mrs. *Broadhurst*, sir? I mean, er . . ."

Gore smiled. "Yes, Thomasina," he said encouragingly, "Mrs. *Broadhurst*. Is she at home?"

Thomasina continued to gape, her lips working pointlessly. She had not been instructed how she was to answer questions such as these. After starting several replies and discarding all of them as being entirely too absurd, she decided to let her betters sort matters out for themselves.

"Yes, sir. Mrs. Broadhurst is in the morning room." At least she was being truthful.

"Thank you, Thomasina." He gave her a puzzled grin. "I shall see myself in."

"Very good, sir," the maid said and scurried off for the kitchen to tell Mrs. Butter the latest news.

The bright sun hit Gore's eyes as he entered the room, where Lillie sat sipping the last of her tea and catching up on the latest news with *The Times,* so, at first, he was unaware of who she was. When Lillie looked up at him, she choked on her tea and coughed. He crossed to where she sat and patted her back.

"Gore!" She finally gasped, looking at him with dismay.

He smiled. "You sound, ah, surprised, Lil . . . Lillie!" His eyes had adjusted to the light, and he stared at her, his face comical with amazement.

It was her turn to grin. "Yes, coz. Who did you think I was?" She teased.

He sputtered. "I—you—who . . ."

"I know. Do sit down, Gore," she said brightly. "If it were only a little later, I would offer you brandy, you look as if you could use it. Tea, then?"

Gore glared, removed the teapot from her hand and said in a low, even voice, "I see your ridiculous, childish game is finally at an end."

Her face fell in disappointment. Damn the man, he had known. That put paid to her plan to quiz him with his gullibility, the only comfort she had hoped to glean from the situation, now that Belle had fled. Too, she, rather than he, being behind times, as it were, also

robbed Lillie of the paltry advantage she had anticipated.

"Oh. You knew, then," she remarked, utterly de-
flated. He leveled his gaze at her. "How long did it take
you to guess?"

"Of course I knew. Do you take me for a complete
flat? And, to answer your second question, *coz*, I knew
it the second I set eyes on her." He would never concede otherwise, no matter that he had been taken in
for no more than a few minutes' time. "Did you honestly think I should not?"

"I honestly thought little about you at all, Gore, since
I believed you resident on the Continent in His Majesty's service until heaven knew when," she finished
sarcastically. "Boney's been locked up safe and sound
for years, and still you remained from home. I was not
at all certain that I would *ever* see you again," she
drawled.

"That won't fadge, so cut line, Lillie. What, in God's
name, were you thinking of? Were you out of your head?
Do you know how worried I was when I realized that
the Lillie Broadhurst I knew was not the Lillie Broadhurst parading before all of London?" He gave her no
time to give any response. "You are the greatest scat-
terbrain on the face of the earth. Running off to Italy
like some damn hoyden—"

"You knew I was in Italy?" Her surprise now stemmed
from his apparent resourcefulness.

" 'Course I did! And poor Matthew . . ."

"Good God, Gore, never say you told my father!"

He paused in his tirade long enough to give her a
pitying look. "Now, do you suppose me such a fool? Of
course I didn't tell him. How could I tell him that his
only child, who hasn't the common sense of a squirrel,
was masquerading as someone else and that this some-

one else had assumed her identity *and* that said less-than-squirrel-brained daughter had gone traipsing off to Italy?" His voice had risen with each condemnation he had uttered. "Did you truly think me *that* stupid?" Sarcasm laced his words.

"Er, well, no, I suppose I did not, but how did you learn where I had gone?"

"I tracked you to The Rose Revived and through that fool Prine—our banker, Lillie, in case you have forgotten." He explained in response to the question in her eyes. "And a less discreet creature I hope never to meet again. Fool to expect better behavior in someone of his profession, I suppose. Anyway, between him and Mr. Hapgood at The Rose Revived," he smiled briefly at his recollection of the garrulous innkeeper, "I learned everything I needed to know."

"But you did nothing about it?" She was clearly puzzled.

He shifted in his chair. "Ahem, yes, well. I thought about it, you may be sure."

Lillie grinned at him. "Did she make a splendid Lillie? I was sure she would. We are so much alike—well, I suppose that you noticed that. And she even found The Bracelet!" She added gleefully, as if that set everything else to rights.

"Never mind that now. Where is Belle?"

" 'Belle' is it?" Feeling more solid ground beneath her feet again, she teased him. "She is not here, you know."

"I can see that, Lillie. Where is she? Your insane game is over, and I have something to say to her," he fairly bellowed, then slammed his fist on the table so that her cup clattered in its saucer.

Lillie blinked. Warner had told her that she was certain he really loved Belle, but if that were so, he was behaving in a most peculiar fashion. Was he angry or desperate at the loss of the woman he loved? She had no way to tell, but he certainly appeared to be furious, just as Belle had predicted he would be. She had never seen him this angry.

"Do stop that shouting this instant! I told you, she is not here." His green eyes glittered, and he thought he might just throttle her. "She has fled, Gore."

"What do you mean? Where did she go? Why did you not stop her?"

"How could I, when she had left before I even arrived here?"

"Do you mean that you have not seen her?"

She shook her head in confirmation.

"But why should she do such a thing? Did she not know when you were returning?"

"Oh, yes, for I wrote to her, you know."

Gore sat for some moments, thinking. Left London, and without even telling him. Clearly, she did not care a thing for him, then. But why would Belle run off now, unless she felt guilty about something? Perhaps he had been wrong about her, after all . . . or, to be more accurate, perhaps he had been right about her in the first place. Perhaps she was nothing but a thief who had absconded with Lillie's possessions, her money, before his cousin came home. He looked at Lillie and asked, "Have you noticed anything missing?"

"Pardon?"

"Has anything been taken, Lillie?"

"Whatever do you mean? Was the house burgled while I was away? Warner did not mention it. Well, I should not know if anything were gone, you know, for I was here for the first time only a few days before I left on my journey." A thought struck her, and she glared at him. "Wait a moment. Are you suggesting that Belle stole from me?" she asked in horror. "How can you say such a thing? I would trust her with my life. I did!"

"You barely know the woman," he shouted. "Now, where is she?"

Lillie waited, staring at him in amazement. She had never seen him in such a rage, never seen him so distrustful, before. What had happened to the charming and rakish man she had known so well all those years ago? She preferred to think that this silly notion was no more than misplaced anger, a stupid reaction because his pride had been wounded at Belle's departure, and without a word to him, it seemed. Surely, he would presently acknowledge his attack on Belle as baseless, for certainly, he'd had time enough to know her even better than Lillie did, and must realize that there was only good in her. Well, if his pride were, indeed, hurt, she would just let him stew in his childish fury until she felt he had suffered enough to tell him Belle's whereabouts.

After a long pause, she said calmly, "I shall not tell you."

"Hah! You do not know."

"I do, but I shall never tell you! You are a foolish, selfish man, and I shall never let you near her again!" Furious now herself, Lillie ran from the sunny room, slamming the door after her.

He knew there would be little point in pressing her further for the information—not just now, at any rate. The answering percussion of the front door slamming behind him echoed throughout the house.

She and Warner were unpacking the last of her many trunks after Gore had stormed out, because Lillie had been too tired to bother unpacking the day before. Although the abigail had tried to take the entire matter out of her mistress's hands, Lillie had wanted the enjoyment of unearthing all the treasures she had collected on her journey.

"I had to purchase so many more trunks to hold everything," she said absently.

"I can see that, ma'am. Is there anything left in the shops at all?" Warner was disemboweling a massive trunk that was full to the brim with clothes and gewgaws.

"Oh, one or two things, I daresay," Lillie replied gaily. She held aloft a midnight blue ball gown trimmed in blonde. "What do you think of this?"

"It's beautiful. Did you get that in Paris?"

Lillie nodded. She pulled out a long rose-hued shawl, so delicate it seemed to have been fashioned from cobwebs, and held it out to her abigail with a smile. "This is for you."

Warner gasped in delight. "Oh, Mrs. Broadhurst, thank you. It is the loveliest shawl I have ever seen."

"I am happy that you like it. Oh! And this, too." She held out a necklace of garnets and pearls.

The maid took it and, sniffing, dabbed a handkerchief to her eyes. "I do not know what to say, ma'am. Truly, you should not—"

"Stuff! You deserve it. Please, put it on."

Warner did so and exclaimed her delight once again. A short while later, with a pile of gowns and spencers in her arms, she asked, "Mrs. Broadhurst, where shall I put these?"

"Why, in the armoires, Warner, where else, you goose?"

"They are full."

"Oh, my, already?" Lillie bit her lip. She had, indeed, been more than extravagant in her acquisitions, but she had not been able to help herself. Lillie and Cecily would get on quite well together.

"Yes." Warner grinned. "Well, you did buy quite a lot, but then, Mrs. Broad—that is, Mrs. Makepeace's wardrobe still is here, you know."

Lillie sat back on her heels and tossed a pair of recently unearthed blue dancing slippers on the floor. "She left it all?" Warner nodded. "Blast! I should have known she would. If you are right, Warner, and Gore does love her, he had better do something about it, else he shall have me to answer to! And, if he does not, I shall not leave her to live her life as a companion, not even to Uncle Aubrey."

They had had this conversation on the previous day, after Warner had filled in all the gaps in Belle's letter. Lillie had vowed that, if Gore did not come to his senses, Belle would come to her in Burford, and that, she swore, was that. Warner had tried to disabuse her of this notion, pointing out that Belle would never live on anyone's charity, but her words had done no good then, and she knew they would do even less now.

She tried, nonetheless. "But, ma'am, you know her, and—"

"No, Warner," Lillie sighed, "*you* know her—ever so much better than I. She is just as proud as ever, obviously." Her maid nodded. "Oh, I could shake him *and* her! Running off like a frightened rabbit. Why did she have to fall in love with him, anyway?"

Warner smiled. "As if we ever plan such things, ma'am."

Lillie grunted and sighed again. "I shall go there, of course, after we see just what Gore plans to do. But, if the worst comes to pass, what can I do? I can hardly drag her back to Burford with me."

"You will contrive, ma'am, you always do," Warner drawled. "Then, you do not intend to tell him where she is?"

"Not yet," she replied smugly. "He will have to cool his heels and his *head* for a while—he deserves no less. *Then* I shall tell him."

It did not take Gore long to realize that Cecily must know where Belle had gone, and on the following day, he presented himself, considerably calmer, at the door of No. 12. He was not surprised that Cecily was from home, must be shopping, he told himself, but he was exasperated. As William, too, was out, he took himself off to his club in a renewed miff.

But Cecily was not shopping. She had delayed calling at No. 7 to give the doubtless weary traveler time to rest but, by the third day, she could stay away no longer. Curiosity about the real Lillie Broadhurst was only secondary, for Cecily was determined that, together, she and Lillie could contrive a way to help Belle, preferably by bringing her together with Gore. Before long, she was seated in the morning room with Lillie and Warner, going over Belle's leaving and the events of the past few days.

"I did try to convince her to stay, Lillie—oh, I may call you Lillie, I hope. I feel as if I have been doing so for ages—well, but I have, haven't I? In a manner of speaking, that is." Lillie grinned and nodded. She liked her neighbor. "Warner and I both tried talking to her, to no avail."

"And what do you think about Gore? About his feelings for her, I mean."

"Well, I cannot be certain, but I do believe that he cares for her." Lillie told her what had occurred on the previous day. "He never did! I am shocked that he would say such things about her. But that must be it—he must love her!"

"The same thought occurred to me, I must admit."
Lillie chewed her lip. "I have been thinking on it, and
such behavior is completely unlike Gore—at least the
Gore I used to know. Of course, I never knew him in
love—except for that awful Matilda Braithwaite. He did
throw his heart over the moon for her, but he was only
thirteen or so at the time. Still, he never acted like this,
for all she treated him like an old shoe, so perhaps there
is something in what you say, Cecily. Perhaps *this* Gore
does love Belle. We must hope that he will come about."

"I expect that he will call on me to tell him her direction, for he must believe that I would know. Don't
worry," she held up a hand to forestall Lillie's warning,
"I shall not breathe a word. But you must promise to
tell me all." Her eyes sparkled with anticipation.

When Gore called the following day at No. 12, he found
that the occupants were once again from home. Disappointed and desperate, he returned to Lillie. On his first
attempt, she and Warner—for he also thought to pry the
information from her abigail—were not at home, but on
his second visit, the following day, Thomasina ushered
him into the drawing room. By this time, his frustration
threatened to vent itself all over again in another burst
of anger, but he knew he must keep his temper.

"Ahem, Lillie, I want to apologize for my behavior the
other day. Inexcusable. Won't happen again, I assure you."

Lillie eyed him carefully. He looked like a man who
had slept and eaten little for days. Good, she thought,
he is doing penance for his sins. She took pity on him
and asked him to sit. Gore's head was pounding. He
had spent the past few days and nights vacillating between believing Belle to be a cunning trickster or the

woman of his dreams, and he was no nearer a conclusion than he had been when he last left Lillie.

She looked at him and said coyly, "Tea, Gore, or something stronger?"

"Nothing, thank you. Just tell me where she is."

"Belle?"

"Lillie, do not push me too hard."

"You do not ask if any of my possessions are missing, Gore. Nothing is gone," she said in a low, even tone. "She left here with nothing."

He flushed. "Then, why did she go?"

Lillie shrugged.

"Will you tell me where?"

She laughed lightly. "Very well. She has gone to Eulalie in Minster Lovell."

He thought a moment. "And she is not returning?"

"No, Gore, apparently not," Lillie said gravely.

What could she possibly want with Eulalie? She had left here with nothing and had little enough of her own to begin with. She could not, or dare not, take anything that belonged to Lillie, so how would she live? Had she gone to Eulalie to talk her into giving back The Bracelet before her masquerade was exposed? If she had, there would be no need to return, for it would keep her in high style for some time. He rose, taking his hat from the Pembroke table. Lillie tried to answer his earlier question, to tell him why Belle had gone to her aunt, but he interrupted.

"Thank you for the information, Lillie. If you will excuse me . . . ?"

"But, Gore, I . . . Are you going after her?"

"I am," he replied so severely that she was not at all certain whether to be pleased.

Filbert had toddled into the drawing room and now sat unnoticed near Gore's chair while the conversation whirred about him. As Gore turned to leave the room, the cat dodged between his feet. From his position on the floor, Gore shut his eyes and twisted his lips in disgust.

"Blasted cat felled me again!" Gore growled, glaring at them both. Filbert had dashed to Lillie's lap, where he sat staring at him innocently. Lillie was unable to contain a giggle, and, as he quit the house, he could have sworn he heard her whisper, "Well done, Filbert!"

By the time Gore arrived in Minster Lovell on the next day, he had convinced himself that Belle's reasons for going to Eulalie were criminal. He had even considered bringing the local magistrate with him, but decided he could not be certain that Belle had not already taken The Bracelet and escaped. For that matter, he could never expose Eulalie and Aubrey to the scene that was certain to result. No, instead he hoped to be soon enough to catch her out—he would have to expose her to her hosts, that probably could not be avoided, but he would simply return the treasure to Eulalie and deal with Belle himself.

Gore's lips were set in a grim, unapproachable line. He was looking forward to that. How dare she try to deceive such good people who had only been kind to her, who cared about her? She had taken them in without a thought, without caring how her actions might hurt them, not worrying a bit about how they would get on after she had left, not . . . Gore stopped in mid-thought. Was he really thinking of Eulalie and Aubrey or himself? To be sure, he was very fond of them and did not want to see them disillusioned, but was that his real motive for going to Minster Lovell? He could easily have contacted the local magistrate and had him handle the matter. That way, The Bracelet would have been safe and *she* would have been routed without his having to see her again. But that was just it, he admitted to himself, he *wanted* to see her again.

"Is Mrs. Singleton at home?" he asked the maid who answered his knock.

"No, sir, although I do expect her and Mr. Singleton presently."

"I see. Is Mrs., er, Broadhurst in?"

The maid looked puzzled for a moment, then recovered herself. "Oh, yes, sir, she is."

He raised his brows in surprise. Clearly, protocol in these parts did not require that she go through the charade of pretending that she did not know if someone were "at home" until and unless that person indicated a desire to receive the caller. In London, this poor maid would have been turned off without a reference for committing such a solecism.

"She is in the garden, sir. I will announce you." The maid ushered him in and turned to lead him in Belle's direction.

He gave her a charming smile. "No need. Actually, I would like to surprise her, as she is not expecting me." *That* was an understatement. "If you will be so good as to tell me how to get there, I shall announce myself, so to speak."

"Well . . . very good, sir. The garden door is just through there."

Gore followed her gesture, and in a moment found himself looking through the glass at Belle. She was just sitting down on a stone bench, a pair of secateurs and some half-blown roses at her feet, testifying to her recent occupation. She was only half-turned in his direction and, thus, could not see him. He watched as she removed her straw hat and fanned herself with its wide brim, for the day was hot. Her cheeks were flushed, and the sun threaded strands of auburn through her brown hair. Gore had never noticed the red before. He found it most attractive.

He opened the door quietly, so that she would not hear his approach, but the sun threw a shadow before her and she turned, one hand shading her eyes.

"Gore!" She was unable, for a moment, to hide her pleasure at seeing him, but his stern countenance and rigid bearing told her that he must know everything. She could think of nothing to say.

"What are you doing here?" he demanded.

"I? I might ask the same of you, you know. How did you find me?"

"Do not play at any more games with me, *Mrs. Makepeace!* Lillie told me where you were."

"So you know, then."

Gore stepped closer, his hands itching to shake her. "Madam, I have known since the beginning."

Belle flushed and her eyes grew wide. "You never did! When . . ." She had risen from the bench, but now sat down slowly and looked up at him.

He cut into her words. "I knew at the Binghams' that you were an imposter . . ."

"Dear God!"

". . . so, I made it my business to learn just who you were, if not Lillie."

"You knew *then* that I was not her." She was trying to work out in her mind the logic of his behavior. "I do not understand. Why did you not tell me? Why did you allow me to continue?" She looked into cold, green eyes and thought she saw the answer, but it appalled her. "You tricked me!" Her embarrassment at having been caught out all along deprived her of the ability to see the absurdity of this remark, but Gore did not hesitate to point it out.

"I tricked *you?"* He threw back his head and laughed mirthlessly. "That tears it! You are a conniver and a dissembler, and you think to denounce me? Have you no shame at all?"

Belle blushed again and bent her head to the hat she was twisting in her hands. "I—I know what you must think of me, but—"

"Do not *dare* attempt to explain your behavior to me, Mrs. Makepeace." He made her name sound like a condemnation. "And you have no conception what I think of you, but I shall enlighten you, believe me, I shall. In time." He sat down close beside her on the bench. "There is a more important matter to be dealt with first."

She gave him a questioning look. "What do you mean?"

"I mean The Bracelet."

"The Bracelet? What about it?"

"It is why you are here."

"I have no idea what you are talking about, sir."

"I told you, no more games. You came here to get it back. Since you are still here, I shall assume that you have not yet been successful, and I mean to see that you are not."

She jumped up from the bench and threw her hat on the grass. "What? How *dare* you? Do you honestly believe that I would be so, so despicable?"

He rose also. "Mrs. Makepeace, let me say that I cannot believe you have any familiarity with honesty. You thought to curry favor with the Singletons before they learned the truth, as they were bound to do, now that Lillie is back, and to steal The Bracelet from under their noses." He sneered. "Or, perhaps, you intended to 'borrow' it, as you so cunningly told Eulalie you might ask to do, and then make off with it." She gasped in horror. "I am here to see that you don't—"

"Belle, is this . . . person . . . bothering you?"

They both turned in surprise, for they had not heard anyone approach. Eulalie stood erect and calm, watching them, as, apparently, she had been doing for some moments.

Gore looked from her to Belle and back again, his mouth agape.

"Yes, Gore," Eulalie said sternly, "is there something you want to say?"

"I—How did you find out?"

"She told me, after she arrived here."

"But your maid . . . I asked if Mrs. Broadhurst was in. She did seem a bit perplexed at first, but—"

Eulalie raised her brows and gave a little laugh. "I suppose she thought *you* were confused, Gore. You see, when Belle arrived, she was, of course, announced as Mrs. Broadhurst. After Belle had told us her story, we told Clarissa that Belle had just wanted to surprise us and, so, had given another name." She laughed again. "Poor thing, she must think we are all about in our heads!"

Gore was not really listening to this explanation. He swung around to Belle. "You told her?" But she would not look at him. "Belle . . ."

He collapsed back onto the bench, shaking his head.

"I collect that he has not given you the chance to tell him why you have come, Belle?" Eulalie asked sardonically.

Belle shook her head.

The older woman's eyes twinkled. "Now might be an opportune time, my dear. I shall leave you to it." She turned to go into the house, then looked back over her shoulder. "Of course, I will not say that *I* probably never would bother trying to talk sense to such an empty-headed creature, much less marry him, but it is none of my affair, after all, is it? My, my, Aubrey never gave me so much trouble when *we* were courting, but manners change, I suppose."

Belle was mortified. Marriage and courting. She had never said a word to Eulalie about anything of the kind. Good God, what would he think now? Well, all she could do was to make her explanation and hope that he had paid no mind to Eulalie's words.

"Gore, once I learned that Lillie was returning to London, I knew I could no longer keep up our, er, masquerade," she said somewhat stiffly. She would never tell him that, from the beginning, Lillie had insisted that Belle remain and had said that the consequences could be easily dealt with. "The circumstances were bound to be . . . awkward," she explained with a wry twist of her lips, "and my remaining could only have made things worse."

He looked at her wordlessly.

"I must tell you that I did not leave London because I was afraid of what would happen. Oh, I do not expect you to believe me. Just a moment ago, you thought me a thief, why should you not now believe me a coward?"

Gore's voice was gruff. "Belle . . ."

"Please, allow me to finish. It is necessary that you know the truth, for we are bound to see one another again." Rather than looking puzzled at this, as she expected he might, he smiled and put his hands on her shoulders. She shrugged them off. "For, you see, I came here to tell Eulalie and Aubrey the whole story, to beg their forgiveness, and to ask them to take me on as his companion. They are the kindest people in the world," she continued, eyes watering, "so you will not be surprised to learn that they have forgiven me, and I am now employed here."

"No, that is impossible."

"I am sorry if it distresses you, Gore, for I do realize

that you must hate me. But I am certain that we can come to some understanding, you and I, that we can deal together civilly when it is necessary." She picked up one of the faded roses from the bench, and was removing some of its withered petals.

"I have no wish to deal *civilly* with you, Belle."

She looked up at him and blinked. Then she lost her temper; she had, after all, been holding it in check for some time. " 'No wish?' As you choose, sir, but let me tell *you* something. You have accused me of deceiving you, and I cannot deny it. Yet what have *you* done, sir? You knew from the beginning who I was and never said a word." She beat at his shoulder with her rose. "You talk to me of deception? Ha! To think what I went through, the guilt, the worry! Why, I even learned to ride for you, and I attended that *stupid* lecture with Mr. Goodwin because I dared not tell you that it would bore me to death. *Which* it did! I did all of that, and you cannot even be civil to me? Of all the—Ouch!" She had pricked her finger on a thorn.

Gore took her hand and kissed it. "Is this civil enough for you? Or this?" He leaned down and kissed her lips softly.

"Oh, well." She returned his smile. "I am not certain. Perhaps if you were to do it again, then I . . ."

He complied. Belle grinned up at him. "No, my darling, there was nothing civil about it at all. The devil take civility," she said, and lifted her lips for another sample. "May I safely assume that you have forgiven me?"

He shook his head, smiling. "No, sweetheart. You must forgive me. Was there ever a greater dolt than I?"

"I want to say that there probably is not, but I fear that I must deserve the title." They sat down together on the bench, their arms about one another. She laughed. "I do forgive you for thinking me a thief, and I even forgive you for forcing me to learn to ride, for I found I love it, but I am not at all certain that I can forgive you for making me attend that lecture! That was too cruel."

Gore laughed aloud. "You see, I was torn. One day I was convinced that you were a schemer, the next that you were an angel. By the time I'd finally made up my mind, you had fled, and all my doubts came back."

She nodded. "I knew that I was only postponing the inevitable. Of course, you would learn the truth once you met the real Lillie again, and eventually, you would visit Eulalie and Aubrey. But I wanted only to get away, I could not face you just then. And I had to find employment, you know. I did not know what else to do; the Employment Registry could find nothing for me, so, in my desperation, I thought of Eulalie and Aubrey." She rested her head on his shoulder.

"Well, as to that, I am not certain that Eulalie will let us back into the house until we are engaged, Belle." He cocked a brow to the French door, where the drapery was just slipping back into place. "I do believe that we are being supervised." He chuckled, then looked at her soberly. "Will you marry me, Belle? I would be the happiest man in the world, if you said yes."

"Yes," she said very promptly. Then she reached up and kissed him.

Once they were inside the house, Eulalie hugged and kissed them, and Aubrey beamed from his chair. "I knew things would work out properly, Aubrey," Eulalie said.

"Took them long enough, though, didn't it, dear?"

The Bracelet sparkled in Eulalie's outstretched hand. "You will wear this on your wedding day, Belle. It is what brought the two of you together after all, is it not?"

EPILOGUE

Filbert jumped into Lillie's lap and began to gnaw on the edge of the letter she held in her hand.

"Filbert! You bad cat! It's lucky I had already read that part, for Belle crosses her letters, and you have bitten off part of her message." She laughed. "Although, now that she is going to wed one of the richest men in the kingdom, I cannot think why she is so concerned about the high cost of postage."

The cat looked at her and yawned, then rolled over onto his back, large tummy waiting.

"I am beginning to think that you have read this." She waved the letter. "For Belle instructs me to scratch your prosperous tummy on her behalf." She did so, and as he purred heavily, she told him the rest of the news.

"Yes, Belle and Gore are to be married, Filbert, isn't that wonderful? The wedding is to be at Eulalie and Aubrey's house in Minster Lovell, and we are invited. Warner, too, of course. Belle has told me the whole story. She has written to Cecily and Warner, as well, so we will have a wonderful coze, the three of us. Thank heaven that Gore finally realized his pigheadedness. And, afterward, we shall go home to Burford, Filbert. Who knows what awaits us there." She took the cat in her arms and hugged him tightly.

He pulled his head back as best he could and glared at her, but she only laughed. Apparently, she had forgotten that he did not like to be cuddled in this fashion. It was undignified. He squirmed from her grasp and leapt to the floor, carefully washing all those places where her arms had touched him. Then, after closely inspecting a bit of lint on the carpet, he jumped back into her lap and began to knead a comfortable space there. Obviously, he needed to begin training her all over again now, and it looked to be a long process. Lillie laughed again and stroked his head, and Filbert fell asleep to dream deeply about the beautiful Columbine and all those mice in Burford.

ABOUT THE AUTHOR

Jesse Watson lives in Waltham, Massachusettes, where she is at work on her third Regency. She can be contacted in c/o Zebra Books.

WATCH FOR THESE ZEBRA REGENCIES

LADY STEPHANIE   (0-8217-5341-X, $4.50)
by Jeanne Savery
Lady Stephanie Morris has only one true love: the family estate she has managed ever since her mother died. But then Lord Anthony Rider arrives on her estate, claiming he has plans for both the land and the woman. Stephanie soon realizes she's fallen in love with a man whose sensual caresses will plunge her into a world of peril and intrigue . . . a man as dangerous as he is irresistible.

BRIGHTON BEAUTY   (0-8217-5340-1, $4.50)
by Marilyn Clay
Chelsea Grant, pretty and poor, naively takes school friend Alayna Marchmont's place and spends a month in the country. The devastating man had sailed from Honduras to claim his promised bride, Miss Marchmont. An affair of the heart may lead to disaster . . . unless a resourceful Brighton beauty finds a way to stop a masquerade and keep a lord's love.

LORD DIABLO'S DEMISE   (0-8217-5338-X, $4.50)
by Meg-Lynn Roberts
The sinfully handsome Lord Harry Glendower was a gambler and the black sheep of his family. About to be forced into a marriage of convenience, the devilish fellow engineered his own demise, never having dreamed that faking his death would lead him to the heavenly refuge of spirited heiress Gwyn Morgan, the daughter of a physician.

A PERILOUS ATTRACTION   (0-8217-5339-8, $4.50)
by Dawn Aldridge Poore
Alissa Morgan is stunned when a frantic passenger thrusts her baby into Alissa's arms and flees, having heard rumors that a notorious highwayman posed a threat to their coach. Handsome stranger Hugh Sebastian secretly possesses the treasured necklace the highwayman seeks and volunteers to pose as Alissa's husband to save her reputation. With a lost baby and missing necklace in their care, the couple embarks on a journey into peril—and passion.

Available wherever paperbacks are sold, or order direct from the Publisher. Send cover price plus 50¢ per copy for mailing and handling to Kensington Publishing Corp., Consumer Orders, or call (toll free) 888-345-BOOK, to place your order using Mastercard or Visa. Residents of New York and Tennessee must include sales tax. DO NOT SEND CASH.

WATCH FOR THESE REGENCY ROMANCES

LOOK FOR THESE REGENCY ROMANCES